Malheur

A Balkan War Mystery

BY

PAMELIA BARRATT

Plowshare Media

LA JOLLA, CALIFORNIA

Library of Congress Control Number: 2016952479
Barratt, Pamelia
Malheur : A Balkan War Mystery

ISBN: 978-0-9860428-9-8   (trade paperback edition)

Cover illustration: Adapted from a photo by Chen-Pan Liao, Wikimedia Commons, under the Creative Commons Attribution-Share Alike 3.0 Unported license: https://creativecommons.org/licenses/by-sa/3.0/legalcode

Published by:
Plowshare Media
La Jolla, California, USA

PUBLISHER'S NOTES

For information about permission to
reproduce selections of this book, write to:

Plowshare Media, P.O. Box 278, La Jolla, CA 92038
or visit PLOWSHAREMEDIA.COM

To my husband, Ken Barratt,
for his patience and understanding.

PREFACE

Yugoslavia
March, 1991

This novel is based on true events occurring during and after the Yugoslav Wars of the 1990s. Yugoslavia was located on the western side of the Balkan Peninsula across the Adriatic Sea from Italy. As a country, Yugoslavia no longer exists.

The western Balkan people are almost uniformly Slavs, and have been so since the 6th century CE, yet their region never became dominant on the world stage. The terrain is 70% mountainous which made travel, communication, and trade difficult. It was thought of as the 'land in between'—between the Western Roman Empire (based in Rome) and the Eastern or Byzantine Empire (based in Constantinople, now Istanbul); between the Roman Catholics and the Eastern Orthodox Church; between the Hapsburgs and the Ottoman Turks; and between the democratic west and the Communist east.

The Balkan Peninsula

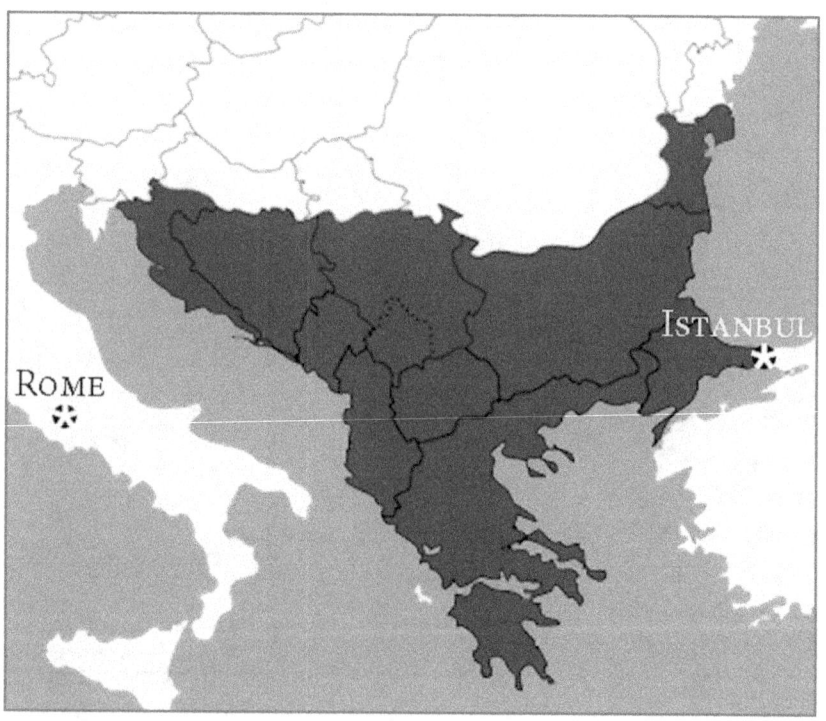

Created first as a kingdom after World War I, Yugoslavia became a Communist country after World War II. Its dictator, Tito, divided it into six republics: Slovenia, Croatia, Serbia, Bosnia Herzegovina [which is shortened to Bosnia throughout this book], Montenegro, and Macedonia. Establishing these borders in such a way meant that one third of all Serbs lived outside of Serbia—half of those lived in Croatia and the other half in Bosnia. Seventeen per cent of Bosnia's population was Croatian.

After the death of Tito in 1980, the federation of republics was beset by economic and political problems. Many republics wanted to be free from the Yugoslav central government in Belgrade. With the fall of the Iron Curtain in 1989, some existing Communist leaders realized they would have to take on new tactics if they wanted to stay in power. By controlling the media, they espoused religious and ethnic pride, while distorting accounts of history. By 1991–1992 tensions had developed to the point that four of the six republics passed resolutions to secede from Yugoslavia. The brutality of the wars of secession rivaled that of World War II. For four years, the people in an area half the size of Oregon were subjected to brutal acts of ethnic cleansing and genocide.

The peace following the Balkan wars could not have been maintained without the dedication and determination of both civilians and the International Criminal Tribunal for Yugoslavia (ICTY) to bring war criminals to justice. *Malheur* illustrates the struggle by so many people of conscience to expose their crimes, as well as the difficulty of apprehending, trying, and convicting them.

CHAPTER 1

ZAGREB, CROATIA

A sallow-faced woman opened the door, wiping her hands on her apron. "Ah, yes, you are Maric." Not waiting for confirmation, she added: "Let me show you to your room."

Maric hadn't met her aunt Alma before. Did she look like her father? There was no time to study her face. Maric had to quickly follow her, passing through the small living room, only briefly smiling at the two children playing there. Alma called out their names, but didn't stop. Up the stairs she went, and Maric, carrying her backpack and small suitcase, tried to keep up. Once on the landing, Alma reached up to pull on a rope. Maric stepped aside as the attic ladder descended.

"Up there is all we can give you. The house key, sheets, and towels are on the table. I put a chamber pot under the cot, so you won't have to come down here often to use our bathroom." Alma excused herself, as she had to finish cooking. "We'll be eating in a half hour. Join us if you would like."

Maric watched her aunt's back as she descended the stairs abruptly. Perhaps it was just the timing of her arrival. Aunt Alma was obviously busy cooking dinner. Picking up her suitcase, Maric climbed the stepladder, opened the door at the top, and saw the attic space where she was to live. The pitch of the roof meant she could only stand up on the left side of the room, or under the dormer window. How fortunate to have a window! With the late afternoon light coming through it, she could scan the room. A cot sat under the eaves to the right of the door, along with a cardboard chest of drawers. There was a straight back chair. A table under the dormer window held a small lamp. Maric put down her suitcase and walked over to turn it on. It worked. She turned it off. Opposite the door at the other end of the room was a rod suspended by chains from the angled ceiling. The few hangers it held revealed its purpose.

She was pleased with the space. In fact, she couldn't believe her good luck. After retrieving her backpack from the second floor landing, she drew up the ladder after her and closed the door. When her dad had told her she would have to live with his sister's family in Zagreb, she had worried that she wouldn't have any privacy. Perhaps Aunt Alma wanted privacy as well. Even so, Maric decided it was best to go down to have dinner with the Dadics this first night.

She had time to unpack her suitcase, but left setting up her ham radio for another day. She was still glowing from the bus trip from Mostar. She had never traveled out of Bosnia before. When the bus reached the coastal highway in Croatia, she was overwhelmed by the deep blue of the Adriatic, shimmering to the west. She had seen the sea as a child from Bosnia's minuscule shoreline, but the view there was blocked by a Croatian island. From the bus, she could see numerous offshore islands, some with white sandy beaches and others mountainous, forested, with rocky shores. They were all part of Croatia. To the east were high mountains. The bus drove for hours along the sinuous coastal route, passing cities and fishing villages nestled in bays and coves. Maric loved the terracotta rooftops.

For the last hour and a half of the trip, the bus turned northeast, away from the sea, up hills and through mountain passes, until it came to the capital city—Zagreb. Once at the Zagreb bus depot, she had to negotiate the local transportation system to find her way to her new home. The Dadics had no car. Even if they had, she would not have asked to be picked up.

All of this was behind her now. She had arrived and would

make this place home as much as possible. On the chest of drawers she propped up photos of her parents, her sister Luna, a group photo of her ham buddies, and Hakim. She put her Croatian-English dictionary on the table. That would have to do for now. She had better go down to dinner.

Lying in bed that night, she wondered why her dad had never talked much of Alma, his youngest sister. It wasn't until the war broke out that Maric heard of her. She knew both her parents had relatives in Croatia, but they never had the money to go there for a visit. Her family had lived in Bosnia all her life. Her father had gone to places all over Yugoslavia to work. For many months at a time, he had to work far from home, even outside of Yugoslavia. Jobs in construction were all that he could get. When he came home to Mostar, he often brought with him a history book he had purchased "for his girls." He loved history. When he was home, he read and shared with them stories of past events. She and Luna devoured whatever books he brought them. From an early age, Maric knew she wanted to study history when she got to university.

The Bosnian War broke out in 1992, just as Maric was entering her third year at the University of Sarajevo. Bosnia wanted to secede from Yugoslavia and become an independent nation. Slovenia had already left and Croatia was in the process of fighting for its independence. She questioned the sense of taking her out of university because of a war in Bosnia and sending her to the neighboring country, Croatia, which was also at war with Yugoslavia.

Her friend, Hakim, had explained that she would be safe anywhere in Croatia, where there were few Serbs. "Yugoslavia, is under the control of Serbs. They are perfectly willing to let Slovenia break away, but not Croatia and Bosnia, where a third of all Serbs are living."

She missed Hakim and was worried about his safety. She didn't want to think about him or she would never get to sleep. Maric also worried about Luna. Her sister was in her first year of medical school at the University of Sarajevo. Their mom and dad had made separate arrangements for both their daughters. "You can't come home to live with us. It's just a question of time before the war spreads to Mostar," their dad had said. So refuge was found for each girl with different relatives who lived in safer areas.

Maric accepted her placement with her aunt Alma Dadic in Zagreb, but Luna begged her parents to let her continue her studies at medical school. With medical training, she argued, she could really help people in need during the siege. After a month of discussions over the telephone, their parents reluctantly gave in and let Luna stay in Sarajevo.

Luna was exceptional, so bright that she had been accepted at the university two years before she finished high school. She was confident, serious, but also intense. When she looked at you, you felt you were being pinned down for dissection.

Many of Maric's friends had also left the university, deferring their plans for the future. The pending danger left no time for regrets, and concentrated their feelings for one another. It was hard for Maric to say goodbye to Hakim. They were two cogs on the same wheel. She would miss Luna, but they rarely saw each other, even though they had both been attending the same university for two years. They tried to have tea together every other month, just to stay in touch. Maric also had to say goodbye to her 'hamster' friends, but that was not as difficult. She knew she could keep in contact with them by radio. From university, she returned to Mostar to have a brief visit with her parents, before taking a bus to Zagreb.

☙

The first morning at Aunt Alma's, she rose out of bed and waited until she thought everyone had left the house before coming down from the attic. After a quick shower, she went to the kitchen to make a piece of toast, after which she intended to leave the house for the day. Before she could finish eating, Aunt Alma returned from walking her children to school. Maric gobbled down the rest of her toast so she could get out of her aunt's way. "Thank you again for making room for me in your home."

"Uh-hum."

"I won't be home for supper. I'll be gone the entire day." Not that Maric knew what she would be doing, she just felt it was wise to give Aunt Alma as much space as possible.

Alma said her dinner would be kept for her in the kitchen, and went upstairs to the second floor.

Maric left the house. She hoped to find the library, a post office, get a map of the city, bus and tram schedules, and she wanted to start looking for a job. But before all that, she wanted to write her parents to say that she had arrived safely, to thank them for providing a safe lodging for her, and in particular, for being such warm and loving parents.

She knew her dad would be sending Alma a stipend each month to cover the cost of her food, so she wasn't going to feel guilty on that account. But in her letter, she thanked her mother for the years of cooking lessons. "Maybe Aunt Alma will let me cook the evening meals."

Within a week, Maric realized Alma would never agree to that. She had hoped to have fun with the children, who were seven and nine years of age. They seemed eager to see her, but Aunt Alma did not encourage their friendship. They were never allowed up in her room. "They might fall off the ladder." Maric offered to take them to the park, but there was always a reason that they couldn't go. Alma did make her a dinner each night, but seemed pleased that she usually came home too late to eat it with the family. When she was in the Dadic house, Maric spent most of her time in her room.

ᏣᏋ

After a couple of weeks, she had had time to explore the

neighborhood. She could see that the Dadics lived in a square building which contained four two-story homes. They must have been built after WWII, she thought. How ugly! The whole neighborhood was made up of the same square buildings, one after another. Two homes faced the street, and two the back alley. None of the homes had a backdoor. Only a sidewalk separated one square building from the next. No grass or trees softened their aspect.

However, having a window in her attic bedsit offered many possibilities. For one, it gave her a means of putting up an effective antenna for her ham radio. She attached a hook to one end of a long wire and threw it up on the roof, hoping it would attach to something. It took several tries, but finally it caught somewhere. Then she attached a second hook to another long wire and threw it until it landed on the roof of the building next door. It was fortunate that the two buildings were little more than a sidewalk apart. Still, it took many tosses before that hook caught on something.

Days later, she received her first ham radio call from Leni, one of her university friends who had bravely stayed in Sarajevo. Not wanting the Dadics to hear, Maric turned down the volume and kept her ear near the speaker. She needed to buy some headphones. She heard:

9-Alpha-3-Mike-Echo-Delta…9-Alpha-3-Mike-Echo-Delta, this is Tango-95-Mike-Tango-Tango. Are you there Maric? 9A3MED, this is T95MTT calling and standing by.

Maric answered, "Tango-95-Mike-Tango-Tango, this is 9-Alpha-3-Mike-Echo-Delta. How copy? Over."

Leni responded, speaking slowly and clearly: *Static crashes take you out but copy OK…. Civilians have few places to hide… snipers pick them off…. Shells are fired from the hills all day until nightfall…. Luna is fine. How copy? Over.*

"Got it. Tell Luna we love her. Are you safe? Over."

Yes, Yes…. So far, no shells have hit the university. Some telephone lines are down. Please write down the following: call

615-284 to say that Fejad is fine, call 615-399 and say Jenita gave birth to a boy named Carnil. Father left 3 weeks ago for Prijedor. No word from him since. Copy that? Back to you. This is T95MTT, I'm clear on your final.

"Good copy on you Leni. Will do. Take care. All the best. T95MTT this is 9A3MED. Bye for now," Maric signed off.

The next morning, Maric waited around until everybody was gone from the house. Her uncle left home at 7:30 in the morning for work and Aunt Alma walked her two children to school soon thereafter. Once they had left, she quickly went down into the living room to use the telephone. Both telephone numbers were local, so the calls would not cost her aunt anything. She got through to the first family. They were so grateful. It turned out that Fejad was a university student in Sarajevo, so she also told them that no shells had hit the school. She had to say goodbye quickly. They asked for her number, but she told them she could not take any calls. No one was home at the second number. She would try again on another day.

No one in the Dadic family knew she had a ham radio, nor did her parents. Why she hadn't told them was hard to explain. She was glad to have a private life. Years ago, she had been all set to go to the university when her mother was hit by a car. Luna was eleven at the time. With her father away, it was up to Maric to manage the family. She had to take care of her severely crippled mother until her dad was able to get a job that kept him in Mostar. The good thing about that situation was that her mother taught her to cook. By the time she started college, she was seven years older than the other entering students. Only Luna knew she had a ham radio. Maric asked her to keep it a secret. Maybe she didn't tell her parents about it because it was something she was in control of, and that felt good.

Her hobby had started at the university when she met Hakim, a student in her history class. They both loved to talk about topics brought up in class. That soon led to more chatting over coffee. She wondered if her being an older woman made their friendship safe for Hakim to pursue. Soon, their discussions strayed into present day politics. Hakim read newspapers and articles in the library every day and explained various issues to her. Gradually, Maric began to understand the politics of Bosnia, and its relationship to the other republics. There was so much she hadn't known.

Most of her friends were people she attended history classes with, until Hakim introduced her to two engineering students. At first Maric wasn't drawn to Majesira. Her hair was closely cropped and she seldom smiled. Majesira was from Maric's home town, Mostar, but she was not interested in reminiscing. It wasn't even that she was Muslim, and therefore lived on the opposite side of the River Neretva. It was more that, until meeting Majesira, Maric hadn't known such a serious woman, except perhaps Luna. But with Luna being her sister, Maric had always felt comfortable. With Majesira, Maric felt like a foot soldier in the presence of a general.

Leni, the other engineering student Hakim introduced her to, was more affable and quite a beauty. She was also a Muslim. She was from further northeast, the city of Travnik, which Maric knew nothing about.

Majesira had been operating a ham radio for years and was teaching Leni how to use one. With Hakim's encouragement, Maric started going to Majesira's room to be taught as well. After several months, she and Leni both wanted their own radios. A few male engineering students helped them buy second-hand sets that were cheap but needed repair. The men seemed to enjoy the challenge of getting the radios to work properly. Maric falsely attributed their helpfulness to Leni's good looks. Later she became aware of the general camaraderie and code of ethics between 'hamsters.' Maric's coining that term went unappreciated. Her knowledge of English was far better than theirs.

She and Leni acquired their licenses, Leni easily, but it was a struggle for Maric, not having an engineering background. When they got their certificates, they put up antennas, and by the middle of Maric's second year in Sarajevo, she was having great fun communicating back and forth, especially at night when reception was best.

When the war seemed inevitable, Majesira started talking about setting up a communication network that they could use no matter where they lived. "The symbol for our network could be CZ, čast žene, ["honor women" in Serbo-Croat]. Our goal could be simply to have women honored."

Maric didn't grasp the need to emphasize women. She went along with it because she recognized Majesira as a born leader. She was several years younger than Maric but seemed to know things that were beyond Maric's awareness. For instance, she didn't want their network to be associated with any one nation, ethnic group, or religion. She told them that she was in contact with women with similar interests from the United States and France.

Maric thought their purpose would be simply to relay information to help families stay in contact, but she could see that Majesira had goals that went far beyond. She called eight 'hamsters' together on the day she was leaving to go home to Mostar. "We ought to agree to a time when we will try to listen and send messages. Nine o'clock in the evening is good for transmission and it's convenient." She stopped to guage if all were in agreement. "Let's aim to communicate on Wednesday evenings starting with the frequency of 7.1." She handed out a list of frequencies they should use, as well as the names and call signs of each of the hamsters. "If that frequency is occupied, move on to the next frequency on the list." She waited until everyone digested what she had said.

Leni broke in, "Thank goodness we're all in the same time zone."

"Yes, we are lucky in that respect," Majesira agreed, "but occasionally it may be important to broadcast so people in other parts of the world can hear your message. Some of you are going home, where fighting is already occurring. To reach other time zones, let's broadcast at 9:00 P.M. as usual, and then again at 6:00 A.M. That way even in the United States some people may pick up the messages."

The siege was in full swing by then. As soon as Bosnia announced its independence from Yugoslavia, Bosnian Serbs took up positions in the hills surrounding Sarajevo and started shelling the capital unremittingly. Serb snipers targeted civilians. Nobody was safe. Many telephone lines were cut. A student they knew had been shot by a sniper. Sorry as Maric was to split up from her friends and to leave her studies, she was grateful she had a safe place to live and a means to stay in touch.

Maric's thoughts again went to Hakim. Throughout her second year at university, Maric and Hakim continued to meet over coffee. Hakim had tried to make her a political activist, but at that time she hadn't felt sure enough of her convictions to join in on protests. She was a student first, so pleased to finally be at university that she just wanted to read and learn as much as she could, not work on a particular cause. Besides, learning Morse code and ham communication had already used up most of her spare time.

Several months ago, Hakim had told her, "One out of every three Bosnians is a Serb. They're still a minority, but they dominate half the area of our country. I'm afraid Serbs in Bosnia will try to form their own republic."

His analysis had been right. As soon as Bosnia tried to secede from Yugoslavia, the Bosnian Serbs proclaimed their area to be independent—the Republic of Srpska—and started to attack the rest of Bosnia. They were assisted by Serbia and the Yugoslav Army, both of which were controlled by Slobodan Milošević.

Hakim was five years younger than Maric, but ten years more mature. She would always be grateful for what he taught her about politics. In fact, their talks were the highlight of her two years at university. Hakim was a Muslim man from Srebrenica. Like Maric, he left the university when the war broke out. He felt he had to go home to protect his family against Serbian aggression.

☙

Maric received her second ham message four nights later, asking her to telephone a Zagreb number and relay a message to a location much further away. The destination was Ljubljana, the capital of Slovenia.

Other nights, the reception was so bad she couldn't understand a thing. When that happened, she wasn't really concerned, because there was nothing she could do about it. But at times, the reception was just poor, allowing the messages to be somewhat, but not completely, understood. Such nights she couldn't sleep well for worrying that she was letting someone down.

Recently, a message was transmitted from Prijedor in northwestern Bosnia:

This is Tango-94-Red-Rose…Members of CZ, please record this testimony."

(Another voice:) *"I am Danira Hodzić. I have escaped Trnopolje concentration camp. In April of 1992, Bosnian Serbs took over our government of the city of Prijedor. Then the army took over the adjacent town of Kozarac where I lived. The phone lines had been cut. Most of us tried to surrender. We were told we'd be taken to a soccer stadium. Serb soldiers separated the men from the women. The women went to Trnopolje and the men to Omarska and Keraterm concentration camps. By May, I heard that 1,500 were deported to these camps and at least 100 people were killed. We were fed one meal a day. Before I escaped, several of us women were taken off to a field at night and repeatedly raped. One night I recognized one of the rapists. It was Nenad Žigić, a taxi cab driver in Prijedor. I learned from others that he had beaten, raped, and tortured many women in Trnopolje. There were other Serb soldiers who did that as well but I don't know their names. I knew Nenad because, before the war, his cab picked up my family every Friday.*

(The original voice came back on.) *Record that, ladies! We'll get that bastard. No impunity for rapists! T94RR. Over.*

Maric tried frantically to write down the testimony in its

entirety, but she missed parts because she just couldn't write fast enough. She realized how much better it would be to have it on tape, so days later, she purchased a tape recorder. What she would do with such a testimony she did not know, but she agreed with the caller: *Rapists should not go unpunished!* Maric checked Majesira's list. Sure enough, the woman with that call sign was Jenica Andreić. She was from Prijedor, Bosnia, and a member of their CZ network.

∝

When she started university in 1990, Maric had a limited understanding of political events in her country. She was born in 1965, twenty years after the Western Balkans unified as Yugoslavia—Land of the Southern Slavs. She learned in school that Tito had organized the country into six republics: Slovenia, Croatia, Bosnia, Serbia, Montenegro, and Macedonia. Her dad always had reservations about Tito. Supposedly, he was a moderate Communist, but he was dictator for 35 years! He ran the country from Belgrade. By the time he died in 1980, several of the republics were tired of the economic constraints imposed by his central government.

Talking with Hakim, Maric learned details that explained more about what was going on. She remembered him telling her that after the Berlin Wall fell in 1989, Communism lost its credibility with the people. Power-hungry politicians had to find a new ideology to rally around. Nationalism met their needs. Although "Unity and Brotherhood" came from Tito's mouth, by dividing Yugoslavs into six groups, he had kept those people thinking of themselves as distinct. Tito had prepared the ground for nationalism to take root.

There were two politicians that Hakim was most worried about. The President of Croatia, Franjo Tudjman, who preached the need for a 'pure' Croatia, implying that Serbs and others should not be living within his country's borders. The other politician was the President of Serbia, Slobodan Milošević, who wanted to unite all Serbs under one nation. Milošević hoped to enlarge the country so it could encompass those other Serbs living outside Serbia.

Hakim had asked her to consider why had Yugoslavia been willing to let Slovenia secede?

She had trouble answering at first. Then she realized that Slovenia had few Croats and Serbs. Its society was homogeneous.

Hakim explained: "That's right, but in Croatia and Bosnia there are many Serbs and they want to be connected to Serbia. Or a better way to put it is that Milošević's rhetoric has encouraged Serbs to think of themselves as Serbs first, no matter where they are living. That's why Serbs in Croatia want to break away and form the Republic of Krajina. Much of this has been orchestrated by Milošević, just like Hitler did with the Sudetenland before World War II."

That made sense to Maric. She remembered their history professor covering Hitler's grab of the Sudetenland. "That explains it," she said. "Milošević's claim that the Serbs of Krajina need 'protection' was an excuse to move Yugoslav troops, the JNA, into Croatia." They both smiled. Maric was becoming savvy. Finally, at age 27, she was coming to understand the politics of her times.

Sadly, her university life had now ended, yet moving to Zagreb was also an adventure. She had never been outside of Bosnia, and all she really knew of Bosnia was Mostar and Sarajevo. Now she had a new place to live and could be on her own. True, her aunt didn't want her, but that in itself was liberating. All she had to do was stay out of her way. Aunt Alma didn't want to know and didn't care what she did. Maric knew she was lucky. All the fighting in Croatia was located in the "armpit," where Krajina was. She was safe in Zagreb; unlike many of her classmates, she did not have to return home to a battle zone.

Finding a job was essential, but how? Starting at the City Library of Zagreb, she hoped to look up the want-ad columns in newspapers, without having to buy the papers, and was pleasantly surprised to find several jobs available, if you spoke and read English. There were even some schools looking for English teachers.

She sought the advice of the reference librarian, asking her if she knew anything about the places listed. The woman looked at Maric and said: "Let me see how well you speak." She handed Maric a book written in English, suggesting she read a passage out loud. After completing a paragraph, the woman took the book from her and said smiling: "You speak very well." She took a look at the list of jobs Maric had selected and ranked them in order from best to worst.

Three days later, Maric was employed as a high school English teacher. With the war going on, some teachers had been killed and others had to leave the city to take care of relatives. Maric wasn't technically qualified, having had only two years of university training, but schools were desperate to fill sudden vacancies. As it happened, Maric was hired by a school of high academic rating.

⅋

Occasionally, Maric received a letter from her parents. The last one was startling:

Dear Maric,

I hope you're enjoying your teaching position. Your mother and I are very proud of you.

Have you heard of this faction of ultra nationalist Croats who have seized power? They have taken over in areas of Bosnia that have a large Croat majority, and did exactly what the Serbs did in both Krajina and Srpska. They've called their area the Republic of Herzeg-Bosnia and are in the process of expelling all Bosniaks and Serbs. They have been known to round up a group, lock them in a house, and set the house on fire.

It is now looking like Serbs are claiming three-fifths of Bosnia for Serbs only and Croats are claiming the remaining two-fifths for Croats only. Muslims will have no place to go. How could the Croats turn against them? War really brings out the ugliness in people.

Your mother and I are so sorry that you and Luna must live your youths through these times. We wish to tell you that good things will come in the future. They will. Nothing lasts forever. We heard from Luna recently. She is doing fine. At least you are safe. We wish we could all be together. Your mother is doing well, still able to make a tasty dish out of a potato, onion, and turnip. We have lots of friends. We all look out for each other. This may be the last letter you will receive from us for some time. We have heard that mail service is about to be cut off.

I just heard that the Serbs don't want the Croats to have Mostar. Shelling has started again.

Love,

Dad and Mom

A mixture of people lived in Mostar, mostly Catholic Croats and Bosnian Muslims, better known as Bosniaks. They had lived together in relative peace for a century or more. From the beginning of the war, the two had fought as allies, resisting the advances of the Serbs. But in 1993, as her dad's letter indicated, Bosnian Croats turned against the Bosniaks. Why? Maric couldn't believe it. Ethnically, the people were all Slavs, they spoke the same language and used the same Latin alphabet.

The Neretva River divided Mostar. Bosniaks lived on the east side and Croats on the west, but for decades, people flowed in and out of both areas, socializing and shopping in any of the numerous markets on both sides of the river. Now, even the graceful old stone bridge, Stari Most, was shelled and destroyed.

This Croat-Bosniak War (The War within the War) was disastrous. Fortunately, it lasted less than a year. American diplomats stepped in to help sort out the problem. Eventually, Croatians resumed being allies with the Bosniaks, and together they fought the Serbs. Maric didn't know why the Croats had switched sides. The immediate tragedy for her was that during this aberration, her parents were killed. Three months after her father's last letter, her Aunt Ada from Mostar wrote:

> *My Dear Maric,*
>
> *Your father, bless him, was working at home to be with your dear mother. They were killed by two shells that destroyed five houses in a row, including yours. That block is now in shambles. You must not come, Maric dear. It is far too dangerous. I'm sorry we can't even have a funeral for your parents. Everything is in chaos. It's not safe anywhere here. You must stay in Zagreb with Aunt Alma.*
>
> *I've written Luna, but I'm not sure mail gets through to Sarajevo. I had to have someone at the Catholic Church take this and the letter I've written to Luna to a nearby town to post. I'll write you again if I have any more information.*

Maric was devastated. She hadn't worried much about her parents, assuming they would always be there. How could she have taken them for granted? She wished she could commiserate with Luna, but she couldn't contact her. She sent out ham messages about her parents' death and asked for news about Aunt Ada. No one responded.

Maric told Aunt Alma that her parents had been killed. For days, her aunt seemed to mourn their deaths. She asked Maric to eat dinner with her family. But after a week, those offers stopped. It may have occurred to her that she might never get rid of this niece, who now had no parents or home to return to. Furthermore, the monthly stipend from her father had stopped, along with the mail deliveries from Mostar. To compensate, Maric started giving money to her aunt each month. Alma accepted that, but not Maric's offers to cook the family dinners. Fair enough; at least Maric could stay in the Dadic attic. Her salary was minimal, but she incurred few expenses, living as she did.

 c⃰

Finally, in the fall of 1995, when it seemed that the war would soon be over, Maric received a horrible message from Majesira:

9-Alpha-3-Mike-Echo-Delta, this is Tango-92-Victor… Luna has been hit with shrapnel from a shell and is not expected to live. She knows her parents are dead. Luna sends Maric her love.

"Oh God, Luna," Maric said to herself, "my little baby sister!" Majesira was still transmitting, so Maric forced herself to continue listening:

Leni disappeared a while ago. More to tell. SF2 SF2 SF2 Over.

Maric disciplined herself to concentrate on Majesira's message. She knew exactly what to do. She spun the dial to 7.2 MHz and began listening intently for Majesira's signal. After a few moments, there it was:

9-Alpha-3-Mike-Echo-Delta, this is Tango-92-Victor. Are you there?

"Yes, go ahead, Majesira." Short of breath, Maric listened carefully. Could there be more bad news to come?

…The other person I told you about will be where I live in four month's time. We expect the war to be over by then. Can you come too? The address is as follows. I'll send it in CW" [radio abbreviation for morse code].

As she tapped out the dits and dahs, Maric carefully copied it down: Šerifa Burića, 23…

Then Majesira's voice came back on. *I hope you got that. Can we meet June 7? I will tell you then about your sister. She is quite a hero. Over.*

"Yes, Roger that…. T92V this is 9A3MED, clear for now."

If only Luna could have lasted four more months. She probably never got the chance to be a doctor. Now there was no one to go back to, no one with whom to share childhood memories. It would take some time for the loss to sink in. They had exchanged letters twice a year, but it had been four years since she had actually seen her sister. Maric's spirits were feeling the impact of these losses. She tried not to mope and feel sorry for herself. Her teaching job helped. Both its unending work and her enjoyable students offered the necessary distraction to keep her going.

ଓ

The Dayton Peace Accords were signed in December of 1995. With the war over, teachers and other professionals were returning to the capital to resume their old positions. Maric managed to hold on to her job until the end of the school year in '96. The principal wanted to rehire her, but schools all over Croatia were obligated to give the returning teachers their jobs back. "I put in a good word for you with the president though," he said.

"The president—do you mean Franjo Tudjman?" Maric asked, expecting a joke to follow.

"Yes, his aide, Primo-something, has been calling schools asking for recommendations of people with excellent English skills, and I mentioned you."

ଓ

By the time she climbed on the bus to go to Mostar to visit Majesira, Maric knew she had been picked for the job in Tudjman's office. Unknown to her, one of her students was the nephew of President Tudjman. That may have been why she was chosen for the position. Her new job would be to transcribe tapes. She'd be working near Tudjman's personal office. The post was only for a year, maybe less, but she was glad to have it. She would start as soon as she got back from Mostar.

The bus trip to Mostar took six hours. She had a window seat. A large woman wearing a scarf and woolen shawl sat next to her. Maric smiled at her but they did not converse. She was lost in thought, looking forward to seeing her friends, but also dreading seeing the destruction of the city that she loved.

Riding on the bus from Zagreb to the beautiful coast of Croatia, Maric saw no destruction of buildings. The towns they passed through were intact. In the last four years, Tudjman had negotiated as many as twenty cease fires which ensured that the fighting, for the most part, stayed outside of Croatia. The exception was in the first year of Croatia's war for independence, when the Croatian Serbs formed the breakaway Republic of Krajina. Hakim had told Maric that the Croats were not sufficiently armed to prevent the breakaway or to stop the ethnic cleansing in Krajina of Croats. The route the bus took to Mostar did not go through Krajina, so Maric didn't see that destruction.

When the bus crossed into Bosnia, it headed northeast. The pastures were the same brilliant green they always had been in mid-summer, but some towns were largely demolished. Only hearths and chimneys were left standing. Other towns seemed untouched. Why? Each had their stories. She hoped there were people alive to tell them. The bus passed through dense forests and over steeply-graded mountain roads. Finally, she started to recognize the names of towns as the bus wound its way down high hills to the city. As they descended, she could see the Neretva River.

Soon, she would hear about Luna. Had she finished medical school? She might have even received her diploma. The school probably dispensed with graduation ceremonies during the war. Not that it mattered now, but she hoped Luna had felt a sense of accomplishment before she died.

Once on level ground, the bus entered city streets. Many buildings were pockmarked with bullet holes. Others weren't so lucky. Hit by artillery shells, all that remained were fragments of their outer walls. Maric was overcome with grief thinking of what her parents had gone through in their last year of life. She quietly tried to wipe the tears from her eyes. It was no use. They kept coming. The woman seated next to her patted her hand. Maric turned toward her to show her appreciation and saw that she was on the verge of crying herself.

Seeing the river lifted her spirits. Its forceful persistence to carry on gave her reassurance. It was still the turquoise blue she remembered, and still on its way to the Adriatic Sea, flowing gracefully past them and their futile wars.

Closer to the heart of the city, she saw that Stari Most, the bridge the Ottomans built in the 1500s, had been blown up. Not even pedestrians could use it. As a child, she'd become spell-bound watching boys jump off of the top of its arch into the river below. Those carefree days were long gone.

As the bridge was out, the bus could not get close to where her home had been, so Maric got off in the Muslim part of town. She decided to go first to Majesira's house. It was difficult to find. Street signs were missing. Majesira had said that the front door of the tall bank building looked in the direction of her house ten blocks away. Maric remembered that bank. It had been possibly the tallest building in Mostar. Walking past it, she saw all the windows had been knocked out. A man on the street told her that Croats had taken it over in early '93 and used it as a sniper tower to shoot at Bosniaks.

Majesira's home was a small room in the basement of a low building in which six families lived. Leni was already there. They had been waiting for Maric's arrival. After warm greetings, hugs, and tears, they got down to telling each other their stories.

Majesira began: "During the war, none of us could leave the building through the front door because of snipers. We had to exit through Mr. Popović's window at the rear. We were lucky, no shell fell on this block. Our windows still have glass because none of them faced the tower."

"Can you imagine, just ten years ago, Sarajevo hosted the

winter Olympics!" Leni lamented.

Maric insisted that they first tell her about Luna.

Leni started to explain: "Luna was embarrassed to tell you that she had dropped out of medical school. She was grateful that you had put off going to university for seven years to take care of your mother. She wasn't sure you'd understand."

"Dropped out, but why? She always wanted to be a doctor. Why would she drop out?" This news was the last thing Maric expected.

"Yes, and that's what she became. She couldn't stand studying, knowing that people all around her needed medical attention. She spent the last year and a half treating people, going to them at all times of the day and night if they couldn't come to her."

"What happened?...Was that when she was hit with shrapnel?" Maric guessed.

"It's difficult to know how it actually started. I believe a Bosnian Serb who had lived in Sarajevo all his life was attacked by a group of Bosniak thugs and left for dead in the street. Luna heard about it and went to examine the man. He was in critical condition but she thought she could save him. Some men helped her take him to where she lived to get him out of the cold. She nursed him back to good health. It took three months. Some said they were in love. He began going out with her when she visited sick people and helped her treat them. Some people didn't like it that they were working together, you know, because he was a Serb. The shell whose shrapnel eventually killed Luna killed this man outright. Some said she died more from a broken heart than from the shrapnel."

Her friends let Maric cry. Then she became silent, almost peaceful. She knew her reaction was strange. But she was actually glad Luna did all those things, glad that her sister knew love with a man before she died. Maric was seven years behind her on that score, too. "What was the man's name?"

"I'm sorry I don't know." After a pause, Leni said: "In

Sarajevo before the siege, not only did Serbs, Bosniaks, and Croats live peacefully together, but the city had an unusually high percentage of interethnic marriages, something like 30%."

A year prior, Leni had been severely wounded by shrapnel herself, and was carried out of Sarajevo in a wheelbarrow, through the secret tunnel that went under the airport. The U.N. had taken over the airport early in 1992, so food and medicine could be delivered to the city, in spite of the siege.

While Leni talked, Maric noticed how thin she had become, and her color was poor. She was still pretty, but no longer the vibrant beauty that she had been.

After hours of catching up, a neighbor brought the three of them *burek*, a favorite dish they all relished before the war. Two hours later, another neighbor brought them *cevapis*.

Maric couldn't help asking Majesira, "How can your neighbors do this when they have so little themselves?"

"I think they have been planning this for days, knowing you both were coming."

"For us?"

"They're grateful for your help with relaying messages throughout the war."

Maric wanted to know if they had any contact with Hakim and his sister.

"I think you can be sure that Hakim was one of the thousands of men massacred six months ago at Srebrenica."

The lump came back in Maric's throat. "Yes, that's what I thought too, but I had to ask. And his sister?"

"No, we haven't heard from her since the second year of the war." Majesira pulled her chair in closer to them. "Our job is not over, you know. We have to follow through on the cases we've documented and make sure that as many of the rapists as possible get convicted of their war crimes. We already have names and poignant testimonies. We have to do our best."

They discussed how, up until a few years ago, rape had not been considered torture by the courts. "One of our next battles is to have the International Criminal Court offer witness protection for victims who are willing to provide rape testimony. Then there's the need to change attitudes. A raped woman is often shunned by the people who formerly loved her. All these things need to be brought to the public's attention.

"Pretty soon telephones will be reinstalled and our ham sets will go quiet. We mustn't become complacent. We owe it to those women who have suffered and died to do what we can to improve things."

Eventually, Maric told them about the new job she would start when she got back to Zagreb.

"My God," said Leni, "you may have the chance to find out some top secrets."

"Yes," agreed Majesira. "Such information could really help us. You might discover who gave certain orders."

"Let me get this straight," Leni asked. "You're going to transcribe the tapes of Tudjman's telephone calls during the war?"

"Yes, and maybe conversations that went on in his office, as well. I don't know exactly. I think anytime he turned on the tape recorder, that is what I will transcribe."

"Are they going to give you a computer?"

"No, just a word processor."

"So, you can't email your transcriptions."

"No." Her two friends were way ahead of her. Ever since she got the job, her mind had been on this trip to Mostar. She hadn't considered that her upcoming work might allow her to gather evidence about war crimes.

"Maric, you could use floppy disks," Leni said. "All word processors have a slot for floppies."

"You must be careful that they don't see you making a copy."

She had to leave Mostar two days later. A friend of Majesira's offered to take her to the street where her home had been, but Maric wouldn't let him. It would have required him to drive some distance to get to another bridge to cross the river, and she didn't think it was fair to have him spend the money on petrol, so she wasn't able to see her old neighborhood or try to find Aunt Ada. There were plans to rebuild the bridge. It might take several years, but sometime in the future she would return to Mostar and honor her parents and visit her aunt. She thought they would understand that she couldn't do it just then.

Chapter 2

In March of 1996, soon after the conclusion of the Dayton Peace Accords, which ended the Bosnian War, there was a telephone call between Zagreb and Belgrade, from the president of Croatia to the president of Serbia, between Franjo Tudjman and Slobodan Milošević:

T: *Hello, Slobodan, congratulations. You must be quite pleased with yourself.*

M: *Franjo, my God, wasn't that hell? I hope I never see that Holbrooke bastard again.*

T: *Well it's over, and you did quite well for yourself.*

M: *How can you say that? Hey, wait, is this line secure?*

T: *It is at my end.*

M: *Well, it certainly is here. That's one thing we're good at, right? [Looking off to the side at his assistant, Grgur, 'It better be!'] Well good. Yah, Franjo. It was an incomplete victory. We all know Srpska should be a part of Serbia.*

T: *It will be, sure thing, it will. I bet you'll have it in another ten years. By the way, I'd like to have the rest of Bosnia by then. There are still so many Croats living there.*

M: *My God you're greedy. You have a huge coastline now, and have successfully driven out your minorities.*

T: *Yes, I did you that favor, Slobo. I knew you wanted our Serbs so I pushed them out of Croatia for you, hee-hee. Now Srpska is fat and juicy with Serbs just waiting for your an-*

nexation.

M: *You phony bastard. You just wanted a pure Croatia. Don't pull that kind of shit with me. You may be a man of culture, a historian, but you're a fascist. You and all the rest of you Croats hate Serbs. Yah, and by the way, I got the pig analogy. You've always thought we were beneath you.*

T: *Easy, easy, Slobo. This is a friendly call.*

M: *Yah, but explain to me one thing. There is something I have never understood. Why do you consider our form of Christianity inferior? ...Hum? You all have got your balls.*

T: *Come on, Slobo. I know you're an atheist. Unlike you, I don't pretend for the public's sake to be a devout Catholic. I saw you on TV practically kowtowing to the Patriarch.*

M: *Hey, with 10,000 people present, what could I do? It all helps with my image. Ha, ha... So what's the purpose of this call: to say that we almost got away with partitioning Bosnia?*

T: *We'll get there, but we have one serious obstacle in our way, as I see it: The International Criminal Court.*

M: *They'll never get me! Those Dutch are pussies. You saw how we managed them at Srebrenica.*

T: *Don't get overconfident. They could get all of us. We must destroy evidence, especially our plan to partition Bosnia.*

M: *Ha, it's going to take them years, at least three, I figure, to start indicting war criminals.*

T: *Yes, but once they issue warrants for our arrest, Interpol will come in and seize documents and tapes from our offices. I think we both made tapes of our telephone calls, right?*

M: *Yah, yah, it helps with the memory....Hum, I see what you mean.*

T: *Well, I'm planning to get our tapes transcribed and then alter them where necessary. Our conversations before and during the war must agree and not incriminate either of us.*

M: *OK, Franjo. Sounds like a good plan. I will do the same. My man, Grgur, will be in charge at this end and he can coordinate with your little guy, what's his name?*

T: *Primo—not so little, Slobo, he's two meters tall.*

M: *That was a joke, Franjo! Croatians: tall in stature, short in humor. Ha, ha...*

T: *Ok, we'll turn this over to Primo and Grgur, then.*

M: *Yah, good idea. You're still a bastard, but good idea!*

T: *Yah, yah, you scrappy mongrel. Goodbye.*

M: *Goodbye.*

CHAPTER 3

In the fall of 1996, Maric began her job at President Tudjman's office. She took the bus to St. Mark's Square. It was probably the most important square in Zagreb, so it was on many bus routes. The square holds the old church, with a roof well known throughout Europe. Its tiles display the ubiquitous checkered shield of Croatia. The shield that was also on the flag, the football uniforms, and every souvenir you never wanted.

The government office building in which she would work was a huge white stucco structure with about 40 windows spanning the front on both stories. Entering the central doors put her in a long hallway that ran the entire length of the building. Numerous doors to offices opened onto this hall. She was told to go to the second floor, room 222. She arrived at 8:00 A.M., a half hour early. She checked her notes. This was the correct office. She stood outside the door, not knowing what else to do. Ten minutes later, a cleaning woman walked by pushing a wide, dry floor mop. When she passed by Maric again, on her return trip down the long hall, she said: "They probably open up at 8:30, or so."

Maric checked: "Is this the office of Primo Grahovac?"

"Oh, yes." She said with a sympathetic smile. "Your first day?"

"Yes."

"They'll check your purse. Don't take offence. They do it to everybody."

Maric smiled and said "Thanks." She judged the woman

was in her fifties, based on her hair, which was turning gray. The next time she came by, Maric asked her what her name was.

"Vesna," she said.

"Really! That's a Bosnian name, isn't it?"

She stopped for a second. "Are you from Bosnia, then?"

"Yes, … although I've lived in Zagreb since the war started."

She looked around. "Lucky you!" Without looking at Maric, she continued pushing the mop, walking off at a quickened pace.

In ten minutes, someone came with keys to open the office, but Maric was not invited in until Mr. Grahovac himself arrived. He seemed pleasant enough. He pointed to a chair and asked her to sit. The room had three desks with swivel chairs and computers. There also was a small table to the far right with no drawers and a straight back chair where Maric was to work. All the desks faced Mr. Grahovac's office. After several minutes, he came out of it carrying a word processing machine. "Do you know how to operate one of these?"

"I never have, but I think it's like a computer, isn't it?"

"It can't do as much as a computer." He put the machine on the table and went back into his office, keeping the door ajar. There was a wall mirror to the left of the door to his office. The man at the first desk, whose back was to her, could see what she was doing by looking in the mirror. She heard what she thought was a tape being played inside Mr. Grahovac's office. When it stopped, he brought out the recorder and placed it on her table, along with headphones. Maric didn't touch any of this equipment, sensing she should wait for further instructions.

"Sometimes we'll give you some documents or articles in English and ask you to translate them into Croatian. Periodically, you will be given a tape recording of proceedings that went on in the president's office when he had discussions or telephone conversations. Such tapes go back as far as 1989, when he first became president. We want you to transcribe them into this word processor. Before leaving to go home each day, you will turn everything in to me: the word processor, the tape, and any other material you worked on. If I am not here, you can give them to Focić.

"In the morning when you come in, please hang up both your coat and purse on that coat tree by the door. Then sit at this table and wait for one of us to bring you your work."

By this time, Maric had noticed that there was a floppy disk slot in her machine. Mr. Grahovac went back into his office and returned with a tape. He showed her how to operate both the tape recorder and the word processor. "When you come in, we'll give you a tape. Fill out this log: your name, the date, and the number on the tape that you will be transcribing. Then start listening and type each sentence exactly as you hear it. If you have to stop to use the rest room or to eat your lunch, just tell me or Focić here."

Focić turned around to look at her and smiled. He was a big man with a thick neck and very short hair, the type of cut the army requires. "Focić, this is Maric."

"Welcome." He smiled again, then turned to face his desk. Before returning to his office, Maric noticed Mr. Grahovac smirk at Focić. In the mirror she saw Focić roll his eyes in response.

She could tell within ten minutes of starting this project that it would become tedious, but it was a job, and she needed it. When she left to go to lunch, she realized she had left her hanky in her jacket pocket so she went back in to retrieve it. She heard Mr. Grahovac and Focić laughing. "Have you ever seen such jug handles?" She had heard that one before from someone at the university. She knew they were talking about her ears. Fine! The more these men viewed her as ridiculous, the less they would be suspicious of her.

Early on in her job, a conversation she transcribed between Milošević and Tudjman was shocking, but she made sure her face didn't reveal her thoughts. Their conversation took place before the war even started. The two presidents were planning on partitioning Bosnia. It was agonizing for her to not be able to expose their deceit, but she had no means or opportunity of making a copy of the tape.

As weeks went by, she noticed people in the office were relaxing their guard. Finally, an opportunity came up. One early afternoon, she was left alone in the office for about fifteen minutes. She was prepared for such a moment. Recently, he had begun carrying a floppy disk in a pocket she had sewn to the inside front of her skirt. She quickly stuck the floppy in the processor's slot, went to the beginning of the document that she had been transcribing, and started making a copy. To her horror, the machine made a whirring sound. She opened the door to the hall so she could hear if someone was approaching. A few minutes went by before she did hear someone coming. She stopped the data recording, put the disk in her pocket, and was typing where she had left off when Focić walked in. He must have realized his mistake in leaving her alone. She kept her eyes down and concentrated. He probably didn't want to get into trouble with Grahovac, so he kept quiet about his blunder. For the next week or so she felt him watching her carefully.

Meanwhile, Maric continued arriving early to her job. She talked with Vesna whenever possible, until the office opened up. Vesna had lost her husband, only child, and home during the war. She became a refugee and slowly made her way to Zagreb where, by some miracle, she landed this job cleaning the state office building.

One day, Vesna said that her boss wanted the offices cleaned before people came to work. She was given a key to all the offices on the second floor. They expected her to come to work at 4:30 A.M. and clean about seven offices by 8:30. After 8:30, she was to clean all the bathrooms. The bathrooms had to be cleaned every day. There were six altogether, two for men and one for women, located at either end of the long halls on both floors.

"Maybe the day of the week you clean our office, I could come in early to catch up. Would that be all right?"

Vesna gave her a long, hard look. Maric knew she was on to her. Finally she said: "As long as you work while I'm in the office cleaning, because after I'm through cleaning your office, I have to lock the door."

That was their arrangement. Maric had to arrive after the doorman started letting people in the building at 7:30. But if she arrived that early, she would be conspicuous. So she and Vesna decided that Vesna would clean Grahovac's office on Tuesday between 8:00 and 8:30. Focić usually left the recorder and word processor on Grahovac's desk.

The next Tuesday, Maric arrived at 8:00 in the morning with both a floppy disk and a blank magnetic tape hidden in her pocket. She figured it would take a long time to copy the tape so she started on that right away. The tape she was in the process of transcribing was still in the tape recorder where she had stopped listening to it the day before. She estimated where the tape had stopped and then rewound it. She put in her blank tape on the recorder side and replayed the original tape. While that was recording, she slipped her blank floppy in the word processor and made of copy of what she had transcribed to that point. Recording on the floppy went fast, so she got the word processor back to Grahovac's desk. By 8:20, the tape recorder had finished making a copy. She fast forwarded the original tape to where she thought she had stopped it the previous day. With both tape and floppy inside her secret pocket, she quickly looked over the room to make sure everything was in place. She left the office to wait outside in the hall. Having locked both doors, Vesna walked down the hall on the way to the bathrooms. She didn't look back at her. In fact, from then on, they rarely spoke to one another.

Maric was nervous all day knowing the copies were on her, but she put the same serious look on her face and just carried on as usual, doing the transcription. Henceforth, she only made copies when she was close to the end of transcribing a tape. It meant that she went in early about once a month to make copies. After work on those days, she didn't go straight home to her aunt's house, but went back to her old school to say hi to friends and to use the school's equipment to make additional copies. All of these she hid at Aunt Alma's, under the mattress at the foot of her bed.

When the war had been over for a year, Maric tried to phone Majesira, but the number was not in service, so she mailed her a letter. She hoped that Majesira's old address was still valid. A week later she began checking the mail at Aunt Alma's daily. Three weeks went by before there was a reply. Majesira had a new phone number. She said the best time to call her was between 7:00 and 9:00 in the evening.

Maric used a pay phone outside a chemist's shop two blocks away. She told Majesira about parts of the incriminating evidence she had acquired against Tudjman, Milošević, and some others. She asked her if she knew anything about a place named Maller. "I think it may be somewhere they are hiding war criminals."

"I'll work on finding out where and what it is. I'll also try to come up with a plan as to how we can get your evidence to The Hague. I think you should stay put, so no one gets suspicious of you. When do you think you'll be finished with the transcription?"

"I'm up to the end of 1994. Of course I don't know for sure, but I think I could have four more months of work, maybe less."

"Have they started to talk about what kind of work they will have you do after the transcription is finished?"

"No."

"I see. You must be very careful. I think we should have an exit plan in place *before* the work is over. I know phone calls are expensive, but could you call me a month before you think you'll be finished?"

"Yes, sure. How's Leni?"

"I haven't heard for several months, but I think she is fine. They have started to rebuild the bridge here. International money has flooded in to get it done."

"That's wonderful."

"Also we have received many testimonies now. Several include incriminating evidence against some of the villains. We're getting there. Your work, Maric, is groundbreaking…"

CR

A couple of months later, Maric thought she was working on the final tape, as the events she was transcribing were leading up to the Dayton Peace Accords. The three presidents, Tudjman, Milošević, and Izetbegović (the President of Bosnia) would soon be going to Ohio.

One day, Focić gave her a piece of fancy chocolate wrapped in gold-colored foil. He just came over and put it on her table and smiled at her. She noticed that he did it when Grahovac was not in his office and the others weren't looking. She thought the smile had been genuine, with no suggestion of sarcasm. She smiled back and thanked him. He said nothing but looked down while he returned to his desk.

The following Tuesday, Maric was making her final copies. She had just slipped the magnetic tape next to the floppy in her secret pocket when she heard a piercing scream coming from the hall. She quickly put the tape recorder back and rushed out of Grahovac's office, then ran from the outer office into the hall. There was Grahovac himself rushing along with other people toward the banister, where Vesna was leaning over the top of the stairwell peering down. "Did you see him? Where has he gone? Did he fall?" Vesna cried hysterically.

Maric realized Vesna was creating a diversion, so she quickly headed for the bathroom at the end of the hall. Partway there, she reversed her direction and hastened back toward the stairwell like the others, hoping it would appear that she had just come from the bathroom and was rushing to join the others gathered there.

Vesna finally calmed down and explained that for over a week she had seen a man "standing just here early in the morning, once leaning over quite far. I saw him again this morning. It was when I got ready to close and lock an office door that I realized he had disappeared. I'm sorry, but I've been worried about him. I don't see how he could have disappeared so quickly." She looked around quizzically at each of the other office workers. "Did any of you see him?" None had.

People kept asking Vesna what the man looked like, his name, where in the building he worked. She described his appearance but didn't know the answers to their other questions. She finally quieted down. One of the building officials questioned her, noting down her answers. By then, the onlookers went into their offices to start their day's work.

Maric realized how close she had been to getting caught, and was very grateful for Vesna's daring ingenuity. The women avoided eye contact with each other. Maric went into the office, sat down at her table and waited to be brought the word processor. Mr. Grahovac hardly looked at her, but she was still on edge the rest of the morning.

After lunch, Mr. Grahovac asked Maric to come into his office. She was certain he had figured out what had happened that morning. She tried to look calm, but she was close to trembling.

"Maric, we're pleased with your work transcribing. You have done a wonderful job, taking no time off and working diligently every day. We are looking for other work that you could do for us, now that this project is finishing. We thought we would give you a little treat. A friend of mine has a ticket to *Nabucco*. Do you know what that is, *Nabucco*?"

"No."

"Have you ever been to the opera before?"

"No." She tried to look excited.

"Well, *Nabucco* is an opera by Verdi, and it is being performed in Ljubljana's opera house this Saturday night. If you would like to go, we will pay for your trip to Ljubljana: bus fare, hotel room, dinner, and opera ticket. No one else here can go, so we thought of you and wanted to give this opportunity to you as a way of saying thanks for your good work."

Naturally, she was suspicious, but she tried to look starry-eyed with appreciation. For the rest of the day she was nervous and worried, but tried to put on a calm façade. When she left the office to go home, she made a detour to the library where, over the past year, she had found she could use both a computer and a tape recorder to make copies of what she was carrying in her secret pocket. Many months ago, while at the library, she had set up a Yahoo account so she could email herself the updated information from the floppy.

On her way home, she stopped off at the chemist to phone Majesira to make plans for the weekend.

"While you're in Ljubljana, I am going to see if I can find someone reliable who will take your tapes to The Hague."

"How can you do that?"

"I am going to try to contact the prosecutor's office in The Hague to see if they will send an investigator to see you at your hotel. What hotel will you be staying at?"

"I don't know yet. I'll call you as soon as I do."

CHAPTER 4

APRIL 15, 1997

Dinko had never been to Slovenia before. He was born on a farm outside of a small town in a section of Croatia known as Dalmatia. It was only when he became a soldier in the Yugoslav Army (JNA) that he got to see other parts of Croatia and a bit of Serbia. When Tudjman became president, Dinko became his proud and loyal supporter. During a series of skirmishes in which Croatian Serbs defied the president's leadership, Dinko performed as a sharpshooter and took out some critical opposition leaders. Tudjman must have heard of his successes. From then on, he was given some vital and secretive assignments. Dinko always hoped to be able to join Tudjman's security team, but the president explained how he had a much greater need for him in these clandestine missions.

He was on such a mission at this very moment. His job was to take out a Croatian traitor while she was in Slovenia. He withdrew three photos from the pocket of his black trench coat to scan the woman's features once again. He sheltered them with his other hand so they wouldn't get spotted by the light rain falling. What an ugly bitch! With ears like those, how could he miss?

He was partially hidden behind a potted bush at the door to the restaurant. People who looked like tourists had already gone inside, but none, so far, looked like Maric. He had been well prepped—she would be staying at the Central Hotel, attend the opera, and if it was raining, she would be wearing a turquoise blue anorak. Five minutes later, the rain had picked up when he saw another bunch of people walking toward him from the direction of the hotel. As they got close enough, he could see a bright blue anorak among the crowd. The hood was up so he couldn't see her ears, but it had to be her.

He thought it would be too risky to go into the restaurant to get a better look. He would head over to the opera house and wait for her there. He had already decided the best opportunity to kill her would be late that night as she walked back to her hotel after the opera.

A family of four was approaching him as he walked off. The two children were laughing, trying not to step on the cracks in the sidewalk. Suddenly the little boy fell. The father immediately stooped to help his son up. He examined his son's scraped knee. The mother said something tender, kissed her index finger, and touched it gently near the child's wound. The lad's tears stopped and the family continued walking.

Dinko's memory stretched back to a similar incident in his own childhood. He had been younger than this boy. He remembered being afraid, and then he recalled the reason for his fear. His father boxed him on the ear for falling. That made his head hurt even worse than his knee, but he knew better than to cry. His father turned to his sister Kira and slapped her on the face, scolding her for not holding on to his hand. Kira didn't cry either. Mama said nothing.

These Slovenes obviously didn't know how to bring up children, he thought. His wife Salina understood. Nothing gets done properly without fear. Dinko himself never dared to say anything to his father until he was 16 and eligible for the army. A real man is a fighter, strong and merciless.

CHAPTER 5

Grahovac told Maric that she would be staying in the Central Hotel, wherever that was. She had never been to Ljubljana before. Imagine that! She was going to Slovenia's capital. The city was supposedly one of the gems of the Balkans. Like Zagreb, it was also located on the Sava River, but closer to the river's source.

Maric had never been to an opera. Mostar was too small to have an opera house. She did remember talk of an opera on tour in Bosnia, but she never saw it. She was looking forward to the evening ahead. Of course, there was more to the trip than *Nabucco*.

Majesira had arranged for her to pass on the evidence she had collected to an investigator from The Hague. She was to take the tapes and floppy disks to Ljubljana, and sometime on Sunday morning, the investigator from the prosecutor's office would meet her at the hotel. Carrying the evidence with her all that time made her nervous, but she planned never to let it out of her sight. That meant carrying her backpack to the opera.

"Do you still have that turquoise blue rain jacket?" Majesira asked. "I remember you wore it all the time in Sarajevo."

"Yes."

"It's supposed to rain this weekend. You should take it with you."

Maric took the two-hour bus trip to Ljubljana early Saturday morning so she would have a chance to see some of the city. The Central Hotel was on Miklosiceva 9. When she checked in there, the room wasn't ready, She had to tote her backpack, since she couldn't risk losing the tapes. It was fairly light anyway. She was glad she had worn her black woolen slacks, as it was a cold day. Majesira was right about the weather. It threatened to rain all day, so she also carried her anorak.

First, she would walk to the opera house. Using the map on the hotel's brochure, she could see it was only 6 or 7 blocks away in Miklošič Park. According to the brochure, there had been a statue of the Austro-Hungarian Emperor Franz Joseph there, but after World War I, it was replaced with one to honor the linguist Franc Miklošič, who was devoted to Slavic languages.

The opera house was pink and designed in the Neo-Renaissance style, probably built over a hundred years before. The brochure said cherubs and frescoes abounded inside. I'll see them tonight, she thought. For now, I'll take the time to admire the marble sculptures on the outside.

Maric next walked past the House of Parliament, known as The People's Assembly before Slovenia seceded from Yugoslavia. It was plain and stark, typical of architecture built in Communist times, but the entranceway took her by surprise. It was sur-rounded by sculptures of naked people of all ages, genders, and occupations. "How strange," was her first reaction, but then she realized that showing people without clothes equalizes them, suggesting the building's true purpose: to represent all the peo-ple. She praised Slovenia for allowing the sculptor to reach ahead of current convention.

From the parliament building, she made her way to the Sava River, only three blocks away. She believed that put her in the neighborhood known as Old Town. By that time, she was re-ally hungry. There were several cafes to choose from, but she had to watch her money, so she just had fish snacks, sitting out near Triple Bridge. She walked along the river until she got to Dinkon Bridge, which she crossed, making her way to the funicular that carried people up a steep hill, on top of which sat a castle. From that height, she could see the whole city. She hadn't had so much fun since her first days at the university. She enjoyed the view while having a late afternoon cup of coffee, before making her way down and back to the hotel. What she had seen of Ljubljana, she loved. The people seemed relaxed and friendly.

When Slovenia won its independence from Yugoslavia in 1991, it had to fight the Yugoslav army for only 10 days. Few people were killed and there was little destruction. Slovenes by-passed sustained suffering, ethnic cleansing, shellings, and geno-cide, all of which left deep scars on Bosnia. She herself escaped such horrendous experiences by living with her aunt in Zagreb. But for Croatians who lived in Krajina, and Bosnians, especially Bosniaks, the wars were devastating.

She had to make sure to get back to the hotel in plenty of time to get ready for dinner, but a heavy cloudburst slowed her walk back. When she asked for her key, the clerk handed her a note informing her to meet the Elderhostel tour down in the lobby at 6:00 sharp. The guide would have her ticket for the op-era, walk everybody to the restaurant, and then on to the opera.

It was already 5:50! She rushed up to her room. She de-cided to keep on her sensible slacks. Anyway, there wasn't time to change clothes. She emptied her backpack of most of her belong-ings to lighten her load. The tapes and floppy disks she left in the inside zippered pocket. She brushed her teeth and combed out her hair from its bun. Then she threw her soaking wet an-orak over her arm, making sure the hotel key was in its pocket, grabbed her backpack, and proceeded down to the lobby.

She was only a few minutes late, and saw a group of twenty or so people, some of whom had red and white Elderhostel tags on their coats, walking out the door. Most were elderly Americans and were smartly dressed, but she didn't care. She no-ticed a middle-aged woman in the group who was just as casually dressed as she was, and had a turquoise anorak on similar to her own, which made her feel more at ease. Maric tried to catch a glimpse of her face, but never had the chance.

As she hurried to catch up to the group, a small woman

lagged behind, struggling to open her umbrella to ward off the rain. Maric stopped to help her, and managed to open it. The woman was grateful, and insisted that Maric walk under it with her. The restaurant was no more than three blocks away. Appreciating the warm cozy atmosphere inside, everyone hung their rain gear on hooks by the entrance, hoping it would dry before they had to leave to walk to the opera.

They were seated at two big tables. Dinner was lovely. The people around Maric were friendly. Once they found out where she was from, they had questions. "Was she happy with the Dayton Peace Accords?" No, she wasn't, but how to explain that briefly over a dinner? So she just answered that she was glad the war was over. They asked if she had lost anyone during the war. She spoiled their good spirits when she answered that question. The tour had recently been to Bosnia, but the country was still so war-torn that they only stayed two nights.

It was still raining as they left the restaurant. Maric walked with an elderly couple, Mr. and Mrs. Childs from Savannah, Georgia. She loved listening to their accent. They walked very slowly so the three of them lagged far behind the others. By the time they entered the opera house, the others weren't in sight. Maric took off her wet anorak, wrapped it inside out, and put it in her backpack.

The Childs showed their tickets to the usher, when Maric spotted her friend, Tara Sultalo, whom she had known at the University of Sarajevo. She excused herself from the Childs and went over to greet Tara with a big hug. It had been five years since they took history classes together. They had so much to catch up on that Tara suggested they sit together.

Tara was from a well-off Slovene family and was used to attending the opera. She led Maric up to the balcony where she had a seat. A middle-aged man was in the seat next to hers. Tara just asked him if he would exchange seats with her friend, whom she hadn't seen in five years. The man graciously obliged.

Tara said the oval-shaped opera chamber held about 500

people. They were seated in the upper balcony, but by looking down, Maric could recognize some of the people she had dinner with. They were all seated in the same row of the orchestra section.

Maric asked Tara if she could look through her opera glasses. It was fun to see what people looked like at close range without their knowing it. There was a tall, bald-headed man standing to the side at the front of the theater. He was also looking through opera glasses at the audience. His black clothes matched his bushy chinstrap beard. Maric handed the opera glasses back to Tara as the performance began.

Tara was excited to hear the performance. All the singers were Slovenian. Maric could understand Tara quite well. Slovene and Croatian are similar languages, both Slavic. Tara helped by speaking slowly with precise diction. When Maric realized that the opera would be sung in Italian, she quickly read the plot synopsis.

Maric's favorite part was when the Hebrew slaves sang *Va piensiero,* longing for their homeland. During intermission, Tara told her: "When Verdi's opera was first performed here, Slovenia was occupied by the Austro-Hungarians, who forbade encores of the hymn, afraid of arousing public protests for Slovene nationhood."

After the opera was over, Tara suggested having a glass of wine at the Grand Hotel, which was fairly close to Maric's hotel. It had stopped raining, so Maric didn't bother to put on her rain jacket.

Tara had left the University of Sarajevo at the same time as Maric and for the same reason—the siege—but she was able to continue her studies at the university in Ljubljana. For the last several years, she had been working for the local history museum as an archivist, and occasionally leading city tours for tourists. Maric tried not to be envious. Tara seemed genuinely impressed that Maric worked for the president of Croatia, although Maric couldn't elaborate on the nature of the job and expressed little enthusiasm for it.

About an hour later, they made their way back to the Central Hotel. Tara left Maric a couple of blocks before the hotel, making sure she knew where to go. The two women hugged goodbye, not sure when they would see each other again.

As Maric approached the hotel, she noticed police cars on the other side of the entrance. Several people were gathered halfway down the block. She went up to them to see what they were looking at and saw a crumpled body on the sidewalk. The police were about to cover it, but Maric was able to catch a glimpse of a blue anorak. Her heart started racing. A fellow on-looker told Maric that a woman had been murdered.

"How dreadful," Maric was gasping for breath.

"Shot twice and nobody heard it."

Maric was almost paralyzed, not knowing what to do. After ten minutes of standing around with the others, she went into the hotel and barely caught the elevator that was going up. She planned to lock her door as soon as she got in her room and then close the curtains, which was silly, as no one could see in a room on the 5th floor.

To her surprise, there were several people milling about on her floor. Most wore police uniforms. She knew her room was #538, but she had to check the numbers on the wall to be sure she was going in the right direction. She got fairly close when she realized that people were going in and out of that very room, #538. She stopped abruptly. Oh my God, they must think it was me who was murdered! She became breathless. A cold shudder rippled through her body. She didn't know what she should do, but instinct told her to get away. She turned around and went back to the elevator.

She didn't want to be noticed. She needed time to think. Why would they think it was her? Then she remembered glimpsing the blue rain jacket. Was it that woman? Was she wearing her jacket? Maric frantically pulled the anorak out of her backpack. In an outside pocket she found a hotel key and a letter addressed to: "Brenda Hines at the Central Hotel, Miklosiceva 9, Ljubljana,

Slovenia." Down in the lower left corner of the envelope was written: "Please hold for arrival." Oh my God, we must have switched jackets when we left the restaurant! For some reason Maric felt overcome with guilt. She hadn't even seen the other woman's face. Finally, common sense took over. Maric hadn't caused her to be killed, but did they want to kill Brenda Hines or her? It was obvious. Maric started sweating and shaking. Someone had meant to kill her but killed someone else by mistake. She didn't have to think long about why anyone would want to kill her. She knew they didn't want her to remember what she had transcribed. When working in Tudjman's office, she had been so careful not to show her disgust. How could she have been so naive! Of course they had to get rid of her.

What should she do? It would soon be discovered that the woman was not her. She had to get out of the hotel. She couldn't go to her room. The murderer may be in the lobby. She had the woman's name and the key to her room, #417. She pressed the "down" button to call the elevator.

When the doors opened, two policemen stepped out and hardly looked at her, hurrying past down the hallway. She stepped into the elevator and descended to the fourth floor. What if this Brenda has a companion? She would have to chance it. What else could she do? When she unlocked the door, she was relieved to find no one in the room. It appeared that Brenda was traveling alone. A medium-sized suitcase was on the luggage stand. It did not have an Elderhostel tag on it. Wasn't this woman on the tour? Had she accidentally switched jackets with someone who was not on the tour, but was at the restaurant and also went to the opera? What were the chances of that?

It was then that Maric realized that the suitcase was locked—with a flimsy little padlock, but locked none the less. How could she open it? She looked for some implement in the desk drawer and then in the bathroom. She tried a bobby pin, then a nail file from the woman's toilet kit, but to no avail. She was sure a man could just pull it off or smash it open. She noticed the shower curtain in the bathroom was hung on hooks. She took one off and tried one end in the lock. She couldn't even get it into the hole, but when she inserted the other end, it turned something inside and the lock opened. She was becoming a shameless criminal. Once they realized they'd killed the wrong person, though, they'd come after her again. She was desperate.

After a minute of poking around in the suitcase she found Brenda's passport. She was an American. According to her birth-date, she was seven years older than Maric, but her picture had probably been taken many years ago. With her hair down, Maric thought she could pass for her. Brenda's wallet was in the suitcase as well. Why hadn't she taken it with her to dinner and the opera? Maybe she didn't need it. Probably, everything had already been paid for. It contained 13,500 Tolars, which could be really useful to her. Searching the suitcase further, Maric found $1,000 dollars in traveler's checks. Why was the woman carrying so much money? She also found some airline tickets. Maric didn't take the time to look at them carefully, other than to note that they were for a flight that left Trieste, Italy, in four days time.

She transferred Brenda's passport, wallet, airline tickets, and traveler's checks to her backpack. Brenda must not have carried a purse or the police would have known the identity of the dead body. Maric remembered the letter she found in the anorak pocket, but couldn't take the time to read it. She had to get out of the hotel!

Every one of Brenda's belongings that she found in the room she put in the suitcase, including the padlock. The case was easily zipped shut. Brenda traveled lightly, thank goodness. Should Maric just leave the hotel? That might make the police realize that there was some connection between Brenda Hines and herself. This idea scared her, but Maric was quickly becoming used to doing scary things. She had all the identification she needed. She left 100 Tolars on the night stand for the maid and proceeded to the lobby to check out. Her suitcase had rollers that squeaked, but she pretended not to mind.

"Yes, I would like to check out," she said in English to the man at the desk.

"Really! Is anything wrong?"

Maric smiled, looked him straight in the eye, and tried to assure him that everything was fine, but that she had just had a sudden change in plans.

"I see Madam, but I'm afraid we have to charge you for the room."

"Yes, of course, I was expecting that."

"Very well!" While he prepared the bill, she wanted to look around to see who was in the lobby, but she didn't dare. She just hoped no one noticed her. The moment of truth came when she had to sign a traveler's check. She had barely had the chance to look at Brenda's signature, but remembered her writing had slanted to the left and her middle initial was "W." Maric signed it quickly, and while handing the clerk the check asked him how she might make a local telephone call, and if there was a telephone book she could use? She hoped her questions would keep him from scrutinizing the signature.

He directed her to an alcove at the side of the reception desk. "Just dial nine to get an outside line. If it's not local, your call will not go through," he replied.

She found the number for a taxi company and ordered a cab to take her to the bus terminal.

❧

The bus to Trieste didn't leave until 7:00 A.M. Maric bought a ticket and asked which gate the bus would leave from.

"Number seven, it always leaves from number seven."

"I see, but…the bus in gate seven says Ljubljana."

"Yes, our driver's gone home to get a good night's rest. He'll change the sign when he comes back in the morning."

She needed a place to hide in case "they" came looking for her. She knew only the people in Mr. Grahovac's office. Would it be one of them? No, Tudjman might send anyone to kill her, she decided. She went out to gate seven and inspected the bus. The bus or its storage area might be a good place to hide until morning, she thought, but both were locked. Twenty minutes later another bus rolled in. Passengers filed out. The bus driver opened the baggage bay. She walked up to him and asked when his bus was leaving next.

"6:40 A.M. sharp, going to Zagreb, but there will be another at 12:00."

"Thanks." When he was through taking out the luggage and busy talking to someone, she crawled in with her suitcase and backpack. She moved to the furthest corner and prayed that he wouldn't look in again. He didn't. He swung the door down and locked it. She was in there for the night and it was pitch black and already cold. She would have no idea when morning came, as no daylight could seep in. She used her backpack as a pillow, and by groping around she found a canvas tarp to put over her. Emotionally drained and physically exhausted, she was finally able to sleep.

She awoke hearing some commotion outside and peeped out from under the canvas. The luggage compartment was open. The driver had his back to her and started walking away, so she crawled out and had just lifted her suitcase out when she heard "Hey, no, no, no. I load bags on to the bus. Just wait over there." She waited where he told her to go, but stood behind a pillar.

A few minutes later, she stole a look around the pillar and saw the bus driver talking to a man. Oh my God! It was the same man she had seen at the opera: tall, bald, and with a thick chin-strap beard. That was too much of a coincidence.

She immediately ducked behind the pillar again and held her breath. Minutes later, she heard more people. She figured they were getting on the Zagreb bus. Finally, that bus started up. In the distance, she saw another bus driver coming. He seemed to be walking toward platform seven. He unlocked that bus' luggage compartment. When she had the courage to look again for the bearded man, she was alarmed to see him walking by the pillar on its other side. He appeared to be walking toward the Trieste bus driver. When she peeked again, she saw him showing a photo to the bus driver. Her heart sunk. His footsteps approached her pillar. Oh no! This is it, she thought, holding her breath again and closing her eyes, but he just walked by.

She waited a full minute before she dared to even move. Finally peeking around the pillar on the other side, she saw the man pull open the glass doors to enter the bus station. She started breathing normally again and gathered the courage to look around the opposite side. The new driver boarded the bus for Trieste. He was followed by a man carrying a broom and trash bag. He must be a cleaner, she thought. Knowing the cleaner would make noise, she hurried over, put her suitcase in, and climbed into the luggage compartment. She hid in the corner, as she had done on the previous bus. Ten minutes later, other suitcases and boxes were thrown in. Finally the bus took off. She knew the first stop would be the Trieste airport. If she could just get off the bus there undetected, she'd be safe. Or would she? Would she ever feel safe again?

CHAPTER 6

ZAGREB, CROATIA

Oz didn't always pay close attention when his parents discussed their next hike. He remembered them commenting that Slovenia's Julian Alps were not as high as the mountains in Croatia. But in the late spring of 1985, Oz was twenty-one and in his third year at the University of Zagreb. The politics of the day and young women were what captured his attention. The night before Boma and Fabela left, they insisted on talking their plans over with Oz. "We're doing a ridge walk starting in Bohinj and ending at Triglar. It will be a two-day trek covering over 80 kilometers with a height gain of only 1,400 meters."

"Sounds challenging," Oz said, trying to appear enthusiastic. He was confident of their skills. They often hiked difficult trails.

"It offers 360° views." Demonstrating by rotating his hand clockwise, Boma said, "The Adriatic Sea on the west, Triglav to the north, then Bohinj Basin, and finally the wooded hills of Primorska."

Fabela, his mother, unfolded the map and pointed to each of the places. "Now that it's late May, the meadows should be awash with wild flowers."

"What about the weather conditions?" Oz asked.

"They're warning that the snow above 2,000 meters is hard and very slippery," his dad answered.

Oz wasn't concerned because his parents were always sensible. It was the views and physical exertion that pleased them.

Taking risks was unnecessary for them to enjoy a trek. The next morning, Oz said goodbye, wishing them a fun adventure. By mid-morning, he was deeply involved with his own activities.

But when they were a day late returning home, he feared something had gone wrong. He called Slovenia's Mountain Rescue office.

"Yes, we were about to call the number they left with us. They should have been back at Triglar two days ago," a young Slovene voice said. "Sometimes people forget to sign out. We'll check at Dom Zorka Jelincica, the hut at the summit where they were planning to spend the night..."

Within hours, their mangled bodies were found, air-lifted, and taken into the rescue center. They were on gurneys with sheets over them when Oz arrived. It was thought that somehow they slipped on a snow patch and fell off the edge of the cliff, hitting a rocky ledge.

Years later, Oz wondered if the afternoon shower on their second day of hiking had made the snow like ice. Oz was sure their deaths were immediate. He could visualize Tata grabbing Mama's hand to stop her, but then not being able to stop himself from sliding.

Oz still remembered every detail of that terrible day.

"How did your parents get here?" he remembered Edi asking him.

In his rush to drive to Triglar, Oz had forgotten about needing to pick up his parents' car. The man who asked this question was tall and blond, around his own age. He introduced himself as Edi Juric. Over the next hour, while Oz was informed that his parents' bodies would be taken to Zagreb's morgue, Edi stood by him and quietly explained other aspects of the process. "This service is free, you know. We are all volunteers here. The helicopter, ambulance: it's all free."

The amazing assistance didn't stop there. Later, Edi offered to drive Oz's parents' car to Zagreb, saying that he could get back to Slovenia in the ambulance. It turned out that Edi was a recent graduate of Zagreb University, where Oz was in school.

Oz's mourning went on for months. Coming home to an empty house was particularly hard. He sometimes collapsed in his father's arm chair and sobbed. While he was in classes, his thoughts were distracted, but at home he had time to savor memories. How could two such kind and loving people be gone forever, so quickly? This difficult period also had its blessings: his new friendship with Edi, and the support of his American relatives, Aunt Vera and Uncle Tom.

Aunt Vera was his mother's sister. Immediately following his parents' accident, she and Uncle Tom caught a flight to Zagreb. They stayed to help Oz get adjusted. Tom couldn't leave his engineering firm for long, but Vera stayed on for three weeks. From then on, Oz and Vera corresponded weekly. She and Tom also paid for Oz to travel to Portland once a year.

That first year after his parents died, Edi called several times to see how Oz was doing. The two capital cities, Zagreb and Ljubljana, were an hour-and-a-half drive apart. Occasionally, they met at a trail head so they could hike a mountain together. Oz wanted to see where his parents had fallen, but Edi told him that particular trail was too difficult for a novice.

Oz was left with a nice house and enough money to finish university, but his life seemed empty. The three-bedroom home echoed his loneliness with every step on its wooden floors. So many items in the house reminded Oz of wonderful moments he had with his parents. Reminders, although cherished, were also burdensome. Living in the family home, he couldn't escape the source of his unhappiness.

He found the social scene at the university somewhat diverting. He managed to kiss a few girls at drunken parties. When he tried to follow up by asking for a date, they usually turned him down. His face was partially to blame. It was covered with pock marks from a long bout of acne as a teenager. His chin didn't protrude. If clean shaven, it made him look weak and indecisive. He finally realized that a beard would take care of both problems. It came in very dark. He learned to trim it, keeping the chin hairs longer. That did the trick. Although still a virgin at age 22, he felt he now had more of a chance with women.

ℂℛ

Not wanting to continue depleting his inheritance, Oz decided to take a part-time job in the evenings while he was finishing his fourth year of university. He became a cook's assistant at Cantinetta, a large restaurant off of Central Square. Besides his daily chores of washing and chopping vegetables, he was in charge of keeping the supplies stocked. On Mondays, he was sent out to buy whatever dry goods the restaurant needed.

About the fourth week of working there, the cook laid into him, telling him he wasn't doing his job right. "Last weekend we ran out of vermicelini, canalini, and tomato sauce. Tonight I found there was only one package of manicotti and two of penne left and not one single jar of Acciughe. Oz, all you have to do is top up the supply of pastas and sauces that I have listed on the bulletin board. You're a university kid. Is that too hard for you? I don't think so. Are you taking some of these things home with you?"

"Absolutely not!"

"If it happens one more time, you're fired."

"When did you notice things missing?"

"What do you mean? When I needed them was when I noticed."

"I replenish the supplies on Monday. Does it happen Monday?"

"No. no, it is later in the week, just when we're busiest."

Oz was puzzled, but had some ideas. There was no sign of a break-in, so it was probably someone who worked for the restaurant. Extra staff were hired for the weekends: an extra waitress, Fiona, and a busboy, Aldo. Perhaps one of them doesn't go home until after everyone leaves. Aldo was a rough-looking young kid, who probably hadn't gone to high school. He was relaxed and joked a lot. Fiona, a woman in her late thirties, was quiet, petite, and appeared nervous. The following Friday, Oz noticed she carried a shopping bag and hung it on a hook with her coat on top. That evening, when Oz had a break, he went by the coat rack and felt the bag under her coat. It seemed empty. By the time she was ready to go home, the shops would be closed, so why the bag?

Near closing time, Oz made sure he was ready to go out the door. When Fiona left, he followed and noticed her shopping bag definitely had some heft to it. He caught up to her and took her bag, saying: "Here let me help. I'm going your way." She resisted vehemently. Oz felt there was much weight in it.

"What are you doing?"

Oz forced the bag open and saw a can of marinara sauce, bread sticks, and spaghetti noodles. Fiona started crying.

"Please, don't tell the boss, Oz. I have four kids and they're so hungry. I thought the restaurant wouldn't miss this little bit of food."

"The boss has to know, Fiona, and it's best if you tell him yourself." She started to make a run for it, but Oz caught her arm and walked her back to the restaurant. Fiona lost her job. He felt sorry for her, but her dishonesty jeopardized his own job. He thought about checking up on her family life to see if she really needed help, but he got distracted by the new hostess that the restaurant hired. She was pretty. Her name was Jelena. To his surprise, Jelena used every opportunity to talk to him, giving him flirtatious looks that even the cook noticed. He didn't ask her out, but kept wishing he could find the courage. Two months later she came to work with a suitcase. At closing time she whimpered that her boyfriend had thrown her out and she had no place to go. Oz offered a room in his house, on a temporary basis.

He didn't have sexual designs on Jelena, he just wanted to help her, but he quickly discovered that she was willing, even eager, to become intimate. Now he had oodles of opportunity. During the day he went to classes and the library. They saw each other at the restaurant, had a quick meal, worked, and then went home to make love. Three months later, she proposed that they get married. They could go to her village outside of Belgrade to have the double-crown ceremony, common among the Orthodox. Oz imagined her relatives discharging firearms as was the custom at Serb weddings. He was in shock and had to tell her that he wasn't ready to marry. Oz realized that he loved the love-making, but not her. He was ashamed and embarrassed that he had led her on.

"Is it because I'm Serbian?" she asked.

"No, of course not."

"Because I'm Orthodox, then?"

"No!"

Those were the only two reasons she came up with. He didn't want to be so blunt as to say that he wasn't in love with her. Had she not realized this could be the real reason? The next weekend, Jelena wanted to visit an old friend, so Oz and Edi went hiking. He didn't miss her at all, in fact he felt liberated. Over the next two months Jelena asked him for the money to buy a dress, then earrings, shoes, and a sweater. It finally dawned on Oz that he had never seen her in any of these new clothes. She could have worn them to hostess, but she didn't. He asked her to leave.

When Jelena moved out, Oz rented out most of the house to a young family. He shared the kitchen with them and kept one bedroom for himself. They were a nice enough family, but the house was never quiet and he was never alone. He felt restless again.

ଓ

In 1990, a year before the Yugoslav Wars began, Oz felt himself adrift without a compass. It had been six months since he split up with Jelena. Now, he had just finished his degree at the university, but he didn't know which way he should direct his life. Staying at home was no fun. The house was usually noisy, and the only privacy he had was when he was in his bedroom with the door shut. He was still working part-time at the restaurant. That took up four hours in the evening, but he was sure he didn't want a career working in a restaurant. He didn't know where to look for a serious job, because he couldn't make up his mind about what he wanted to do.

He worked on his English during daylight hours. At the library he would read books on English grammar and make lists of vocabulary words he tried to master. When he tired of that, he'd wander over to his favorite bookstore, carrying his little notebook and his Croatian/English dictionary. The store had a fairly good selection of books in English, some for children and many more for adults. A step stool in the back of the store served his purposes. He could sit there for a few hours, surreptitiously reading books, avoiding the eyes of clerks. Occasionally he bought a book, but usually he pretended the book he had been reading was not right for him, after all. He returned it to the shelf and walked out, not proud of himself.

He was a week into reading *The Mysterious West* by Tony Hillerman. He had to look up so many words that he only read about eight pages a day. His dictionary was inadequate. 'English' meant 'British English.' There were no translations for words like *crowbait*. His aunt wrote him later and told him it meant *an old horse*. Another expression was *to dry gulch*. That one took even Aunt Vera a couple of weeks to find out. "Evidently, it means *to ambush*," she wrote. Oz was enjoying this book and didn't want to give it up, so when he got the proprietor's evil eye, he decided to buy it. He was in the process of paying the clerk when he saw Edi leave the store and walk away.

What was Edi doing in Zagreb? Why hadn't he said he was coming? The clerk took his time, so that when Oz was free to leave the store, Edi was nowhere in sight. It was then that Oz realized that Edi had been wearing army fatigues.

In 1990, Yugoslavia was still a Communist country and still composed of six 'republics.' They were republics in the sense that the 'Socialist Republics of the Soviet Union' were republics. Aunt Vera told him that all of Yugoslavia was the size of Oregon, so each republic was very small. Seeing Edi in uniform got Oz thinking about enlisting. He thought that the Yugoslav army (JNA) might be interesting because its soldiers came from every republic. All spoke Serbo-Croat, with slight variations. "It would be a way to get to know people from the far reaches of Yugoslavia," he told his aunt and uncle on the phone. Oz could hear his uncle Tom snicker. When they called him, they used both of their phones so they could have a three-way conversation.

Oz had been told that military service would make a man out of him. The general feeling in Yugoslavia was that army service was like a rite of passage. Oz decided to join the army.

He was ready for a passage, as long as it didn't include combat. Once in the army however, combat is what they trained him for. Oz appeared to be a pushover. He was unusually thin, his shoulders were narrow, and his posture was slightly hunched. Fellow soldiers were surprised to discover that he was actually agile, strong, and fast. The other soldiers started calling him Žica, meaning wire or bean, like a string bean. He didn't take offense. Derisive though the name seemed, he knew it also carried affection.

When it was time to be assigned to a regiment, Oz spoke up for the job as an assistant cook. He became doubly lucky: he had restaurant experience and superiors took one look at him and thought he wouldn't be good as a soldier, so they went along with Oz's request, thinking they had "better get some use out of him."

Soon after becoming a cook's assistant, Oz found himself lucky again: Edi was in his regiment. The two would see each other when Edi was in the cafeteria line and they exchanged friendly banter. Sometimes, in the evening, they could talk privately, swapping subversive remarks about the army and discussing their nervousness about current politics.

Yugoslavia had been a Communist country for close to 45

years. When its long-time dictator, Tito, died in 1980, the government teetered and tensions surfaced. Unable to use Communism
to secure their power, new leaders spurred their people to nationalistic aspirations. One-third of the Serbs at that time lived
outside of Serbia. Trouble was brewing and everybody knew it.

It first came in 1991, when Slovenia proclaimed its independence. Yugoslavia's central government in Belgrade didn't
want Slovenia to secede. It ordered Yugoslav soldiers to cross
into Slovenia to put down the rebellion. Oz was pulled out of the
kitchen to be sent on this mission. He found himself next to Edi,
and both were expected to fire at the Slovene National Guard.
The two friends agreed to fire well over the heads of the Slovene
guardsmen. Fortunately, this awkward situation came to an end
before their defiance was discovered. It took only ten days for
Slovenia to become an independent country. Edi was ecstatic. He
no longer had to fight. He could leave the JNA and return home
to Slovenia as a civilian. Oz was ecstatic for Edi and Slovenia, but
his problems weren't over.

The same day that the Slovenes claimed independence, the
Croat Assembly passed a resolution to secede from Yugoslavia.
Croatian Serbs, however, did not want to come out from under
Yugoslavia's umbrella. When Serbia and the JNA supported the
breakaway Republic of Krajina, Oz decided it would be an excellent time to leave the army. His term was up. Once again, his
superiors took a look at him and thought he wouldn't be of much
use anyway, so they let him go.

Oz settled back in his house, or one room of his house,
and applied for a job at Zagreb's Police Department. Croatia was
fully engaged in the war with Yugoslavia, Serbia, and its own
breakaway state of Krajina. Several policemen had left the force
so they could join the Croatian army, leaving vacancies just at the
time that Oz applied.

Oz was hired. As a novice, he was given menial tasks for
over a year. He was impressed with the chief, Ivanovich, and how
he handled his staff without showing favoritism. During his pro-

bationary stint, Oz could study the different personalities of his fellow 'men in blue.'

Eventually he was promoted to work under Captain Calich in the homicide department. That was exactly what he wanted. His aim was to become a detective. However, Oz soon found the captain to be lazy, careless, and possessing a mean streak.

During the investigation of a drowning in the Sava River, the captain wanted to label the death as suicide, but Oz made a scrupulous examination of the man's clothes and found what appeared to be a small cleaning stub stuck in the pocket of the man's suit. Furthermore, in spite of being water logged and muddy, the suit was obviously well made and stylishly tailored. The man had dressed with care. Oz took it upon himself to locate the cleaners in question. The proprietor was shocked to hear that Mr. Trobich had possibly committed suicide. The gentleman had picked up the suit in the morning of his suicide and remarked how bright and sunny the day promised to be. "He was smiling as he left."

When Oz returned to the police station, Captain Calich had left for the day and would not be in to work on the following day as well. A note was left on Oz's desk to write up the report of the suicide and hand it in. Oz didn't know what to do, so he went to the deputy chief. When he walked into his office the chief himself was also present. Oz briefed them and asked if he could continue the investigation, as it did not appear to be a suicide. They gave Oz the go-ahead.

By Monday morning, Oz had found the murderer and the police were about to arrest him. When Captain Calich walked into the station, he was furious, called the arrest off, and was in the process of firing Oz when the deputy chief intervened. Within a few days, Captain Calich was demoted and switched to another division. By 1995, Oz became a detective, the job he had wanted.

CHAPTER 7

PORTLAND, OREGON

Vera and her sister, Fabela, had grown up in Split, a prosperous city on the Dalmatian coast. It was the second largest city in Croatia, one with a long history. Greeks, Romans, Byzantines, Venetians, Austrians, and Italians all took turns ruling that area. Diocletian built a walled palace so large that today it is like a town within the city. Densely-packed, stone buildings with red tiled roofs open directly on the streets. Day and night, people were out walking.

For centuries, Split had been a sophisticated tourist destination. Growing up there, the sisters were exposed to a wide variety of Mediterranean people. Their father, a pharmacist, insisted that his girls get a liberal education. He was a man of strong opinions who liked to argue politics. Vera could recall his ranting against Croatia's Fascist regime for its cruelty against Serbs and Jews during the Second World War. He was determined to steer his daughters clear of the right-wing mold that many Croatians fell into. "Don't listen to people who tell you that Catholic Croatians are superior to Orthodox Serbs. That's nonsense!" he would say.

Both girls learned English. Fabela was five years younger and more athletic than Vera. However, Vera had their father's pluck. She was able to land a job in the tourist industry, where she met Tom, an engineering student from Portland, Oregon. Once she and Tom married and moved to Portland, Vera rarely saw Fabela, although they wrote each other monthly.

Tom and Vera had only one child—a girl named Emily.

Vera delighted in motherhood. From play groups, she and other mothers started their own preschool. Vera was a Brownie and then a Girl Scout leader of Emily's troops. It was only after Emily went to college in California that Vera had to deal with separation. Perhaps if she and Tom had had more children, or if she wasn't so far removed from her roots in Croatia, it would not have been such a problem to her. For the first time, she fully sympathized with what her parents had had to go through when she had moved to the States twenty years ago.

Tom was always fully engaged in his engineering work. He tried to discuss projects with her, but they were difficult for her to understand. When he became vice president of the firm, he took up amateur radio as a hobby. At that point, Emily was in her second year at college. He installed a ham radio in their third floor room, and asked Vera to keep him company when he went up there after dinner. "You can read your book while I work on the radio," he suggested. Vera went along with that. She wanted to be with him, especially since he was gone at work all day and Emily was no longer at home. Several times a week, they climbed up to the third floor together. Over time, he showed her how the radio worked, and Tom became fully licensed as a general class ham operator.

ларь

Emily was raped and murdered in her fourth year at UCLA—a month before her graduation. The guilty man was never identified. Vera wondered if the separation she felt during Emily's early college years was to prepare her for when it became permanent. At first, she did all she could to help the police. She interviewed Emily's friends. She even crashed some campus parties, just to get ideas of what to follow up on.

When it looked like the murder would never be solved, Vera knew she had to stay busy. She continued leading a Girl Scout troop, although the work became a strain. She found herself jealous and resentful of the other parents, whose complaints about their teenagers' antics seemed ungrateful. She decided to study, with Tom's help, for the lowest grade ham license. She eventually passed the exam. Two or three times a week she and Tom went on air.

After Fabela's fatal hiking accident, Vera became determined to keep in close contact with her sister's only child, Oz, through whatever means possible: letters, phone calls, and occasional visits, in spite of the great distance separating them. She and Tom were happy to pay for Oz's flights to Portland.

The sisters had not seen much of each other over the last thirty years. The passing of Fabela wasn't the devastating blow to Vera that Emily's death had been. Years later, she still had not fully recovered from losing her daughter. She would never say so, but oddly enough, her sister's tragedy was helping her. Now at least, Vera had an excuse to mother another child, not that Oz was a child, really.

She knew that Tom thought she used Oz for an 'Emily-substitute'. She wrote him weekly and traveled to Zagreb to visit him each year, in addition to his annual trips to Portland. It meant so much to get letters from Oz, even though it reminded her of getting letters from her daughter when she was away in college.

☙

There were days when Vera backtracked into mourning their daughter's death.

"It's been seven years, Vera. You've got to move on," Tom implored.

"If we just knew who killed her—why he picked her." Emily's body had been found among the trees surrounding a campus pond, a place she frequently went to walk. But the police were convinced that she had not been murdered or raped there. In the spring of her freshman year, Vera had strolled with Emily around that same pond. It was as if the murderer wanted to spoil that memory for Vera, as well.

Now that there was a war in Croatia and Bosnia, Vera noticed that Tom used it to divert her attention away from Emily. He kept suggesting that she try to contact her distant relatives.

"Why bother, the phone systems have been cut off."

"What about your cousin in Osijek? And don't you have your uncle Premil somewhere remote? I remember he came to our wedding."

She and Tom lived in a narrow three-story house set among cedars and oaks. Vera loved the trees. They offered much needed shade in the summer months, when the air was heavy with humidity, and they attracted many birds, which she enjoyed watching. All she could see while sitting on the patio most days were Stellar Jays and towhees. When she wanted to see other birds without craning her neck to look up, she climbed up to the third floor where she could sit on a wooden chair in front of a large window. She was more likely to spot them when eye-level with top branches. If she was lucky, she would spy shy birds, like MacGillivray's Warblers.

A year ago, Tom purchased their first telescope. He set it up on a tripod in front of that same third-floor window. In good weather, Tom would slide the upper part of the window down and rest one leg of the tripod up on the windowsill. That way, the scope could protrude slightly out the window, giving them an almost 180° field of view. They had a little black notebook in which they recorded the date and whatever they saw of interest.

At 9:00 one night, Vera was looking out the window through the telescope while Tom sat working with the ham radio. He became insistent that she send out a message requesting information about her relatives.

"You just want to look through the telescope," she teased him as she went over to the radio and sat down in front of it.

"Is this frequency in use?" Vera waited for a reply. There was none. She asked again, with the same result. She knew the frequency was hers, so she called: "CQ Europe, CQ Europe, this is Whiskey-Bravo-7-Hotel-Echo-Golf. Looking for Croatia or someone with a friend there. Seeking news about my relatives in war torn Croatia. WB7HEG calling CQ and listening."

Vera knew this was a long shot, but the band seemed open, and she had heard other EU calls coming in from Italy and Germany on it earlier. She was determined to keep trying and continued with the same approach: "CQ Europe, CQ Europe… seeking news about Croatia…WB7HEG listening." After about a dozen times, there was finally a weak but clear reply:

WB7HEG, please copy Oscar-Echo-2-Zulu-Delta, OE2ZD. Over.

Vera had already begun scanning her world map for an OE prefix, thinking aloud: "OE, OE, OE…a-ha, Austria, great!" Then she squeezed the mic and said: "OE2ZD, thanks for the reply. Name here is Vera, Vera in Portland, Oregon. I copy you fine. Good signal so far. I hope the band holds up. Over."

Very good, Vera, nice to meet you. The name is Hans, Hotel-Alpha-November-Sierra, Hans, near Graz in Austria. I heard you were looking for someone in Croatia. I have a ham friend there that I talk to regularly. I could pass your traffic to him if you like. Otherwise, how can I help you? Over.

My goodness, Vera thought, the generosity of ham operators always impressed her. "Thank you so much. I'm looking for any information about Edita Tomić who is from Osijek or Premil Jurić from Virovitica. My telephone number is 1-503-242-2401." She repeated the message slowly, just in case any fading took her out. "Thank you Hans. How copy? Over."

Dead silence greeted her on the return. "Rats, did I lose him? Did he get my message?" She waited a few more seconds then spoke into her mic: "OE2ZD, this is WB7HEG, are you still there? Over." This time he came back. What a relief!

Yes, yes, I'm here Vera. I think I got your message OK. The band is shifting so I don't know how much longer we can talk. I'll pass it along to my friend tomorrow when we speak. If you get a phone call, maybe you'll get some good news. I hope so. Best

of luck. I'll sign off for now. Nice to meet you. 73, Vera. This is
OE2ZD. Over.

"Thank you, Hans. 73, I hope we can talk again. This is
WB7HEG. Bye bye. Clear for now."

Being a ham was like belonging to a tribe. "73" was ham-
speak for "best regards."

She put down the microphone and turned toward Tom,
quite pleased with herself. "That was fun. Of course it will do
no good. No one will be able to call me. They can't afford it, and
even if they could, they'd never find a telephone that works."

"It doesn't hurt to try. You never know."

That night they received two crackly messages. One they
thought was in Russian and another was in some indeterminable
Asian language. The new system Tom had installed was much
more powerful than the old one.

On most nights after that, Vera and Tom climbed the stairs
to their third-floor room around 9:00 P.M. They took turns sitting either at the window or the radio. They often heard static,
but sometimes messages were broadcast from locals in Idaho,
Washington, or Montana, and sometimes from much further
away. Hearing the variety of accents and languages was definitely
fun.

"What is that language?"

"That sounds like a kid!"

One clear night they heard:

I am Sebiha Jakupovic. I am a refugee from Kozarac.

Vera could understand this language. She thought the
woman was Bosnian.

I am hoping for news about my brother, Munib Bahongic. No
one has seen him since the soldiers took him away.

The woman seemed close to crying.

If only he is alive. We have heard nothing.

Vera and Tom couldn't help her, but hearing the woman's
despair brought home to Vera the bigger picture: terrible things
were happening in the part of the world where she had been

born.

Tom was so pleased that Vera seemed to be coming out of herself. She liked to listen to the ham radio now. She received no news of her relatives, but Vera had become interested in the war. She read what she could in the newspaper and magazines. The images coming in on TV about the siege in Sarajevo were horrific. The ham messages were making the war seem real to them both. They found frequency 7.1 gave good reception from the Balkans.

One night, however, they heard a message which Tom thought would undo all the progress Vera had made. It went something like this:

This is Tango-94-Lima-Xray … Here is the testimony from a 16-year-old girl from Foca, Bosnia:

> *My name is Sanela Jancic. One night in April, 1993, soldiers forced many of the people of my village to go to a camp outside of Foca. The men and women were kept separate from each other by barbed wire. That first night, soldiers came for some of us young girls. They took us to an apartment in town and told us to take off our clothes. I fought, screamed, pulled the hair of the first soldier who grabbed me. He hit me on the mouth. My lower lip started bleeding. I fainted. When I came to, I was raped again. I can't describe it. Another man was running the blade of a knife over my breasts. He seemed to be playing.*

Tom dreaded Vera's reaction. He tried to turn the radio off, but Vera wouldn't let him.

> *While I was still conscious, I was raped by eight more soldiers. I don't know what happened after that. In the morning I was led, along with the other girls who were still alive, back to the camp. The next night we were taken to the apartment again. I begged them to kill me.*

The narrator finished the broadcast by urging whoever was

listening: *Thousands of women are being tortured in this war by being raped. We must restore their honor. Insist that these evil men are brought to justice. There never should be impunity for rape. Join our effort. Join CZ. Over.*

At the end of this message, Tom put his arm around Vera expecting her to collapse in tears. To his surprise, her reaction was quite the opposite.

"You know, Tom, I've been reading about this. Rape is being used as a weapon of war to destroy communities. It's not just an attack on the woman, but on her family and culture. Emily was attacked by an individual—by a masochist. That was terrible, but this is different. This is systematic. I've read it's a tool of ethnic cleansing. Fear of it makes people move away."

He agreed with her, and was so delighted to be getting his old Vera back.

"Did you hear her say: 'honor women?' That is *čast žene* in Croatian. And do you remember there have been a couple of the messages that ended with CZ before the call sign."

Without waiting for his answer, Vera got on the radio again using the same frequency: "Tango-94-Lima-Xray, this is WB7HEG. I am Vera Whittier from Portland, Oregon, U.S.A. I want to help CZ. What can I do? WB7HEG. Over."

Almost a year went by and Vera still hadn't heard from anyone as to how she could help the group that called itself CZ. The Peace Accords were signed, marking the end of the Bosnian War. Maybe people were no longer using ham radio. Telephone lines must be fixed by now. She was glad the war was over, but she missed the excitement of hearing ham broadcasts from the Balkans. Maybe the people there no longer needed help.

Nonetheless, at least three times a week she climbed the stairs to the third floor to listen at 9:00 P.M. She still hoped she would be contacted.

One night in early February, Vera heard this broadcast:

Tango-92-Victor ...Does anyone know about a place called Maller? It may be a hideout for war criminals. If you have any suggestions, please let us know. T92V member of CZ. Over.

This female speaker said "CZ" before saying "Over." Vera fantasized that the caller was really trying to reach her, but couldn't afford a long distance telephone call. Even if lines are fixed, people would still be desperately poor after the war.

Vera wanted so much to help. *Maller, a place called Maller.* That meant nothing to her, so she forgot about it until the early spring, when she started making plans to go to the annual Bird Festival in Burns, a town in eastern Oregon. Most of the spectacular bird sightings would be around Lake Malheur. Vera, like other Oregonians, pronounced the lake's name as "Mal-hyure." Recalling her high school French, Vera remembered that the word should have a silent *h*. Then she remembered 'Maller.' Maybe the person in the ham broadcast had a third way of pronouncing the French word *malheur*. She had to admit that it was highly unlikely that people from the Balkans would choose to hide in a place like eastern Oregon. It's almost on the other side of the world. How would they get here? Once here, how would they fit in?

She knew she was being ridiculous, but in her eagerness to help, she made plans to drive to the lake—a six-hour drive from Portland. She could investigate the area surrounding the lake and see if she could find anything like a hideaway. If nothing of interest came up, the trip would not be a waste. She would take her spotting scope, binoculars, field guide, and notepad with her. Even though the bird festival was a month away, it would be fun to look for birds on her own—her own wild goose chase. Actually, some Snow and Ross Geese had probably already arrived. Being on the Pacific flyway, Lake Malheur was a choice spot for migratory birds to fatten up before moving on.

Tom reminded Vera of recent news from Eastern Oregon. There was mention of an unusually rapid snow melt. He said that the Weather Channel spoke of possible floods, but she didn't take them too seriously. Tom wanted her to drive his Ford Explorer with four wheel drive, but she insisted on her little Honda hatchback. Tom's car seemed too big for her. To please Tom, she conceded slightly and threw her rubber boots in the trunk before she left home.

She got to Burns around two in the afternoon and decided to push on. She'd wait to book a motel room until after it got dark. She wanted to use what daylight was left to investigate the area. Heading south out of Burns on Highway 205, she found the lake came into sight much sooner than she had expected. She remembered it to be more a freshwater marsh than a lake—shallow, and ideally suited for breeding waterfowl.

She drove over the bridge that separated the saltier Harney Lake from Lake Malheur. Off to the left she saw an RV Park in an unincorporated community called "The Narrows." As it was so near Lake Malheur, it might be a convenient place to spend the night. She'd at least check it out. From the office she got a brochure: "41 RV spaces, in addition to yurts and tent sites." It had a small restaurant and grocery store. She didn't book a place because she wanted to save daylight time.

She continued driving south on 205 for twenty more minutes. There was no sign of human life until she spotted a ranch on a rise to the left. The arched sign over the driveway read "Stoka Ranch." *Stoka*, that means 'cattle' in Serbo-Croat. How curious she thought. That definitely sounded promising, but she would have to check it out later. She drove on.

After a few minutes, she looked in her rear view mirror and noticed water had seeped close to the edge of the road behind her. The lake must be rising. Rising fast! Quickly she turned her Honda around and hoped she could make it back to the ranch she had seen. Soon she was driving through two inches of water. Then it became three. She noticed the surface of the water was roiled and writhing. Why? With what? Good grief, they're fish. She hit something, and a minute later she hit something else. Unbelievable! She was running over fish—big fish!

Finally, she reached the arched sign and turned right to pass under it, hoping that she was on the driveway. A frame house and large barn were both perched ahead on high ground. As she approached them, her Honda rose out of the water. Other structures came into view, smaller buildings, and even a helicopter.

She drove as close to the house as she could and got out just as the front door opened. A golden retriever ran out toward her.

"Cooper, Cooper!" A young man hurried after the dog. "He won't hurt you. He's just happy we have a visitor. It's such a rare event. I guess it takes a flood," he said smiling. He was scruffy looking, like he needed to shave three days ago. A gray-haired man stepped out of the front door and remained standing on the porch.

"Looks like you'll be a-staying here for a bit. Come in. My

name's Luke."

Vera introduced herself, feeling shaky. She was not comfortable thinking she had killed something. She told Luke what had happened.

"Those carp are such a problem! They're changing the ecosystem of Malheur Lake. Have you had lunch?"

"I'm fine."

"We'll be rustling up some dinner in a couple of hours. We'd love you to stay. I guess you don't have much choice, do you? This is my dad, Joe Gutić."

The older man gave a weak smile and mumbled something like "Come in."

Gutić sounds like a slavic name, Vera thought as she followed the men into their two-story house. She was guided to the living room. Luke went off to make some tea. She and Joe asked the usual introductory questions. Then Joe left the room saying: "Luke will be back with some tea for you."

This gave Vera a chance to look around. What impressed her was the stone fireplace, crudely made but large enough to hold a wrought iron hanger and pot to cook soup in. Strings of red peppers and garlic were hanging from hooks set into the mantel. When she got up close, she realized they were plastic. Of the several pictures on the mantel, there was one which must have been of Joe's wife: a short, slightly plump woman with dark curly hair. Joe was tall and had been quite handsome in his younger days. There were three photos of Luke at various ages. He had Joe's cleft chin.

Joe came back into the room. Vera got him to answer some of her questions. He was originally from Croatia.

"Oh really? So was I. I grew up in Split." Joe looked away. Vera thought she detected a brief sneer. "Where in Croatia were you from?" she pursued.

"Krajina," he answered. He stood to leave again.

"When did you emigrate?"

Walking out of the living room he answered, "Right after

World War II."

He disappeared from Vera's sight. Why right after the war, she wondered? He may have been from a disgraced Fascist family, one associated with the Ustase regime. But he said Krajina—wasn't that where many Serbs were persecuted by Croatian Fascists? So many questions, but at least now she knew why their place was called 'Stoka Ranch'.

When Luke brought the tea, she learned that his mother was from Mexico and that she had passed away a year ago.

Joe reappeared and suggested to Luke:"Why don't you take Mrs. Whittier with you in the helicopter and check on the cows while there's enough daylight?" Turning to Vera he said: "I think you'll find it interesting. Being from Portland, you probably don't know much about ranching."

"Oh, I would like that. I've never ridden in a helicopter before."

A half hour later she climbed in and buckled up next to Luke. The helicopter was small.

"It can only carry two people because of the high altitude," Luke explained.

Vera hoped she wouldn't get sick. She had heard that nausea was a problem for people riding in helicopters. When they started to lift off, she wasn't sure if she should look out the window. Maybe that's what makes you sick. She took a quick look out of the right side of the craft. She could see nothing but water. The flood made the lake look tremendous.

"See that mountain ahead of us? That's where we're going. It's Steens Mountain." Vera said she had heard of it. "In spring and summer our cows graze on it."

To be polite, she had to look for the mountain. That meant looking out the front window. She wasn't sure she was seeing it. It was more like a big, long hill. Luke's chatter about ranching was interesting, and made her less conscious of being queasy. Unlike his father, she didn't have to pump him for details.

"Some of the land is BLM [Bureau of Land Management],

some is State of Oregon land, and some we own."

"My heavens, do you need all this land for grazing?"

"Yes, it is a huge area, but you need ten acres of grazing land for every cow."

"I had no idea."

"Yes. We have about a thousand cows and fifty bulls. I think we use about 84,000 acres up here."

"Good heavens."

The chopper started climbing. "We're on the western side of the mountain now. It doesn't look very high, does it?"

"No. In fact, it doesn't appear like a mountain at all."

"It was formed 16 million years ago, when a single gigantic fault-block occurred. From this side of Steens it only seems like a hill. But when we climb to the top and look over the other side you'll see there's a mile drop down."

From this overhead view Vera saw a beautiful patchwork of juniper and sagebrush. On up the mountain, she could see cows swishing their tails and flicking their ears as they happily grazed.

Luke landed the helicopter in several places and put out cakes of salt for the cows. She climbed out to breathe the cold air. "That looks like an Indian Paintbrush." He didn't hear her. She saw thistle with purple flower heads. She couldn't remember the name. Then another plant caught her attention. The leaf looked familiar.

"That one is Timberline Penstemon. It's beautiful when it's in bloom. In July and August you can see great swathes of purple." As they flew over pools of water, Luke commented that the cattle had plenty of water with the snow melt.

"OK, that's my work done. Now let's give you a look at the other side of the mountain."

"Oh, my heavens!" Vera gasped as they cleared the top of the mountain and the valley appeared 5,000 feet below them.

"The fault-block shows that the entire mountain consisted of basalt. Before the mountain was formed, many layers of lava, each hundreds of feet thick, covered this land. Can you imagine the forces within the earth that could lift such a huge block of rock almost a mile high?"

"It's hard to fathom. The land below down there is so flat, and it looks like it's covered with snow. No, that cannot be."

"It's the Alvord Desert," Luke said. "It's not snow, but salt. The desert is ringed by fault-block mountains. It's like a basin without drainage. The run-off from the mountains has no place to go. The water evaporates and we're left with salt. People actually go land-sailing and drag race on that salt bed."

"You're kidding! I'd like to see that."

"The plates—you know about them?"

"A little bit. Tell me."

"Let's see if I can explain this. As I understand it, western Oregon is pulling away from eastern Oregon."

In more ways than one, Vera thought.

"That stretching of Earth's crust allowed great blocks to uplift and adjacent ones to fall. That's how the basin and range topography formed."

She was becoming impressed with Luke's knowledge. "Have you been to the university?"

"Oh, yeah, I majored in ecology, but I also have a minor in geology. OK, let's go back over the mountain and I'll show you some other features of our area before it gets dark. You said you are planning to come back for the bird festival? I think I heard you say that to Dad, right?"

"Yes, right."

"Down there's the little town of Frenchglen. Dad owns the hotel there."

"There's a hotel there?"

"Um-hum. In fact, the season will start soon. I work as the cook and manager. We are hoping to find a replacement, someone who can really cook. No one wants to work in a town that has just eleven people."

"Did you say the town has only eleven people living in it?"

"Yep."

"I'm thinking: this is the most remote area I have ever been to."

"Yeah," he laughed, "actually, the most remote area in the lower 48."

"Incredible!" Vera thought this *would* make a wonderful place to hide war criminals. Then she reconsidered. Where would they live?

"There's Highway 205 again. It goes from Frenchglen, past our ranch, all the way to Burns, only today you'd never know it. Much of it is still under water. Normally there are three distinct lakes there: Harney on the west, Mud, and then Malheur Lake. It looks like the area under water is double what it should be."

"Tell me about the fish—carp did you say?

Luke banked the helicopter to the east.

"Here's the problem. Carp are bottom feeders. They eat every plant that tries to grow on the bottom. They even suck the mud to eat little creatures. In fact, they churn up the bottom so much that the lake is no longer translucent. Without light, plants can't grow. You know the lake is very shallow. It used to have vegetation for other fish and birds. Now, only 10% of those birds stop here in the spring on their migration north."

"That's terrible. How did carp enter the lake?"

Luke started to explain but interrupted himself to point out something. "See that down there? That's Harney Field Station. You can take courses there during the bird festival, if you want."

"Interesting," Vera thought. She would remember that.

Flying back to the ranch, Luke pointed out several canals and channels coming out of the lake. "Each of those diversion streams is a place that carp like to spawn. We've been putting in little dams with traps so we can catch them. In fact, we're still mapping the area to locate all of the diversion streams."

For a few minutes Luke was quiet. He's probably looking for more diversion streams, Vera thought.

"I would like to show you where I went to school, but it's too far. It's a boarding school in Crane, an unincorporated community sixty miles from the ranch." Luke turned north again.

"Boarding? You had to board?"

"Most of us did, once we were in high school. The students come from so far away, 100 miles in every direction. Well, we'd better get back."

Vera asked him where he had gone to college.

"Oregon State University, in Corvallis."

"Oh, I see. Did you like it?"

"Yes, it gave me great respect for the natural environment."

"You're not interested in ranching?"

"No, but don't bring that up in front of Dad."

"Couldn't you do both?"

"No, I have two problems with ranching. I'm not comfortable with the way cows are treated, and I feel the way beef is produced is not sustainable."

"How do you mean?"

"Just consider water, for example. The water needed to produce a thousand-pound steer would float a battleship."

"Good grief!"

"That's grain-fed beef, of course."

"That's hard to believe."

"Yeah, what we should be doing is trying to get people to eat less meat. Here's another statistic straight from my college textbook: 'If a person switches from an ordinary meat diet to a vegetarian diet, it would save 1.4 million gallons of water.'"

"No! That's hard to believe."

"I know. I felt the same way. The amount of water saved is enough to fill two Olympic-size pools."

"Swimming pools?"

"Yep."

Vera thought of the delicious steaks Tom cooked on the grill. She could never give those up. She wanted to ask Luke about the need for protein, but before she could, he continued: "Most ranchers are more interested in making money. They haven't had to think about what's good for the planet. Out here, there is so much freedom. You can get away with doing many things. Anyway, I want to try to convince them to consider the environment more. That's my long-term goal."

Banking the helicopter and looking out over his shoulder, he added, "I think the flood water is receding now, don't you?"

Vera couldn't tell until she managed to pick out the ranch buildings below. "Oh yes, your driveway is no longer submerged." She thought she should not question him further as he was coming down to land.

Joe was quiet during dinner, but Luke was pleasant and had a lot to say. By the time Vera could safely leave the Stoka Ranch, she was well fed and it was 7:00 in the evening. The sky was dark, but Highway 205 was clear of water.

"Don't speed. Make sure you go slowly until you reach dry pavement. The flooding tends to leave mud on the road and that can be slippery."

"Also fish!" Vera decided not to stop at The Narrows and drove all the way to Burns for a motel room. What should she do tomorrow? With the flood conditions, searching for a war criminal hideout wasn't practical. On the other hand, now that she had come all this way, she shouldn't just immediately return to Portland. She and Tom had talked about renting a cabin on a river somewhere around here, so they could get away and really relax. Tomorrow, maybe she would drop into Blackburn Real Estate and see what was available.

Oz was assigned a missing person case in mid-April. Such cases were usually straightforward, but his two years of experience as a detective had taught him the advantage of keeping a low profile, so he told his assistant, Urban, to wear plain clothes when they drove an unmarked car to interview Mrs. Dadic.

Alma Dadic had called the station to say that her niece, Maric Andrich, had been missing for four days. Looking at the map, Oz muttered under his breath, "Vrbanicevaul 233, hmm, the home must be in the Trnje district of Zagreb."

Oz anticipated the unattractive, dark grey stucco building, square in shape. As a boy growing up, Oz had a friend who lived in that type of building in the same area. They were built fifty years ago, when additional housing was quickly needed to accommodate Zagreb's burgeoning industrial sector. Each building consisted of four two-story homes, one at each corner. Each house had a small attic on top.

Mrs. Dadic opened the door and invited them in. Both men introduced themselves and handed her their cards. Mrs. Dadic looked the two men over and directed her comments to Urban. Oz smiled. He knew being round-shouldered and needing a hair cut limited the respect a policeman would garnish. But he wasn't after respect. He wanted information, and to decipher honest reactions. He felt his appearance should be neither threatening nor distracting to serve that purpose best.

The house was neat but sparsely furnished. A few toys and

children's books were scattered about. A pair of men's slippers was in front of the sole easy chair. Oz knew the layout. There would be two small bedrooms and a bath on the second floor.

Still looking at Urban, Mrs. Dadic explained, "Maric was supposed to return Sunday night. Even if she decided to stay longer, which she wouldn't have done, because she could only afford to stay one night, she would have called." She took a breath, looking down to read the cards she had been handed.

Oz asked if Maric was a relative. She looked at Oz, hesitated, then turned to Urban before launching into a full explanation: "Maric's the daughter of my older brother. He and his family were Croatians but have always lived in Mostar. When the war broke out, they sent Maric to live with us. We all expected it to be a temporary arrangement, but he, his wife, and their youngest daughter were killed."

"*Three* of them?" Oz inquired.

"Yes,"

Urban was taking notes. How often Oz had heard stories of entire families being killed or displaced! The war had only been over for little more than a year, and even though he personally hadn't suffered any losses, the stories he had heard still gave him nightmares.

"Did Maric work?"

"Oh yes, she had an important job, too. She worked for the president. In fact, it was in gratitude for all the work she had done that she was given a ticket to the opera and dinner, and, and, oh yes, a room at the hotel, the one that's near the opera house."

"But I thought the opera house hadn't re-opened yet?"

"Not the one here in Zagreb, but the one in Ljubljana."

"Oh, I see. So your niece went to Ljubljana. The president's office paid for the entire trip?"

"Everything, I believe."

"What was playing?"

"Playing? Oh, at the opera? Heavens, I don't know. I think Maric told me, but that sort of thing doesn't stick with me. I know nothing of opera."

"Do you know which hotel she stayed at?"

"No. Oh wait! She wrote it down for me." Mrs. Dadic retrieved a piece of paper sticking out from under a table lamp. "Here it is. She was staying at the Central Hotel."

"Have you called the hotel to ask them if she is still checked in?"

"No. I was expecting Maric to call us."

"Mrs. Dadic, it would really help if you could give us a picture of Ms. Andrich."

She looked quite pleased. "I thought you would ask for one." She went to the desk and opened the top drawer. "I have two." She said Maric was 32 years old. One picture made Maric look older, Oz thought. Her dark brown hair was pulled back into a bun. Perhaps she was trying to look older, to give herself more weight working in the president's office. He noticed her elongated face with a pointed chin. She had a typical Slav nose: long, narrow at the bridge, but flaring out at the tip. Her ears stuck out. Not exactly a beauty, but she looked intelligent. The other picture showed Maric smiling, while apparently playing with Mrs. Dadic's two children. Maric's teeth were crooked.

Mrs. Dadic led the men up to the second story. At her suggestion, Urban pulled down the step ladder to the attic. She let the policemen go up on their own. Oz climbed up first. A door opened into the tiny room that was Maric's private quarters.

The room had a peculiar shape, like a lean-to. The ceiling was highest on the left and went down to about a foot above the floor on the right. A single bed was tucked in under the eaves to the right. Between the bed and the door was a skinny chest of drawers. A table with a rickety wooden chair was against the left wall. It held a small lamp. The chair had a cushion on it. Oz made sure Urban took notes of all these items. There were books on the table, along with a tape recorder, papers, pens, and pencils. He imagined her sitting at the table with daylight from the dormer coming in over her back.

There was only one electric outlet. It was by the table. Maybe that's why the lamp had such a long cord. It could reach the chest of drawers and serve as a reading light in bed. There were more books on the chest of drawers, among which were *A History of the Balkans* and an English novel. Oz picked up the alarm clock and noticed the alarm was set for 6:00 A.M. He wondered why there was no Croatian/English dictionary in sight. Was she so fluent she could read Jane Austin without help?

Inside the chest of drawers, under a supply of sanitary napkins, Oz found a ham radio set. Being kept there indicated that she was no longer using it. Maric must have a variety of skills, he thought.

At the back of the room was a bar that was suspended horizontally by two chains of unequal length hanging from the same rafter. This served as her closet. A few blouses and skirts hung there on hangers. One skirt reminded Oz of one that Jelena used to wear. Oz remembered enjoying watching her get dressed in front of a long mirror. No mirror here.

Everything was cleverly positioned according to the pitch of the roof. There actually was little in the room, nothing in the dormer to obstruct daylight. The dormers on the identical building next door were offset. Was that design intentional to give privacy? The space between the buildings was only wide enough for a sidewalk allowing access to the two homes at the rear. The window could be opened for fresh air. There was a gallon-size metal can on the floor in front of the window. Oz's first guess was a chamber pot. He had already thought of the difficulty of negotiating the ladder in the middle of the night. He opened the lid, which was quite snug, and found the can half full of seeds. Was she hiding something in the can? He stuck his hand in and sifted through the seeds and found nothing.

Oz wondered why Maric didn't put the table under the dormer for light. Maybe she wasn't here much in the daytime. Other books were stacked in a pile on the floor next to the table.

He descended the ladder, impressed with a woman who

had made an efficient room out of such a small space. Mrs. Dadic said she hadn't been in the room for months. Oz thought that showed a lack of feeling. Was she resentful that she was stuck with Maric now that the girl had no home or family to return to? Perhaps. Was it hard for the aunt to climb the ladder? No, she could do that easily. It showed, perhaps that she was confident that Maric kept her space tidy. She didn't need to check on it. Waiting four days to report Maric missing? No, that's not strange. It's about the usual time that people wait. But why didn't she call the hotel in Ljubljana?

Oz got back to his office and began writing up his report. He hated writing reports. They slowed him down. It would be one thing if he could just write it up in his own words, but no—there were forms to fill out, the questions were often unimportant, not getting at the significant items of inquiry. He was distracted by his thoughts concerning the girl's aunt, Mrs. Dadic. Why didn't she call the hotel in Ljubljana? Why hadn't she even gone up to Maric's room before calling the police? Oh, to hell with it, just get the forms filled out so I can get on with the case, he thought.

Uh, oh, he had better be careful with these questions. He could imagine his chief taking the case away from him if he knew Tudjman was involved. How could he answer the questions so as not to set off alarm bells?

Employer: *Croation Government*
Place of Employment: *St. Mark's Square*
Position: *Typist*

Oz handed in his report.

He called the Ljubljana Police Department to see if it had any information about the missing woman. He was told that about four days ago, a woman had been murdered outside of the Central Hotel, which is near the Ljubljana Opera House. The LPD had not been able to identify the body yet.

"Would you like to speak to Detective Edi Juric, the detective assigned to this homicide?"

"Yes, I would."

"I'm sorry, I see he won't be back here until 10:30 this morning. Could you call him then?"

Oz couldn't believe his luck: his missing person has probably been found, although unfortunately dead, and his best pal, Edi, was handling the case. Oz got permission from the chief to go to Ljubljana. He called the LPD back and left a message for Detective Edi Juric that Detective Osbart Zagar from the Zagreb Police Department would be at the LPD around 10:30 A.M. to meet with him about his homicide case.

ॐ

Two years prior, Oz had decided to rent out his entire house so he could make more money, but mostly so he could have privacy. Sometimes he'd get home from a case at four in the morning and he'd have to sleep until ten before going into the office again the next day. His tenants had children that woke him up. Also, he didn't want it to get around that he lived in a somewhat fancy house. That didn't go with being a cop. So he moved to a third-floor walk-up in a working-class part of the city.

He had spent a long time selecting an apartment. The one he finally decided on had a window overlooking the street and one with a view of the sidewalk. Perhaps more important was that, in case he ever needed one, he had a hidden escape route. There was a door at the end of the third-floor hall that opened into a closet. A ladder was kept there so that one could climb up and open the hatch. Getting out through the hatch put you on the roof of the building. His plan was to pull the ladder through the hatch and put the hatch back in place. And, just in case it was still too dangerous to remain on the roof, he would use the ladder to bridge the gap between his apartment building and the neighboring one to get away from whoever was after him. He explained all this in a letter to his aunt Vera.

He liked to tell his aunt secrets like that, even if it made his uncle think he was paranoid. With detective work there were so many things you had to keep to yourself. Aunt Vera was a friend who would always listen, and who lived too far away to cause him problems.

Driving to Ljubljana gave him more than an hour to luxuriate in random thoughts. It was a treat to get away and to see the verdant countryside in April. His mind returned to the purpose of this trip. He compared having a missing person case to a homicide. With the missing person case, you get to know a lot about the person right at the outset. You get emotionally involved in their well-being. Then, when you find them dead, as you usually do, you can't help but feel partially responsible. With a homicide, you may end up knowing a lot about the person due to your investigation, but you were emotionally detached from the beginning. He didn't want to find Maric Andrich dead.

Edi was at his desk waiting for Oz with a big grin. "Good afternoon Detective Zagar—the famous Žica." Edi introduced Oz to two other policemen, who seemed to have heard some stories about Oz from when he and Edi were in the army together.

"My God, you almost look respectable, a fairly recent haircut and shave!"

"Yes, I'm undercover now. Don't give me away." After handshakes, pats on the arm, and some more banter, Edi took Oz to a storage area where the police kept objects pertaining to open cases.

"The dead woman had a hotel key in her pocket. Here are the items we found in that room: a book, pjs and underwear, brush, twist to hold up hair, tooth brush and paste."

Oz picked up the book, wearing gloves of course. It was a paperback edition of *For Whom the Bell Tolls*.

They planned to spend the rest of the day visiting important places the dead woman had gone on her last day. The first stop was to be the morgue.

"Why don't you drive, then I can direct us," Edi suggested.

But when Oz tried to start his car, the engine wouldn't turn over. He couldn't believe it. He had driven all the way to Ljubljana without a sign of trouble. Edi loved it. He ran inside and came back with an official permit that gave Oz permission to park in front of the police station all day, if necessary. So they transferred to Edi's car and drove to the morgue. On the way, Edi filled Oz in on the details of the murder. "She was shot a half a block from the hotel, the Central Hotel, on Friday night, between 11:00 and 11:30."

Oz thought it was too much of a coincidence: the murder victim must be Maric Andrich.

"We think the woman was walking back from the opera because there was a ticket stub in her pocket. We think it is probably Maric Andrich because also in her pocket was the Central Hotel key to room 538, which was registered to her."

"That seems reasonable," Oz responded. "I have photos of Ms. Andrich, so that will nail it down, until we can get a relative or acquaintance to give us a positive I.D. Tell me about the shooting."

"She was shot from behind into her backbone. We speculate that she immediately fell on the sidewalk. Then a second shot was fired through her left shoulder blade. A silencer must have been used, since no one heard the shots and people only reported coming across a body on the sidewalk."

"Sounds like a professional killer's work. What type of gun do you think?"

"They think it was a .38 special." said Edi. "We've searched the neighborhood, of course."

"Most professionals take their gun with them."

"The killer could be a woman. It wouldn't have required much strength to do all that."

"Yes, and a woman wouldn't have alarmed the victim, as much as a man coming up from behind her at that hour of the night," Edi said.

"Yes, but female assassins are rare."

Before they got to the morgue, Oz just had time to tell Edi about Maric's job in Tudjman's office.... "She was given the opera ticket and a night in the hotel as a gift for doing such a 'fine job' at work."

"Hmm," nodded Edi. "That does sound suspicious."

"And here's the other thing: my new chief of police is a political appointee of Tudjman."

"Oh great, this could be a nightmare!"

Edi and Oz were led into the morgue's refrigerated room. The attendant explained that it had to be chilled to 9°C to slow down decomposition, thinking that Oz was a civilian. Oz gave a little shudder to play along with his misconception. He of course knew that unidentified corpses had to be kept under refrigeration, sometimes as long as two years. Most were kept on shelves, but since this body was a recent arrival, it was still on a gurney. The attendant rolled it out into the other room where there was good lighting and unzipped the bag.

Oz knew immediately it was not Maric, but didn't say so. "Do you have the body weight and height?"

"Yes," the attendant answered, picking up a clip board hanging from the gurney. "Let's see, she was 165 centimeters tall and weighed 61 kilos, blue eyes, brown hair, short unpolished fingernails, no lipstick."

"Her age?"

"About 40."

"Thank you. I don't think this is the woman who is missing from Zagreb, but would you mind if I took some pictures of her?"

"No."

Oz took out the camera that he always carried in his jacket pocket and snapped three photos from different angles, then asked if he could see the personal effects. The attendant pulled out a box resting on the gurney's under shelf and spread the items out on a white metal table. Oz took out his notepad and recorded the number on the ticket stub from the opera. He noticed it said *Nabucco* on it. The jacket, anorak type, he noted, was turquoise blue. "She was wearing this?"

"Yes," the attendant said turning the jacket over so Oz could see the holes, encircled by blood, where it had been pierced by two bullets.

Oz examined the shoes: black walking shoes. They were expensive, but too casual for a woman who lived in Ljubljana to wear for a night at the opera. The woman may have been traveling. There was a watch, again expensive looking, but simple. "What's this?"

"It's a hair clip. Her hair was pulled back in a bun."

"No earrings, necklace, or bracelet?" Oz thought of all the jewelry Jelena used to wear. The LPD had notes on all this and pictures, too, but Oz was grateful to be able to ask questions himself. Oz knew from Edi how she died, but he had to ask: "Would she have died quickly?"

"Yes. The examiner said within seconds."

Later, Oz and Edi sat in the car to talk in private before they pushed on to the opera house. Oz showed him the pictures of Maric. "The missing woman from Zagreb is smaller with darker hair."

"She doesn't have blue eyes, but she does wear her hair in a bun. That's a mistake. Look at those ears! Best to keep them covered," Edi said.

"At night, the difference in hair color may not show up. I'm wondering if the killer didn't murder this poor woman thinking she was Maric."

"Yes. It's a possibility. What do you think about this woman?"

"Traveling alone. Has anyone reported a missing person?"

"No," said Edi. "She certainly didn't doll herself up to go to the opera. In fact, she's awfully plain in every respect."

"I agree," said Oz. "Is that the usual way she dresses or was she purposely trying not to attract attention?"

CHAPTER 10

APRIL, 1997

Although there were many signs of spring in Portland, it was still too cool and damp to sit out on the patio in the early evening. Tonight they would have to have their glasses of wine in the library before dinner. In any case, indoor or out, Tom and Vera always met before dinner to relate the day's events. Supper was light, as usual—quiche and a tossed salad. Vera was in no hurry to serve it as she wanted to share a letter from Oz which had arrived in the morning mail. It worried her. She wanted to see what Tom had to say about it.

"Tom, would you please read this. I hope Oz isn't going to get into trouble. He may need some legal advice. That may be why he addressed the letter to you as well as me."

Dragi Teta Vera i Tetak Tom,

At last I have an interesting case to investigate. A Zagreb woman is missing. Her name is Maric Andrich. Evidently, she had been given a bonus which had consisted of a trip to Ljubljana's opera, dinner, and a night's stay in a nearby hotel. Who was her boss? None other than the president of Croatia: Franjo Tudjman.

On the same date (Saturday, April 15) that Ms. Andrich was to go to the opera, another woman was murdered in Ljubljana near the opera house. Edi and I consulted and thought the coincidence was suspicious, so I drove to Ljubljana to work with him. We now suspect that someone tried to murder Maric Andrich

*but killed the other woman by mistake. Here's why:
The Slovene police gave me the details of their case and
showed me the pictures of the crime scene. The woman
was shot with a silencer, walking on the sidewalk about
50 yards from The Central Hotel entrance at about
11:00 P.M. They believe that the woman was walking
back to the hotel after seeing the opera.*

*The woman carried in her jacket pocket a ticket
stub to the opera and a key to a hotel room. It was
booked to Maric Andrich, who had a Bosnian passport.*

*By the time I got to Ljubljana, the Slovene police
had already found that Ms. Andrich's immediate family
had been killed during the war. That correlated with
what I was told by Ms. Andrich's aunt, Alma Dadic,
with whom Maric was living in Zagreb. No one has
come forth to identify the body.*

*Prior to the opera, the dead woman had dinner in
a nearby restaurant, as did the people on the Elderhostel
tour, who also had opera tickets. The police interviewed
all tour members the next day before they left Ljubljana
early Monday morning. Of course, by the time I got to
Ljubljana, it was already Wednesday, so I got this information secondhand. The tour guide is Hungarian and
her office is in Budapest. It will take some time before
we can follow up with her.*

*Edi and I went to the coroner's office. I had come
with a photo of Maric and took several pictures of the
corpse. The features were different from Maric's. The
dead woman had longer hair and different eye color.
The coroner pointed out that her hair had been arranged in a bun but they had removed the clip that held
it up. According to the pictures we have, Maric often
also wore her hair in a bun. The personal effects of the
deceased indicated that she wore very plain clothes and
substantial walking shoes—unusual choices for someone*

*going to the opera. Her only piece of jewelry was a
watch.*

    *I'm too tired to write more tonight. It's been a
long day. Hopefully, I'll have more energy in a few days
to continue. Please don't talk about this with anybody.
My police department (luckily, not Edi's) is probably
controlled by Croatia's national security. I need to tread
carefully with this case. I'll tell you more in my next
letter.*
Lijëp pozdrav,
Oz

    "Well," Tom said after he was finished reading Oz's letter,
"I'm glad he didn't put all of that in an email. He's got to be ex-
tremely careful."

    "I think he knows that." It annoyed Vera that Tom thought
Oz wasn't smart enough to be careful.

    "Yes, he probably told us all of this because he likes to get
you involved with his cases. I think you would like to be a detective yourself. Am I right?" Tom said teasing.

    "Why not?"

    "Yes, *you* should have gone to the police academy and *Oz*
to drama school. He loves making his work sound so dangerous."

    She wished, just once, Tom would say something favorable
about Oz. Vera wondered if Tom felt engineering was a better
occupation. Yes, it was dependable and paid better, but it certainly lacked adventure. Besides, there was virtue in police work:
promoting social order and justice, while often putting yourself
in harm's way. She had said such things before, but held back
tonight. She didn't want to get into an argument.

    Before going to sleep that night, Vera hoped Oz had re-
corded the seat location on the stub of the opera ticket.

CHAPTER 11

APRIL, 1997

Following their visit to the coroner, Oz and Edi went next to the Central Hotel. It was a four-star hotel in a nice section of Ljubljana. They elected to park Edi's car several blocks away. Had they driven in a police car, they could have simply pulled up to the entrance and left the car there, but this might alarm people— both guests and management. Edi was of the same opinion as Oz, that a policeman learns more when no one knows he's a policeman. Even though they were in an unmarked car, parking a distance away gave Oz a chance to walk a bit in this beautiful city. For the most part, the streets were narrow. The shops were intimate. Small squares with outdoor cafés reinforced the fact that Slovenes knew how to enjoy themselves.

Once inside the hotel, they located the manager and identified themselves. "Did any of the staff see something out of the ordinary on the night of the murder?"

"You can ask Filip Cupic. He was at the front desk late that night." The manager got hold of Filip, who told them that a young woman did check out at midnight. He thought it was a strange time to check out, but was pleased that she didn't try to weasel out of paying for the room that she had booked but no longer needed.

Edi and Oz both tried to conceal their excitement over this revelation. Edi asked casually: "What was her name?"

"Brenda Hines," Filip said as he looked at the hotel ledger for that date. "Yes, she was in room 417."

"Was she part of the Elderhostel group?"

The manager stepped in: "You know the Ljubljana police have a lot of this information, no?"

Oz replied, "Yes, but they still have not been able to identify the body. So this is important."

Filip said: "It appears that the tour members were in rooms on the second and third floors."

Could this mean that Brenda herself was not on the tour? The manager continued to show signs of impatience, with Filip caught in the middle. They thanked him and asked the manager if they could talk to the cleaning staff that worked on floors two through four.

"Filip, would you telephone up and ask the cleaners on those floors to be ready to receive two policemen for questioning?"

It seemed apparent to Oz that the manager didn't want the questioning to go on around the front desk. They eventually tracked down the cleaning staff for all three floors. The chambermaid on the fourth floor, whose name was Nika, acted like she had something to say, but was embarrassed to reveal it. Finally, she came out with it: "The hotel always puts foreign tourists, especially those on a tour, on the second and third floors. That means that Lana and Anita, assigned to those floors, tend to get larger tips. But that day, I remember being happy because I finally had an American on my floor. I was looking forward to seeing a 200 Tolar note tucked under the desk lamp, but when I went into the room to clean it, only the usual 100 Tolars was left for me."

"How did you know she was an American?"

"The suitcase, she wheeled it herself. It's funny they always want to take their own suitcases, unless they're really old. But they always leave a nice tip for the cleaners. Europeans tend to do the opposite."

"Anything else?" Edi asked.

"Yes, she wore trainers and dressed casually."

Oz made a note that Brenda must have changed into her walking shoes to go to the opera. That must be as far as she was willing to go to get dressed up.

"Color of coat?"

"Don't remember."

Edi and Oz went back down to the lobby and decided to get a quick lunch in the hotel restaurant while they considered what else they should find out before they left the hotel. They sat at a small table and looked at the menu the waitress handed them. In a snooty voice Edi said to Oz, "The pumpkin gnocchi with rabbit ragu should be quite good."

Oz was eager to discuss the case. He readily agreed with Edi's choice, grinning when he noticed it was the cheapest thing on the menu. "We have to contact Orsolya Somogyi, the guide of the Elderhostel tour. That won't be easy. Those guides are run ragged. As soon as they get back from one tour, they are sent out the next morning on another."

"Also, their policy is not to divulge information about any of the tour members," Edi pointed out.

"How is your Hungarian?"

"Awful," said Edi.

"Mine too. Well, they have to be good at English, so I guess I had better make that call." They both knew that Oz was the better English speaker of the two.

The lunch order came. They would now have time to talk uninterrupted. "Where did Maric go?" Oz wondered.

"She must have taken all of what belonged to Brenda Hines with her. The chambermaid said only the 100 Tolar tip was left. Where would she hide?" Edi asked. "She's in a strange country and probably doesn't speak the language."

"She may speak the language. She's good enough to read novels in English and she worked as a translator for Tudjman. Languages may come easily to her." Oz paused long enough to consume several forkfuls of the delicious lunch. Barely swallowing the last, he continued: "Of course, why didn't we think of it?" He put his fork down for emphasis. "Maric may have gotten what she needed to leave the country. Her way out was to assume Brenda's identity. That's why she paid Brenda's hotel bill."

"All right, but she did that because she didn't want to draw the hotel's attention to herself, so she pretended to be Brenda. Hmm, now that I think of it, how could she *afford* to pay for Brenda's room? The aunt said she had ..."

"She must have Brenda's credit card," Oz interrupted. "And that means she probably has Brenda's passport."

"But there is one thing we keep ignoring," Edi said, "and that is that Maric may have killed Brenda just so she could leave the country. The missing person is the murderer."

"I suppose that's possible, but I just don't see Maric as the criminal type."

"All we found out about Brenda Hines is the chambermaid thought she was American. We've got to get in touch with Elderhostel. I hope the hotel will know where Ms. Hines was from, that will give us something to work with before we talk to the tour guide."

After paying the bill, the two detectives went back into the lobby to speak to the desk clerk again.

"The hotel makes a photocopy of the first page of each passport. Ms. Hines was American, but, as you know, the passport never gives the person's address."

"Where was the passport issued?

"Los Angeles," the clerk answered.

Edi turned to Oz and said: "Oh, good, she probably lives on the West Coast. Well that narrows it down!

Oz and Edi's next stop was the opera house. They learned from its manager that many tour companies buy up a row of seats for a performance to give their travelers something entertaining to do when their tour is in Ljubljana. For the Saturday night that *Nabucco* was playing, Elderhostel had purchased 14 tickets in row D of the orchestra. "We do not know who actually used the tickets."

"Do you know when the performance ended that night?"

"Not exactly, but probably about 10:30 P.M."

"What were the numbers of those seats?" Edi asked in Slovene. Edi recorded the manager's answer: "Seats 10 through 23 of row D."

Oz's mind drifted. He realized how easy it was for Edi to get information out of Slovenes. People are much more helpful if you speak their language, and Oz could understand only half of what was being said between Edi and the opera's manager. He remembered reading about the struggle both Slovenes and Croatians had in previous centuries maintaining the use of their languages. Under Austro-Hungarian occupation, the German language was required. Oz recalled his mother telling him: "Once a native language is degraded, the native culture soon follows." How he wished he could be with her now. If he just had one more day with his parents...

Edi was looking at him. Oz realized he had not remained focused. Pretending that he was deep in thought about the mystery he said: "Futile though it may be, I would like to go into the theater and look at the layout."

Oz was stunned by the beauty of the chamber. It was oval in shape, with two tiers of balconies above the orchestra level. The style was perhaps predictable: gilded wall reliefs, red upholstered chairs that fitted the slimmer bodies of a hundred years ago, but Oz appreciated the small scale and intimacy that this theater afforded. He had been to the opera twice. He grew up in Split, which was renowned for the arts. His parents took him to see *Die Fledermaus* in the charming National Theater. The building was yellow and had entranceways and windows narrowly arched. Oz was eleven.

Five years later, on the occasion of his parents' 20th anniversary, they took him to Zagreb so they could see *The Magic Flute*. Oz didn't like Zagreb's Opera House. It was enormous, pompous, monumental, and set off the street, so that back in the early days, horse-drawn carriages had room to line up to drop off their patrons. His father blamed its construction on Emperor Franz Joseph, who probably intended it only for the upper classes.

This theater in Ljubljana was just right, Oz thought. He looked up and noticed the lovely frescoes on the ceiling. Edi was already walking down the aisle. Oz rushed to catch up and ask him to sketch just where the seats were in his notes.

They decided next to walk to the Central Hotel from the opera house. They timed it as 15 to 20 minutes. "Brenda should have been back to the hotel by at least 11:00 P.M., but the time of death was 11:00-11:30 P.M. She should have been walking with the others from the tour, don't you think? She wasn't on the tour, but she had dinner with them and sat with them through the opera. They must have started walking together, but then she separated from the others. She had to have been walking alone when she was murdered or there would have been witnesses. I'm having trouble imagining someone sneaking up on Brenda, shooting her, she falls down on the sidewalk, and the murderer walks away without other people witnessing the act."

"Or with someone who had lured her away from the group," Edi suggested.

"Was it raining?"

"Not according to the police report, at least, not at that time, earlier in the evening, yes. Yet she wore her rain jacket."

"You've got to admit, it was a pretty clumsy operation. If Tudjman's people ordered the murder, someone who didn't actually know Maric must have shot Brenda Hines."

Oz and Edi next walked from the hotel to the restaurant three blocks away. Restavracija Neboticnik was noted for its Central European cuisine and its roof garden. It had been raining earlier the night Maric was there, so they wouldn't have eaten on the roof. The restaurant was casual and small, and the tables were close together. There were hooks on the wall to accommodate coats.

They were now ready to go to the airport. It made it so easy to have Edi drive. He knew right where to go. Oz worried about his car. Would it start again when they got back to the police station? He had to get back to Zagreb.

The approach to Aerodrom Ljubljana was dramatic with the Julian Alps in the background. Oz thought of his parents enjoying their hike until its tragic end. He wondered where they were, how they were feeling, but he was pretty sure that what remained of them was inside him—their gifts to him. He felt their closeness and was grateful.

He and Edi spent an hour and a half at the airport. Edi, being a Slovene policeman, was able to get the answers they wanted, but it took time. They finally found out that Brenda Hines did fly into Ljubljana on the morning of Saturday, April 15, but she had a ticket back to Portland from Trieste on April 19. "Was she planning on spending more time in Ljubljana or Trieste? And why Trieste?" Oz wondered. "At least we know Maric didn't fly out of the airport here. Did she go to Trieste by bus or is she hiding somewhere? Maybe she has a friend in Ljubljana." They both thought about those senarios.

"We need to find out if Brenda Hines did take a flight out of Trieste, but I'm afraid it will take too long right now. I'd have to get clearance with Italian airlines and we don't have time," Edi said. "Oz, I'm going to have to report in at headquarters. I have to get there before the chief goes home. And we have to see if your car starts."

Back at LPD, Oz found his car still wouldn't start, so Edi arranged to have it towed to his mechanic, whose virtues he extolled. While they waited for the tow truck, Oz asked Edi how much he was planning on telling Chief Mlakar.

"Everything," Edi answered.

Edi said that he would like his chief to meet him, so Oz accompanied Edi while he gave his report. Chief Mlakar seemed bright and reasonable. He understood that the two cases were intertwined. "Whoever killed Brenda meant to kill Maric. The LPD is responsible for finding Brenda's killer, but I don't see how we can do that without fully understanding why the killer wanted Maric dead. When you are ready to return to Zagreb, Oz, I would like Edi to go with you. Two heads are better than one."

"Yes, Sir. I would like Edi to go with me while I search Maric's bedsit again."

While Edi drove them in his car to Zagreb, Oz explained that he wanted to write a quick note to his aunt in the States while Edi was driving. "She likes to hear about my cases. I like her to have a record of what's going on. That way, if something goes wrong, she'll know what to do." Oz wrote in his note pad:

> *Dear Aunt Vera,*
> *The woman murdered in Ljubljana is not Maric*
> *Andrich, but possibly an American woman named*
> *Brenda Hines. We suspect that Brenda was killed by*
> *mistake, instead of Ms. Andrich. We want Zagreb PD to*
> *think the two cases (Maric's disappearance and Brenda's*
> *murder) are unconnected in order to delay Tudjman's*
> *people from discovering that they have killed the wrong*
> *person. That will give Edi and me more time to investi-*
> *gate what really happened. We're not 100% sure of the*
> *motive.*
> *Love,*
> *Oz*

With the note finished, Oz and Edi went back to discussing the case. How would they proceed?

"We should speak to Mrs. Dadic. She may have heard of a woman murdered in Ljubljana, and will be relieved that the victim was not Maric." Or would she? Oz wondered. He himself was relieved. He had begun to fantasize knowing Maric. He imagined a young woman of courage and conviction. Now that they knew she had not been murdered, their task was greater. They also had to find a missing person.

It was 7:00 at night when they reached the outskirts of Zagreb. They were famished, so Oz directed Edi to his favorite fast-food restaurant—Pingvin. They grabbed two chicken burgers on ciabattas and ate them on the way to Mrs. Dadic's. They couldn't delay the visit, because Oz had to report into ZPD the next morning. Although they had to tell her that the woman who was murdered in Ljubljana was not Maric, Oz didn't want to tell her over the phone. He wanted to see her reaction. He was glad to have Edi with him for a second opinion.

Mr. Dadic was in his easy chair, slippers on, looking at a match on the TV. He stood up and shook their hands but sat back down to continue watching the game, muttering something like "Alma can answer your questions."

Mrs. Dadic led them into the kitchen, so as not to disturb her husband. She asked them to keep their voices down because her children had gone to bed. She took the news quite calmly, as Oz had expected. "Maric is the last of the Andrich family to be alive, except for me, of course." The woman shed no tears nor did she request further details. Then Mrs. Dadic burst forth with news of her own: "Two men from President Tudjman's office came to ask me when Maric was coming back," she stated almost proudly.

"Really!"

"They asked to see her room and left it in such a mess: birdseed all over the floor! I had to sweep it up so it wouldn't attract mice. Maric was always so neat."

It sounds like Mrs. Dadic must have gone up the ladder after the men left, Oz thought. "Did they say what they were looking for?"

"No, but they were there a long time. I think they had trouble both fitting in the room. I heard them grumble but couldn't make out what they said."

"I remember the can of birdseed," Oz commented. "Why did Maric have it?"

"She always fed the birds in the park on her way to work."

"Did the men take anything away with them?"

"Yes, they took what they called 'the office tape recorder.'

But I'm sure that tape recorder was Maric's. She spent a lot of time using it. I remember she bought it long before she started working for the president. But I didn't say anything to the men. I mean, after all, they work for the president. If they want the tape recorder, how could I object?

"Maric always said she was not allowed to discuss her work. I know she used a tape recorder at work. Then sometimes she used her tape recorder when she was at home. I could hear her talking out loud. Once I asked her what she was doing, she said she was practicing a speech."

Her face took on a solemn, pensive expression. She was quiet for a few moments. Oz and Edi didn't rush in with more questions. She needs time to process the fact that Maric may not be coming back, Oz thought. Then Mrs. Dadic perked up. She seemed to remember something else: "They also asked if I had reported to the police that Maric is missing. I said of course. I expected them to ask me more questions about what the police said, but they were through with their questions."

To Oz, this meant Tudjman's men had already talked to the police.

"Oh, when they were leaving to go out the door, the big one said: 'If she still hasn't returned in a week, I'm afraid the president will have to hire a replacement.' The little guy added that they hoped Maric would show up."

Edi asked if the men left their cards. "No," Mrs. Dadic answered.

Oz asked her to describe the two men if she could.

"Yes, well, one was tall, almost 2 meters, light brown hair, strong looking. His nose may have been broken at one time. He did most of the talking. The other man was thin and of average height, with dark hair which came down over his forehead on the right side."

Oz was surprised at how observant she had been. She had no idea what Maric wore to Ljubljana, but she was able to describe the president's men's appearance in detail. Oz regretted his next request due to the lateness of the hour, but he had to ask permission to take another look at Maric's room. "Yes, all that I ask is that you will be extra quiet so the children don't wake up," she answered.

On their way up the stepladder, Oz whispered to Edi that what Tudjman's men were looking for might still be in her room. The bedsit was totally ransacked. "Why did they have to toss the bird seed on the floor?" Oz asked in disgust. He brought out his flashlight from his crime bag and shone it systematically around the room and ceiling. The little dresser drawers had been taken out and dumped on the floor. The ham radio was turned upside down on the floor.

After a half hour, Edi said, "Maybe she fed the birds on her window ledge." When they pushed up the window they saw a long clear plastic box resting on the window ledge. It fit exactly on the ledge. With the window closed, it was hidden by the sash. It seemed to be full of bird seeds. The indent in the lid held some seeds to tempt the birds to land. Oz tried to remove the box but something was holding it firmly to the ledge.

Edi, who was standing right by Oz, said, "Try taking the lid off."

Oz removed it. Inside appeared to be nothing but more bird seeds, but Oz stuck his hand in and discovered a plastic bag as long as the box. Inside the bag were eight cassette tapes lying end to end. "This is probably what they were after."

The two men smiled at each other—a smile of both pride and fear.

"No question about what those goons would do to us if they knew we had these. We have to listen to them."

Shining the flash light around the window frame one last time, he saw a length of wire bunched up and held in place by duct tape. "What's that?" he asked.

"It could have been the antenna for her ham radio," Edi guessed. "She would have needed one to get good reception."

Oz wondered what else they could learn here. Maric had no

boyfriend that Mrs. Dadic knew of, and she had never brought a girlfriend home.

Edi said, "I wonder if Mrs. Dadic's children might know something."

"Her aunt told me that Maric usually left for work at 7:00 A.M., before the children got up for school. She rarely ate with the family. Most nights, she got home after the family had already eaten. I don't think she got to know them well."

"That's strange," said Edi.

"What's strange?" Oz asked.

"I mean it's strange to be living here for over four years and not know the children well. She probably is self-absorbed, cold, and unobservant."

Oz laughed. He knew Edi was egging him on. They went downstairs and showed Mrs. Dadic the tapes. Proper police procedure dictated that they couldn't just take what they wanted without telling Mrs. Dadic. Also they needed her awareness that the tapes had been found in Maric's room, so the police could not later be accused of fabricating evidence. They offered to let her hear them, but she was not interested. Oz and Edi said they would take them back to the station to listen to them.

"If Tudjman's men come back, it would be best if you don't tell them about the tapes, we think that was what they were looking for."

Mrs. Dadic blanched. "Just take them. I don't want to know anything," she whispered.

Oz and Edi were anxious to listen to the tapes, but Oz didn't have a recorder in his apartment, so once they left Mrs. Dadic's house, they decided to drive to the police station, where Oz knew there was a recorder in the equipment closet. Being late at night, they hoped that few policemen would still be at the station, and that those who were there would not take notice of them. Once inside, Oz took Edi to the end of the hall and into a small room at the back of the building. They hung up their coats on the door pegs.

Oz saw Edi scanning the room before he sat down quietly at the small wooden table. The room was bare of furniture except for a table and two wooden chairs. Oz hadn't turned on the overhead light, but left the door open for now, so the hall light enabled them to see. "Wait here. I'll get a tape recorder."

When he returned, they lifted the table and chairs quietly over to the wall sockets so the recorder's cord could be plugged in. An ashtray, half-filled with cigarette butts, contributed to the room's smell of stale smoke. Oz soon wished he could open one of the windows but knew they were sealed shut. The room was used for interrogation. Every police department has such a room.

Oz finally shut the door. If they needed light, he would use his flashlight. It was important not to attract the attention of the others in the building.

Without talking, Edi took the top-most tape and inserted it in the recorder. They both froze when they heard footsteps coming up the hall. Fortunately, whoever it was stopped before getting to the end, where they were. Probably he's using the toilet, Oz thought. They waited until they heard a flush and the footsteps returning down the hall before proceeding. The tapes were not labeled, so they didn't know what the chronological order might be.

They bent over the recorder so the volume could be turned down low. Each section on the tape was preceded with a date. They realized they must have placed one of the last tapes in first, because the first date mentioned was August 18, 1995.

Tudjman appeared to be talking to his aide, Philip Cupric about U.S. Ambassador Galbraith driving with columns of Serb refugees leaving Krajina. "What arrogance for him to think that his presence could protect them." They spoke in Croatian, which was not very easy for Edi to understand, so Oz kept summarizing for him as they listened. Later in the tape, Tudjman spoke about the Dayton Peace Accords, complaining about "the Americans' 'superior' attitude." He felt that Slobodan made things worse by objecting to every concession the Yanks were encouraging him to make. "That bully never learned how to grease the wheel. He's his own worst enemy. You could tell by the body language how uncomfortable he made the people at Dayton feel."

Edi interrupted, "This has nothing to do with the tapes, but I was thinking that Tudjman wanted to get rid of Maric in Slovenia, that is, in another country, so the crime couldn't be linked to him."

"Yes, you're probably right. We'd better keep going, or we'll never get through all these." Oz played more of the tape. "Did you get that?"

"No."

Oz summarized: "Tudjman is saying that Milošević came out of the war better than we did, 'we' meaning Croatians. We gained our independence and kept our original borders, but we didn't achieve the greater Croatia that we had hoped for. Our Croatians in Bosnia are still separated from us. Cupric's comments are not that important. He's really just a sounding board for Tudjman, so I'm just going to tell you what Tudjman says."

Oz listened some more then said, "Tudjman thinks the Americans were trying to protect the interest of the Bosniaks.... He feels Milošević had maneuvered himself quite well. The Accords legitimized the existence of the Republic of Srpska. Even though it is part of Bosnia and everybody knows, in time, it will be annexed to Serbia.... So Milošević will definitely get what he wants. It will just take more time, but he's going to be able to unite all the Serbs."

"Why would Tudjman make tapes like this?" Edi was interrupting again.

"I have no idea. So far, this tape isn't very incriminating. Everybody's known for a long time that Tudjman wanted a greater Croatia, just like they knew Milošević wanted a greater Serbia."

Edi continued, "If Maric was a typist, was she simply transcribing these tape recordings of Tudjman's conversations in his office?"

"Yes, but I would imagine she typed out what she heard, then gave the tape back and turned in what she had typed each day. They certainly wouldn't have allowed her to take the documents or the original tapes home."

"That's what I think too, but how did she get copies of the original tapes?'

"Who knows? This woman has guts, she's clever, and has learned to stay under the radar."

"Her looks help her with that!"

Oz smiled. Obviously, Edi was feeling somewhat relaxed, whereas Oz kept worrying that someone was going to walk in on them. "What's her purpose? Is she working for anybody or for any organization? Well, we better get on with it."

"She could be tried for treason."

"No, not treason, she's a citizen of Bosnia. She could be tried for espionage, though. She probably feels more loyalty to Bosnia than Croatia. Anyway, if she was a witness, she would be protected by the ICTY." He continued playing the tape.

The more Oz listened to them, the more he was convinced that Tudjman needed to get rid of Maric because of what she knew about him. Edi could be relaxed about all this. He didn't have Oz's problem. Oz couldn't let on to his chief that they were suspicious that Tudjman had ordered Maric's assassination.

They continued listening: "The trouble is that most Croatians who live in Bosnia live among Bosniaks. It was always going to be harder to extract them. Looking back now, I can see that our turning against the Bosniaks was a mistake. I thought we had a good chance of absorbing Bosnian Croatians, but the Serbs overplayed their hand. They did such wretched things to the Bosniaks that the world started to have pity for them and we had to bend to American pressure," said Tudjman.

After listening some more, the tape went silent for about 30 seconds. Then they heard a woman's voice, clear but quiet. She spoke in English, with a Croatian accent, announcing that she was Maric Andrich. Oz almost stopped breathing, so as not to miss a word she said. Usually, when you meet someone for the first time, you concentrate on what you see. This seemed more personal, just listening to her voice. He didn't have to worry about any impression he was making on her. He had the luxury of really being able to concentrate on her words and the way she expressed them. He thought he detected fear, a slight shortness of breath.

She explained that this was the end of the information that she had been asked to transcribe. She gave her full name and said that she had transcribed the eight tapes for Franjo Tudjman. She gave the office number and address of where she did the transcribing then named all the people who worked in the office with her.

So it turned out they had indeed been listening to the last tape that Maric had recorded. Oz's nerves were getting the better of him. "We've got to listen to these tapes elsewhere, because someone could walk in on us at any time and what will we say? This will take us many hours. Let's continue this at my apartment."

Oz signed out the tape recorder. He didn't know if he was allowed to take it home, but at this time of night, who was going to care? They wanted to listen to as many tapes as possible before Oz had to report in the next morning.

Once in his apartment, Oz put on a pot of coffee, even though it was already 11:30 at night. They made themselves comfortable, Oz on the couch with the recorder and Edi in the arm chair, holding a pad of paper and pen. After a few minutes, they started resting their feet on the coffee table. It had been a long day for both of them.

Edi asked, "Do you have any thoughts as to *why* Tudjman wants the tapes transcribed in the first place?"

"No, unless he is trying to avoid what happened to Nixon. Maybe he wants to clean them up. You know, take out the incriminating bits."

"Yeah, that's what I was thinking, but it's hard to do. Can't they tell when the tape has been tampered with?"

They worked into the night, finally going to bed at three A.M. Oz went to the station in the morning as usual, but driving Edi's car, which he parked several blocks away. He slipped the letter to his aunt in a post box on his way.

When he settled in at his desk, he noticed that the others didn't ask him about his case. He figured they had all heard that the corpse in Ljubljana didn't match the missing woman in Zagreb. They were all busy, so he didn't bother telling anybody that his car had broken down in Ljubljana. Even the chief did not ask him into his office for an update. He probably has more important things to attend to, thought Oz. Sometime during the morning, Oz slipped away and tried to erase his signature where he had signed out the tape recorder. He had signed in ink, which couldn't be easily erased, so he gave up trying.

Left to himself, he thought he should try to chase up the tour company, Elderhostel, headquartered in Budapest. The guide wasn't in, so he left a long message, not expecting to hear back for days. But much to his surprise, the guide called him back mid-afternoon. She, of course, remembered the murder outside the hotel, but she had already told the Slovene police that the woman had a ticket for that seat. "Then you know who was in which seat?" Oz asked.

"No, I just know that that seat was sold to an official in Croatia. The others we sold to people on the tour who wanted to see the opera. I didn't keep track of which seat went to which tour member. When they bought a ticket, I just gave them one."

"Did you go to the opera yourself?"

"Yes."

"Did you notice anything unusual?"

"No…yes, actually, there was a man in one of the seats who was not on the tour. But that will happen. Sometimes someone decides not to go and sells their ticket to someone else."

That interview got him nowhere.

Earlier in the day, Oz had searched the internet for newspaper articles with pictures of Tudjman. He found one taken a year ago of him in a crowd of people walking down a street in Dubrovnik. During Croatia's War of Independence, Dubrovnik had been shelled by the Yugoslav army. After the war, many of the old buildings were successfully repaired. On the day that the picture was taken, Tudjman was paying tribute to the restoration of Dubrovnik's Old Town area. Walking near Tudjman were two men who appeared to be bodyguards, and one of them fit Mrs. Dadic's description, but Oz could not find his name mentioned anywhere.

Oz didn't think that this man was Brenda's killer, because contract killers never wanted to be caught on camera. Tudjman wouldn't choose an assassin who had been shown with him. But in case Tudjman's thugs someday came after him, Oz thought it would be a good idea to know at least what some looked like. In another photo, there was a small man opening the car door for Tudjman. He had dark hair which fell over the right side of his forehead. The man appeared to be a chauffeur, but no name was given.

About 3:30 in the afternoon, Oz called home to check on Edi.

"It's been an interesting day," Edi reported. "I have to confess I slept until 10:00 this morning, and you're out of cereal, but as soon as you come home with my car, I'll go buy us some, and some stuff for dinner."

"Don't worry, I'll pick some things up on my way home. All I have to do now is write up a report of what we learned in Ljubljana. Then I can leave."

"Don't mention what we found at Mrs. Dadic's."

"I agree, but why do you say that?"

"About noon, there was a knock on the door to your apartment. I hadn't buzzed anybody in the downstairs door, so I'm not sure how he got through that one. I was on the throne taking a crap."

"Too much information," Oz said smiling.

"Wait a minute. It's relevant. Thank goodness I didn't flush but just stepped out in the hall. The door to your apartment opened and a man peeked in. When he saw me, he said: 'Oh, excuse me I've come to fix the plumbing. I hear you are having trouble with your toilet.' While he said this, I saw him put his keys away—a whole bunch of keys. He backed out, pardoned himself again, and said he must have the wrong apartment. Anyway, Oz, my instinct tells me he was going to tap your phone. He just didn't look like a plumber. I mean, he was dressed for the job all right, and I saw through the window he had a van that said "plumbing" on it, but his hands were too delicate. And letting himself in is a bit irregular."

"… to say the least! Good grief! Thank God you were there."

"Can you spare more time? I have something else to tell you."

"Sure, but I'm going to go to another phone to call you." Oz left the office and found a payphone on the way back to his car.

When Edi picked up, he told Oz that he had spent the rest of the day speaking to people at the Italian Airline Association. "Don't worry! LPD will reimburse you for the calls. It took me more than an hour just to get clearance." Edi's excitement came through when he told Oz that he had found out that Brenda Hines had made another trip to Trieste, Italy, from Portland, Oregon, on June 30, 1996.

"Why Trieste? What was Brenda's occupation? We still don't know that, do we?"

"No! But wait! There's more. On July 30, 1996, two men flew one-way from Trieste to Portland. Then on November 11, 1996, four men made the same flight. Finally, on April 16, 1997, another three men flew from Trieste to Portland."

"How could you determine that?" Oz asked.

"Portland's smaller than Zagreb and Trieste is only one third the population of Portland. You've got to admit, it would be rare for so many people, all middle-aged men, to fly from Trieste to Portland without a return ticket. There must be a connection."

"OK."

"Also," Edi continued, "Brenda Hines flew on the same flight with the last three men. Of course that wasn't Brenda, because she was already dead. It had to be Maric Andrich who made that flight using Brenda's ticket and passport. But here's something interesting: Brenda's original ticket had her flying out of Trieste two days later, so Maric must have had her ticket changed so she could get on the next flight. That's important because it means that Brenda wasn't necessarily intending to fly with the men. She may not have any connection with them."

"What's going on with all these men from Trieste? Did you get their names?"

"Yes, but I had to get the chief to verify that it was necessary for the murder investigation."

"Are they Italian?"

"Italian nationals, but I happen to know there is a fairly large community of Serbs that have lived in Trieste for at least a century," Edi replied. "OK, I'll let you go."

My God, this is getting murky! Oz couldn't wait to tell Aunt Vera about this turn of events. What is luring men from this part of the world to Portland?

After Oz got back to his apartment, Edi started in: "Getting back to who had a motive for killing Brenda, we mustn't overlook Maric. I've been thinking, she probably hated her job, but didn't know how to get out of it without getting her head chopped off."

Oz smiled to himself, knowing he was being teased, but loving the camaraderie between himself and Edi.

"And we still haven't ruled out blackmail. She probably already tried to blackmail Tudjman and it backfired, so now she's running for her life."

Oz couldn't help but laugh. Here he goes again, suggesting several scenarios which would explain why Maric killed Brenda. Of course, Oz didn't agree with any of them.

Edi finally said what was on his mind: "Oz, you are falling into your usual trap of putting a woman on a pedestal, and not analyzing the case objectively. Remember how long it took you to realize that Jelena was taking advantage of you. Yet all the signs were there: coming home late, buying clothes that you never saw her wear."

"All right, all right! I really missed the signs with Jelena."

Edi mimicked Oz's deep voice: "'Maric is not the criminal type.' It's funny. You don't do that with men, older women, or even children. But once you're exposed to a young woman, you seem to lose your objectivity. Besides, she's uglier than sin," Edi said laughingly. "You saw her picture!"

"She is not."

"Oh my God! That proves you're biased."

CHAPTER 12

APRIL, 1997

Vera read Oz's most recent letter and immediately planned to telephone him at his apartment. She knew Zagreb time was 9 hours ahead. It was 10:00 in the morning in Portland, so it would be 7:00 in the evening there. That should be perfect. He should be home from work.

Vera could picture his apartment building, with its beautiful beech tree at the front. He had a studio apartment on the top floor. She had been there once. She stayed in a hotel four blocks away. Oz was particularly pleased that he had a way to get up on the roof. She could imagine him sitting up there during good weather, having a lovely view of the city, while enjoying the peace of being alone outside, away from smokers. Being eye-level with the crown of the beech would be a good place to see birds, she thought.

As she dialed his number, it crossed her mind that if he were sitting out on the roof he wouldn't hear his phone ring. Maybe that's where he was, because he still hadn't picked up. Finally he did, after six rings.

"Ozbart, hi. It's Vera...I just got your letter."

"Oh, hi, Aunt Vera." He seemed relieved to speak to her.

"Guess what? It has just been reported that Brenda Hines is missing. It was on TV last night and in this morning's newspaper." Without giving him a moment to respond, she went on to explain: "She is the daughter of Edwin Hines, of the lumber family from Portland.... I think the article said that she had been traveling somewhere in Eastern Europe but had not been heard from in a month."

Vera caught her breath, and was shocked when Oz responded quickly: "I'll call you tomorrow night at this time," and then hung up, without even saying goodbye.

"Oh dear," she told Tom later that evening, "I hope he's not in danger. Why would he hang up so suddenly?"

"Perhaps he thought the phone call was being monitored."

"Maybe so, oh dear!"

"Aren't you glad you got away from that part of the world? Everybody has to be so careful and suspicious all the time."

"Yes, then, but surely not now! Tito's death put an end to all that."

"No, not really."

"Tito's been gone for 17 years!"

"The leaders now are just as devious—same tricks. Three wars! OK they're independent nations now, but was it all worth it? Look at Bosnia. The Peace Accords left the country unmanageable."

Vera shared Tom's disgust with these events, but this was not what she wanted to talk about. She wanted to get off the topic of politics and steer the conversation back to Oz. But Tom went on: "The wars that they engineered may have been over for almost two years now, but they still have to cover up the truth. There are people who want revenge, others who want war criminals brought to justice. Those deceitful leaders have plenty of reasons to thwart the efforts of an honest policeman." He was quiet for a bit, but then started talking about what she didn't want to hear. "On the other hand—now, don't jump on me for saying this—but don't you think your darling Osbart likes to over dramatize things? It makes him look important. He loves to get you excited about what he's doing."

Here we go, Vera thought. She tried not to show her annoyance. Since Emily's death, Tom had had Vera all to himself. He was unaccustomed to sharing her attention with someone else. She wondered too, now that he was a senior member of his engineering firm, had he risen to the top only to find it's rather dull up there? Was he even envious of Oz for the mysteries his nephew's life unfolded?

Lying in bed that night, Vera couldn't fall asleep. She kept thinking of Maric—or whatever her name was. That was probably not her name now. If she was marked for murder, where would she go? What would she do in Maric's situation? Vera couldn't imagine.

Her thoughts passed from Maric to Tom and his manner earlier in the evening. He tried to do whatever he could to please her. He brought her a cup of tea, even got down on his knees so he could rub her feet that were resting on the footstool. He must have realized his comments about Oz went too far. He rarely said he was sorry for anything. Apologies always helped Vera to forgive, but they were too hard for Tom to utter. Nonetheless, she realized that he was sorry. His actions said so.

How would Oz call them tomorrow night? He'd probably use a pay phone. That would cost a lot of money. She planned to ask him the number of the phone, hang up, and then call him right back. She must remember to have pencil and paper at hand, so she wouldn't waste his money.

Late that afternoon, Oz parked Edi's car on the back street behind the adjacent building and walked to his apartment with a bag of groceries. He was really tired, but on guard and expecting trouble. He found Edi on top alert too. He described his hidden escape route to Edi. Just in case they would have to use it, they decided to take only Edi's little carryall with them. Oz packed his personal papers and the tapes in it. Edi suggested that they go ahead and put the bag on the roof and leave the hatch open.

Oz said, "What the hell, why wait for them? Let's just go now. We can listen to the rest of these tapes anywhere."

"I'm with you, let's get out of here."

But the phone rang. Should he answer it? It had to ring six times before Oz made up his mind: "Hello…. "Oh, hi, Aunt Vera." …"I'll call you tomorrow night at this time." Oz hung up and said to Edi, "Let's go."

Oz didn't even have to explain that Tudjman's people could be watching the building now. Edi said, "Let's definitely use the escape route. God, you're fun. I guess we're having fun…"

They left the apartment with a few dirty dishes in the sink and fresh groceries in the refrigerator. Oz thought it looked like they had just left and would soon be back. Oz locked his apartment and they proceeded to the closet. Once on the roof, they drew up the ladder and closed the hatch. Oz worried that the ladder wasn't long enough, but with its extension, it overlapped the gap between the buildings with a foot to spare at either end. Oz insisted that he go first. It had started to drizzle. The rungs of the ladder were cold and slippery. Since Edi weighed at least ten kilos more, Oz decided that he should take the carryall and push it along in front of him. This took much more time than he thought. He was so afraid of letting the bag slip off that he forgot to be afraid for himself. It turned out fine. Oz got across with little difficulty. He held his end of the ladder down so it wouldn't slip off the parapet while Edi was crossing. This should be easy for Edi, Oz thought. For years he hiked in the Alps of Slovenia.

When they both were across, they pulled the ladder after them, laid it down on the roof and went to look for a door that would allow them entry into the building. There was a door, but it was securely locked. They would have to get down by the fire escape. It looked pre-World War I and never repaired. They had no choice. Oz went down first with the carryall strapped over his neck and shoulder. Oz waited for Edi to reach the lowest platform. The last ladder needed someone standing on it for it to swing down to reach the street. Edi went first. The ladder swung down. Once Oz was on the ground the ladder swung up.

Now if they could just get to Edi's car without being noticed. Did Tudjman have men watching this far away from Oz's building? Maybe no one was even after them. When they got to Edi's car, Oz and the carryall just fit into the trunk. Edi drove off. Oz forgot to tell him which way to go. Later, when they reached the outskirts of the city and Oz could get out of the trunk, Edi told him that, by mistake, he had driven down Oz's street. Two dark cars were double-parked right in front of the door to Oz's building. He had calmly driven by them, but said he didn't start to breathe normally until he was sure they hadn't followed him.

When they arrived at the police station in Ljubljana, Edi called Chief Mlakar. Everyone on the force knew the chief disliked being contacted at home, but when Edi explained the evidence that they had brought with them from Zagreb, the chief willingly gave up his quiet evening meal with his wife. Twenty minutes later, he, Oz, and Edi were seated around a tape recorder. The chief needed to hear the tapes for himself. Oz was already convinced that the tapes should be delivered to The Hague, and delivered immediately. But it was important that Chief Mlakar thought so too. His own Chief Grgić wouldn't want Maric's tapes to get anywhere near the International Criminal Tribunal for Yugoslavia.

It only took a few hours of playing the tapes for Chief Mlakar to agree that they contained damning evidence of a conspiracy to commit war crimes. Although Oz wished he could fly the tapes to the Hague and deliver them himself, there were far too many complications to such a plan. After discussing all the alternatives, it was decided that they should call the ICTY prosecutor's office and ask them to send an investigator to the Ljubljana Police Department to pick them up.

The phone call was put on speaker mode so they all heard the prosecutor's voice. "Yes, but less than three weeks ago, we sent someone to Ljubljana to pick up these tapes and nobody met our investigator at the other end."

This was complete news to all of them. Who asked for an investigator to come pick up the tapes three weeks ago? And, thought Oz, it must mean that Maric took a copy of the tapes with her to Ljubljana, not only to Ljubljana, but to the opera, because she didn't go to her hotel room after the opera. And that means that she still has that copy with her. For a split second, he wondered if she had been trying to make her way to The Hague ever since Brenda was murdered. No, no, someone used Brenda's return ticket to Portland and that must have been Maric.

He heard the prosecutor ask: "What guarantee do I have that someone will actually be there this time?"

To answer that question Chief Mlakar got on the phone and explained some of the details of the case.

The prosecutor asked further: "What was the reason the evidence wasn't turned over to us three weeks ago?"

"A woman was murdered," Mlakar answered.

It occurred to Oz that the prosecutor probably already knew the answer to his own question. He was simply trying to get more information out of them. What should they do? If they couldn't trust the ICTY prosecutor, who could they trust? Oz thought he had better fill in the details to convince the prosecutor of the seriousness of the situation. "We think the killer intended to kill Maric Andrich but killed Brenda Hines by mistake." He went on to explain their dual investigations of the murder and the missing person case. When he was finished, there was a pause at the other end.

Finally, the prosecutor said, "OK, I will send Bastiaan Blomme again then, but tell me, why are the Ljubljana police turning over the evidence to us and not the Zagreb police?" Mlakar nodded to Oz for him to answer the question.

This really put Oz on the spot. It was one thing to state it to his Aunt Vera, his best friend, Edi, now to Chief Mlakar, but to tell the ICTY that Chief Grgić of the Zagreb Police Department was the puppet of President Tudjman was putting his head on the block, with an ax nearby.

When he was finished with his explanation, the prosecutor made no comment and asked no further questions, but said that Blomme would arrive at the Ljubljana PD sometime in the morning.

Later that night, while trying to fall asleep on Edi's couch, Oz rehashed the phone conversation. The prosecutor simply listened to Oz's explanation, no gasps, no: "Really!" no: "Humph," in disbelief. He just listened. He'd heard this kind of thing before, for sure.

The International Criminal Tribunal for Yugoslavia cannot arrest the people it indicts. It has to rely on local police to do that. Some governments won't own up to war crimes that can be easily traced to its politicians. The ICTY must be inured to this difficulty, Oz thought.

Every agency has its problems. For the police, it's always the people at the top that are the hardest to arrest.

Oz was all wound up. Would he ever fall asleep?

He considered how Interpol has a problem similar to the

ICTY. It does not act as a world police force, as people often think. It simply collects data on international crimes, criminal trends, finger prints, and photos. It's supposed to be politically neutral, but it has to deal with the corruption of some of its member states. Countries that are members can use its extensive database, but they can also abuse the system. Oz remembered the case in which a government used Interpol to locate a whistle blower who was in hiding. The government made false accusations and gave Interpol fake evidence against this so-called 'criminal'. Interpol had to issue a world-wide alert. Eventually, the poor guy was found hiding in another country. He was extradited to his own country and done away with.

In spite of his deep yawns, Oz still couldn't fall asleep. His mind wandered to Milošević. He had read that both Serbia and the Republic of Srpska were avoiding sending its war criminals to The Hague. Before the wars, Serbia, with Milošević at the head, was the dominant force that controlled Yugoslav policy. But after the wars, Yugoslavia was nothing more than a federation of Serbia and Montenegro. It must be difficult, Oz thought, for Milošević to accept any shrinking of his sphere of influence. Now, Serbia's southwest province wanted to secede, and no wonder. Close to 90% of Kosovars were Albanians (not even Slavs) and many were Muslim.

It seemed to Oz that world opinion had turned firmly against the Serbs. Although both sides were guilty of ethnic cleansing, the Serbian genocides at Srebrenica and Foca had established Serbia as the supreme evil force. Now, Milošević was fully engaged in not letting go of Kosovo, in spite of world opinion. His rhetoric had whipped up such nationalistic feelings among Serbs that many of them viewed their war criminals as heroes and wanted to hide and protect them.

God, what a mess! His last thoughts were of Maric. Where was she? Was she safe? Would he ever find her?

He was due to call Aunt Vera tomorrow night. He hoped she would understand why he had hung up on her. Uncle Tom was not so tolerant of dramatic situations. He didn't want to take advantage of his aunt, but he knew she was keenly interested in his cases. She was always happy to help him financially, as well. Something told him he may need her help soon.

∞

After Bastiaan Blomme secured the tapes for the ICTY, Oz finally picked up his car and was able to drive back to Zagreb. When he walked into his apartment, he knew immediately that someone had been there. Cushions on the couch weren't put back right. Underwear and socks were just thrown back in the drawer. Whoever did this made no effort to cover up what they were doing. That could only mean that they didn't have to worry about being detected and must be Tudjman's men. Oz sank down on the couch, discouraged and feeling vulnerable.

What should he do? Tudjman probably knows about the tapes and that's what he wanted his men to find. Will they try to hurt me? He could just hear Uncle Tom accusing him of being paranoid, but hell, he was not going to trust any of the perishable food in the apartment. You never know. He collected a small bag of items which could contain poison and went out to eat. He would throw them away when he had an opportunity. There might be someone watching his every move.

Before coming back for the night, he walked several blocks out of his way to find a pay telephone so he could call Aunt Vera. She asked him for the number and immediately returned his call. He apologized for hanging up on her the last time and explained everything that had happened. He told her if she called him, to hang up after one ring. He thought if his phone was tapped, one ring wouldn't give them enough time to trace her call. Then he would call her back when he got to a pay phone.

That night he felt lonely. His home was no longer a sanctuary, and he dreaded going to work the next day. He would have to tell Chief Grgić that the tapes were taken to The Hague. How would he respond? Oz would be fired on the spot, that's how. Oz needed witnesses. There wasn't one person in the police department that he was sure he could trust. His strategy would have to be to let everyone know the truth at once.

The next morning, he purposely parked a few blocks away from the station. He took his time entering the building, waiting to be sure Grgić's car was in the parking lot first. Just as he expected, Oz was told that the chief wanted to see him in his office. Before obeying this order, Oz went to his desk, put a small tape-recorder in his pocket and clicked it on. Three of his fellow police officers were nearby. Oz began telling the men about the latest development in the case. He ended by saying that he found tapes that incriminate Tudjman and they are now at The Hague. He went on explaining crucial aspects of the case. Two men looked at him wide-eyed. The third looked down then slipped away. A few minutes later, Chief Grgić came out of his office saying: "Well done, Oz. Obrad here tells me that you found tapes in the missing girl's apartment. Is that right?

"Yes."

"Obrad also says that you took the tapes to the ICTY. Is that right?"

Oz had long suspected that there was a snitch that reported things to Grgić, but he never knew who it was. So, now he knew it was Obrad. Oz clarified: "Actually, an ICTY investigator picked them up at the police department in Ljubljana, yesterday."

"And why were you in Ljubljana yesterday and not here?"

The Chief's tone had hardened. Oz knew he was about to get the ax. "My car broke down in Ljubljana a couple of days ago. My friend Edi drove me back to Zagreb. That same night we found the tapes in the girl's apartment. We thought they may shed light as to where she had gone. So we listened to them. I borrowed the tape recorder from the department. Edi had to get back to Ljubljana and I had to go with him to pick up my car. When we arrived at the LPD, Chief Mlakar was there so we gave him as full an explanation of the case as we had. He listened to the tapes with us and we all decided that they had to be taken to The Hague without delay. An investigator came…I'll write all of this up."

"Ozbart, you don't have a job on this force any more. Clear out your desk. I'll take your badge. You're fired."

"On what grounds, sir, am I fired?"

"For leaving the country without permission with evidence pertaining to a Zagreb case; for removing equipment from the department without permission; and for not reporting on the case in due fashion. Your friend, who is your friend?"

"Edi Juric of the LPD."

"Why in hell is he involved in a Zagreb police case?"

The chief's face was a bright red by now. Oz went on to explain about Brenda Hines being killed instead of the intended Maric Andrich.

"You failed to inform me of something as vital as all this? How dare you!"

"I think you probably already knew this, sir. When I came back from Ljubljana I found my apartment had been searched. As you probably also know, the tapes implicate President Tudjman in war crimes."

"Get your pocked face out of here! Your police career is over—done for!"

CR

After being fired, Oz left the police station and drove back to his apartment. His first thoughts were for his personal safety. He didn't blame Grgić for firing him. He had cause, but the man was dishonest. He clearly put pleasing the president above police work. Knowing he failed to do what the president wanted was worrying him. Would he try to hurt him? No, he didn't think so. There were three fellow officers who witnessed his argument with Grgić. He also could count on Edi and Chief Mlakar in Ljubljana to back him up.

What about Tudjman himself? Would the president send

his thugs after him? No, Oz didn't think he would. What Tudjman wanted was to find Maric and silence her. Oz had been taken off the case. He was no longer investigating Maric Andrich's disappearance. There was nothing more Trujman could learn from Oz, and he didn't represent any further threat to him.

For the moment, Tudjman still might not know about the tapes. Oz remembered Investigator Bloome saying that until a person is indicted, the prosecutor doesn't have to share its evidence with the defense. Tudjman had not been indicted yet, so he won't find out about the tapes from the ICTY. However, it would look better for Grgić if he told Tudjman himself. There might be a stooge in the ZPD who would inform Tudjman anyway, or Tudjman might have a mole inside the ICTY itself who would tell him about the tapes. Oz thought that Tudjman would not fire Grgić over this because Tudjman had appointed him. Firing Grgić would only draw attention to the case.

What turned out to be Oz's real problem was that he couldn't get a job. Every potential employer wanted a reference from Oz's former employer. When the Chief of Police blackballs you, there is no hope for employment. After two months of job searching, Oz called both his aunt and Edi to tell them his problem. Chief Mlakar said he would hire him if he could, but currently there was no opening, and, if there were, he would be obligated to hire a Slovene first. Oz gave up looking and asked his aunt if he could come to live with her and Uncle Tom for a while. Thank God he had them to fall back on!

But to be honest, Oz also had another motive for going to Portland. He wanted to continue working on the case. He and Edi thought that Maric probably landed in Portland. Where she went after that, they had no idea, but they shouldn't stop looking for her. Bloome had said that Maric's testimony, in addition to the tapes, would seal the case against Tudjman. Also, once in Portland, he may be able to help Edi find Brenda's murderer.

It took Oz three weeks to make the move. He gave notice on his apartment lease and moved a few pieces of furniture and equipment back to his house, after making arrangements with his tenants to reserve a room for his things. The rest he sold, except for his car. His tenants were nervous about his moving out of the country, so he struck a bargain with them. He wanted to leave his car parked in the garage, but he would hire a firm to manage the property while he was gone. Finding the right property manager was difficult and time consuming, but after inquiring with several companies, he found one who would take care of the property for a reasonable cost and didn't require him to present a financial statement before accepting the job, which was good, since he was currently unemployed.

The Ljubljana Police regretted that Oz was no longer able to work on the Hine's murder case, but his moving to Portland could be advantageous. Chief Mlakar called the Portland Police Department to explain who Ozbart Zagar was and asked them to allow Oz to assist with their investigation. He gave Oz a formal letter of introduction to hand to the Portland police when he arrived.

This prospect was exciting to Oz. He stopped shaving, so that by the time he arrived in Portland, his beard would cover the lower part of his face and neck. He liked himself in a beard. He was still feeling the sting of Chief Grgić's final retort.

One problem remained and it seemed insurmountable: he would be forced to return to Zagreb if he couldn't find a job in the U.S. before his visitor's visa expired. But, at least for now, he could look forward to assisting the PPD.

CHAPTER 14

APRIL, 1997

Brenda's ticket was for a flight from Trieste to Portland, Oregon, but it was scheduled to depart two days after Maric got off the bus at Trieste Airport. She didn't want to wait. By then, whoever was after her may figure out where she was. She had Brenda's money, so she decided to pay the penalty and change her ticket to the flight that left that day. Maric checked 'her' bag and went to the gate to wait.

Most of the people were speaking Italian, but she heard Serbo-Croat from some men sitting behind her. She didn't turn around to look at them, but with nothing to do, she did try to listen to their conversation. They spoke in low tones. She thought she heard them say "Portland." When they boarded the short flight to Rome, she got to see their faces. All three were big men who looked strong. Two were clean shaven, but the dark-haired one had a long mustache. Another looked like his nose had been broken. She thought: ex-military. On the flight, she picked up a few more fragments of conversation. She thought they were Serbs.

The stewardess handed her a customs form, which she filled out immediately. Maric wondered why Brenda's ticket was to Portland? It was then she remembered the letter. She took it out of her pocket and read it. It was from Brenda' parents and, although there was no return address, it was postmarked *Portland, Oregon*. For most of the rest of the flight she gratefully slept, knowing that once she landed, a whole new set of problems awaited her.

At Chicago's O'Hare Airport, all passengers had to go through customs. The hall was very crowded. Maric got in the line for American citizens. She really worried that the officer would check her passport closely and notice that she didn't resemble Brenda Hines. She needn't have worried. He hardly looked at her. Her bag had been checked through to Portland, so all she had to do was get herself to another gate, one that was in a terminal for domestic flights. She spotted the three men. They seemed to be turning in circles looking bewildered as to what to do. They don't know English, she surmised, but she mustn't try to help them. They did finally arrive at the correct gate, just as Maric was boarding.

When the plane landed at Portland Airport, Maric felt exhausted. The three Serbs were at the baggage carousel, now talking loudly to each other. Maric perked up when she heard them say something about a man who was going to take them to their job. She watched the first man retrieve his bag. He waited for the other two. Finally, Brenda's suitcase came. She grabbed it and quickly followed the men through the exit doors. They walked up to an older man holding a sign with "HFS" printed on it. Maric walked right up to the man herself. The four men were speaking Serbo-Croat. Maric stood right next to them and listened to the discussion about their jobs.

She spoke up to get the man's attention: "I want to work." She had decided to speak only in English. Showing her facility in the language just might help her get a job in America. Of course, her accent was obviously Slavic. The older man turned to look at her with an expressionless face, and then turned to the men to ask them if they knew her. They said no. He ignored her and went on talking to them. She kept saying that she wanted to work. Finally, he asked if she could cook. She told him she was a fabulous cook. He burst out laughing, and within a few minutes, agreed to let her try to cook at his hotel.

The man's name was Joe. She told him her name was Mary Andrews. He led the four of them to his van. Broken nose tried to take the passenger seat next to Joe, but Joe asked him to sit in the back with the others. With three rows of seats there was plenty of room. Joe drove out of the airport. Maric had no idea where they were going. She listened carefully to the men's conversations and looked out of the window. She was in America! She was excited, but on edge.

Being amongst four strangers was scary, but she was distracted by the scenery of pine forests and farmland. They kept on driving. After two more hours, the terrain changed to scrub land with just an occasional farm and a few trees. Small jade-colored bushes were everywhere. They couldn't still be in Oregon. Surely they must be in the next state. She could tell by the shadows that they had been driving east. What was the state east of Oregon? U.S. geography was hardly mentioned in school. Imagine 52 states! As she had observed from the air, this country was enormous.

Maric had never seen landscape like this. It was not appealing to her. She found its barrenness intimidating. If she had to escape, where would she go? Where could she get help? Joe must have sensed that the men also found the landscape unusual. "We call this 'The Big Empty,'" he said in Serbo-Croat to the men in the back of the van.

After five hours, they finally reached a town that Joe said was Burns. They passed through it and must have turned south. Still, the little jade-green bushes were everywhere. Maric started seeing huge patches of elevated land with flat tops and steep sides. The flat tops fascinated her. Might they be made of dried lava? Then they passed by lakes on both sides of the road. She wanted to ask questions, but thought it was best to stay silent. Maric felt another spike of alarm.

Joe informed the men: "These lakes are called Malheur and Harney. You'll be removing barbed wire around here. This whole area is the Malheur Wildlife Refuge."

Gazing over the lakes, the number of birds was astounding—birds of all sizes and in every direction. Her fascination helped to ease her anxiety.

Finally, Joe turned off the paved highway onto a gravel road for a mile. He parked in front of a series of low wooden buildings. Maric caught the name of the place on a sign as they drove in: "The Harney Field Station." Nothing made sense to her. Joe told her he was dropping the men off here, she should stay in the van, and he would come back and they'd go on to the hotel. How could there be a hotel out here?

He came back a half hour later and drove further south on the same straight highway for another fifteen minutes. Then the road bent west, wrapping around an elevated ridge. A group of small buildings was nestled in the bend in the road. As they approached it, a sign read: "Frenchglen, population eleven." Huge trees lined both sides of the road. A few sheds were dilapidated, but most of the other structures were well kept. The Frenchglen Hotel was one of these, white framed, with a screened-in front porch.

⅏

Three weeks later, Maric opened the squeaky screen door and descended the wooden steps of the Frenchglen Hotel. It was a chilly morning but bright and clear. In the distance, she could see the rise in the land that they called a mountain. Otherwise, there was nothing much to see in that direction. No wind stirred the leaves in the trees on the other side of the road. Highway 205, was it called? Highway—ridiculous!—she crossed it without looking, to walk to the school.

She was starting to 'get the hang of' her job. She recalled Joe's exact words the day she first arrived. He was looking at Luke, his son, when he told her that she would be the "hotel's cook and cleaner." Joe also told her that if ever there were many guests, Susie, from down the road, would stop in to help out. "That might happen on the ocassional weekend. Luke will show you where everything is and break you in."

So many new expressions to learn: "getting the hang of," "help out," "break in." She had started a list. From her studies of English in Bosnia, she had learned that trailing prepositions could alter a verb's meaning. So many idioms were completely new.

Susie was friendly and considerate. Of course, her first question was: "Where are you from?" Maric didn't want to be rude, but she had to keep her past private. Her default answer was: "The Balkans." Susie, perhaps, was too embarrassed to reveal her ignorance (a city? a country?), which gave Maric time to ask a diverting question. "Is there a computer anywhere in Frenchglen?"

Susie suggested that Maric use the school's computer. She was one of two school teachers in Frenchglen, the one who lived in town. So this fine, crisp morning, Maric walked the 200 yards to the school, passing three other small buildings, one possibly a home, and a bush of squawking blackbirds with yellow heads. Most of the big trees she had learned were cottonwoods.

Susie greeted her holding a floppy disk. "If you need one of these, Mary, please take this. It can be yours to keep. The school will never miss it." Maric thanked her. She actually had a blank floppy in her room at the hotel, but kept it hidden with the others. She gratefully accepted Susie's gift.

Susie led her into the school. They passed through the center room quietly, where the other teacher was reading a story to a group of young children seated on a rug. "To get to the office, we have to go through this center room," Susie whispered. "The school has only three rooms. We call this our main one, as it serves as a classroom, library, art, and music room."

After Susie saw that Maric knew what to do, she left her alone at the computer.

While she waited to get online, Maric could hear Susie talking to the students in the other classroom. She seemed to have much more intimate knowledge of each child than Maric could remember in Bosnian schools. That might be an advantage, she thought, of such a rural setting as this.

Once online, Maric checked her Yahoo account. "Please, please show me I haven't lost anything," she muttered under her breath. Someone in Croatia had told her that if you don't use Yahoo for a month, they erase their record of you. By then, it had been well over a month. Her account opened—hooray! All her emails to herself had come through. This meant she had all the transcriptions—a year and a half of work. Relief! Now she had three types of copies of this vital information: email, floppy disks, and tapes. The tapes were hidden in her room along with the floppys. If someone stole both from her, she would still have her email records.

She eased her muscles and leaned back in the computer chair. She still had another hour before she had to go back to work at the hotel. What should she do on the computer in this free time? Now that she was becoming accustomed to her job and living in the Frenchglen Hotel, her present challenge was keeping her spirits up and coping with loneliness. She was so isolated here and a long way from Croatia, with little hope of ever returning. There was no family to write to. She didn't dare write her few friends, as her whereabouts might be traced if she did. Sometimes she'd meet a few guests who came to the hotel, but usually she was too busy to say more than "Hello." No one from home knew she was in Frenchglen, or in the United States, for that matter. Secrecy kept her safe.

About all she could think of doing was to write her memoir. It could be kept secret on a floppy. Reviewing her life over the past ten years would bring friends and family close in her memory. It would be the next best thing to having them there. There was no one she could talk to about her past, but focusing on her memories would help her feel whole.

She had to admit she had been awfully lucky that Joe, the owner of the hotel, had needed a cook. By this time, Luke seemed more at ease with his replacement. He still lived in a cabin behind the hotel, to be available to lend a hand, she supposed. She was given an upstairs room, situated in the back of the hotel, with a view of a few run-down sheds. Her salary was $50 per week, with free room and board. Sweet! (Another new expression.)

So now, she lived on the high desert of Eastern Oregon. The nearest place to buy groceries was Burns—a larger town, 60 miles away on Highway 205. Maric had never been there, except when Joe had driven through it on his way to the Harney Field Station and Frenchglen the day of her arrival.

The procedure to get supplies for the hotel went as follows: on Thursdays, Joe drove thirty miles from his ranch to the hotel. He checked on the accounts. Then he drove sixty miles into Burns to get the hotel supplies for the following week, using the list that Maric prepared. He drove back to Frenchglen to drop them off before he returned to his ranch. Just to do all that, he had to drive 180 miles. Maric could tell Joe was disgruntled at having to do the shopping. Luke had other work to do and Maric couldn't drive. Her family had never owned a car, so she had no idea how.

One Thursday afternoon, she was putting groceries away when she heard Luke say to Joe: "Well, you hired her! What's her name? *Mary Andrews!*" She could tell Luke was being sarcastic. Now she was afraid she might lose her job.

On a morning in mid-May, Maric had finished cleaning up after breakfast. She sat down at one of the dining tables to write out the grocery list. It was an impossible task because she never knew how many guests they would have for dinner or on what night they would come. She had made up her mind to serve *sarma* one night. A Croatian dish every now and then would be good for the guests.

Her thoughts were interrupted when a man and a boy of about fourteen walked in wearing baseball caps. She hadn't heard a car drive up, so she thought they were probably people she hadn't met yet who lived in town.

"Howdy," the man said grinning, "we're here for a cup of belly wash."

Maric opened her mouth but she had no idea how to respond.

"Ah, good. I see you still have some already hot," looking at the flask of coffee on the hot plate.

Relieved to understand what 'belly wash' meant, she smiled and hopped up to bring out two mugs from the kitchen.

"Would you like some breakfast to go with the coffee?"

"No, we ate a couple of hours ago. We're just out target shootin'. Junior here wants to get in some practice before huntin' season."

Maric thought she heard neighing out the front door. After serving them, she took a peek out the window. Two horses were tied up to the post in front of the porch.

"You're new here, are you?"

"Yes, I came five weeks ago."

"Where are you from?"

Maric hesitated before answering, "Croatia." She abandoned her usual answer of "The Balkans" as it never got her anywhere. She didn't want to say "Bosnia," because they may start asking questions about the war.

"Crowley?"

"No, Dad, Croatia! ...Where's that?"

"Eastern Europe."

"By golly! ...I'm Steve, by the way and this is Junior, my son. "

"Nice to meet you. I'm Mary."

She watched them climb back on their horses. Scabbards were strapped to their saddles to carry their rifles. Maric smiled to think that she had become the cook and cleaner for a hotel in the 'wild west.'

Later that day, Luke asked: "How would you like to learn to drive? ...I can teach you. Don't worry, it's a piece of cake out here and it should be good for laughs," he said.

Maric mentally put 'piece of cake' on her list of expressions to learn. She had been in the States all of five weeks, landing in a town of just eleven people. The nearest larger place was 60 miles away. As a hiding place, Frenchglen couldn't be beat. And now she was going to learn how to drive.

It was hard when she first came because she could tell that Luke didn't want his father to hire her. Maybe he thought she couldn't cook. Well, she could cook, she told him: "We eat differently in Croatia. We eat lamb, not beef so much. Many of our dishes involve seafood."

"Fat chance of getting much seafood around here," Luke said. "Maybe a few fish out of the lakes and rivers. What'd ya expect, this is cattle country...."

She quickly learned to cook roast beef, pot roast, and pork chops—dishes people out west loved. Recently, however, she started adding a few dishes of her own. The first time she made *grah*, she decided not to tell anybody what was in it. Food was served family style at the hotel. That night, the bowl of *grah* was the first to be emptied. She heard Luke answer the guests that it was a stew of some sort. After he was questioned further, he said: "Darned, if I know what's in it." That was the first night Luke helped her wash dishes. Later she made *bosanki lonac*. The guests liked that, too.

ॐ

Living on the high desert was definitely strange. Maric had always thought of deserts as oceans of sand, like the pictures she had seen of Saudi Arabia. The ground here was more like small-grained gravel. There were all sorts of holes: big and small. She liked looking for them each Tuesday when she took the trash to the dump, a mile outside of town. She wondered what animal or insect might live in each one.

She was now driving Joe's old Pontiac each Tuesday with bags of trash in the back. The dump was a big pit surrounded by a chain-link fence, but it couldn't be seen from where she had to park the car. She had to carry each bag down a path and between some lava boulders before she came to the gate. Once all her bags were there, she unlocked the gate. Throwing the bags in was the fun part. Little creatures, mostly lizards, skittered for cover under rocks. The fence was to keep big animals, like cougars and bobcats, out. That's what Luke had told her.

When she was at the dump, she liked to check the various holes in the ground near the fence. One was so large that she asked Luke about it. "Badger," he said. "A burrow entrance that large must be that of a badger." Evidently, according to Luke, badgers were fierce animals and wouldn't hesitate to attack anything. Luke liked to scare her. "Watch out for rattlesnakes. They'll strike without warning when you're right near where they're hiding."

Occasionally, she could hear something moving behind the fence, before opening the gate. She tried to convince herself it was only a vulture or raven eating the remnants of the pot roast she had cooked a week before. Lizards were everywhere. They were small enough to pass through the links. Maybe the badger had another exit to his burrow, one that allowed him to enter the dump with ease. Luke told her they were nocturnal and solitary. Perhaps it had moved on and dug another burrow somewhere else. Digging would be hard here. The soil was rough and abrasive. Luke told her this part of Eastern Oregon was within the Great Basin. That meant it had been covered with lava hundreds of feet thick thousands of years ago (or was it millions of years ago?).

CHAPTER 15

EARLY JUNE, 1997

Back in mid-April, when Joe held his "HFS" sign up at the airport, waiting for the men to emerge from the baggage claim, he was perplexed to have a small young woman walk up to him rolling a suitcase. What is this he thought? There were supposed to be only three men. But there she was. She acted as if she was doing exactly what was expected of her. She didn't answer any questions, but just kept saying that she was Mary Andrews and that she wanted to work. She sure didn't look like she'd be up to cutting barbed wire in icy cold water. She was so small, she must have weighed all of 110 pounds. He figured the guys in Trieste must have forgotten to tell him about her because she was only a woman. They were probably giving her to him as a way of saying thanks for taking care of the men. Well fine, he thought. He'd find some way she could be useful.

They had a six-hour drive from the Portland Airport to Frenchglen, plenty of time to find out about her. Joe found that she would only answer him if he voiced his questions in English, yet he was pretty sure she understood Serbo-Croat. He had the feeling she was listening carefully to what the men were saying.

He always chuckled remembering how she answered him by saying: "I'm a fabulous cook."

She was so serious and confident, which became comical when she took off her scarf. She looked like a little monkey, with those ears. What could she have done to have them send her here?

By this time, Joe had to admit that Mary had been an excellent cook and she managed the hotel well. He couldn't have asked for anyone better. Still, he didn't like her past being secret from him. Where was she from? By coming with the others she had to be Serb, but he wasn't even sure of that.

Joe started thinking of ways he could get her to open up. Yesterday, he had driven to the hotel so he could give her two history books: one on U.S. history, and the other on the history of the Balkans through World War I. "The book about the U.S. I used to teach myself when I studied to become a citizen. That was about forty years ago," he said laughing.

"I'll never get citizenship," she told him.

Ah ha, he thought, maybe I'll get something out of her. He waited, but she didn't expand on her comment. She was deep in thought.

"Thank you for the books. I will enjoy reading them." She offered him coffee and cookies, then asked him some questions about the hotel. When the conversation began to lag, she said she had to start preparing the dessert for dinner. "I know eight people have made reservations and six are spending the night."

That's good, he thought. Business is starting to pick up. He knew he would have to try again at another time, but couldn't help himself from making one last probe. "Whenever you want to tell me about things, I'm here to listen." No response. He opened the door to the porch to leave, turned back to look at her, and smiled. He thought her eyes were glistening more than usual.

CR

Joe gave it a month, hoping Mary would loosen up. By this time, he knew that she was Croatian or Bosnian but nothing more. He telephoned Zoran in Portland to see if he knew anything about her. "Why was Mary sent from Trieste with the men?" he asked. Zoran sounded alarmed. He asked Joe to describe Mary in detail. What was she doing now and where was she living? A week later, Zoran called Joe back and told him not to worry about Mary, then he hung up.

Great! Joe wasn't worried so much as he was curious. He was also annoyed. He didn't like a woman to keep a secret from him.

Now he had a new plan of attack. He drove to the hotel on a quiet morning, hoping he could have her undivided attention. She offered him coffee and a piece of toast. He started to tell her what he described as 'his dark secret.' "Luke doesn't know this. I'm trustin' you not to tell him. You and everybody else around here know me as Joe Gutić, but really I am Joakim Pavelic." He paused to check her reaction. There was none. She showed no change of expression. Good grief, he thought! Maybe she's never heard of him. Nonetheless, he soldiered on.

"I am the son of Ante Pavelic." He noticed that she raised her eyebrows. He waited. Finally she started to talk.

"I know Pavelic was Croatian, an extreme fascist, and the leader of the Croatia puppet state of the Nazis during World War II. That person was your dad?"

"Yes!"

"He was responsible for horrible atrocities against the Serbs, so horrible that even hardcore Nazis cringed. My father told me there were several concentration camps to torture and kill Serbs, Jews, Gypsies, homosexuals, and Communists."

"Yes, yes!" There was a little smirk on his face. He went on: "I was my parents' last child, born in 1934, Joakim Pavelic. When WWII was over in 1945, Dad quickly left the country to go into hiding. By the time I was eleven, we were all safely living in Argentina together. I grew up on ranches and worked as a vaquero. I knew what my father had done in Croatia, and was ashamed. He was cold and harsh. I left Argentina and made my way north to the States.

"I spoke Spanish, and in those days, it was easy to slip in and out of countries. My high school diploma and vaquero experience helped me land jobs. I worked my way to eastern Oregon and ended up on the RR Ranch.

"Several years later, I heard that my family had been dis-covered hiding in Argentina, but before they could extradite my dad, he escaped with my mother to Spain."

"Yes, I remember my mother saying how disgraceful it was that Franco's Spain had given him asylum."

"In the meantime, I had fallen in love with Rosa. Her fa-ther, Rudolfo Romero, owned the RR Ranch. We got married and when her parents died, I became the owner of the ranch."

"I thought your ranch was called Stoka Ranch."

"Yes, we changed the name."

"Why?"

"I thought Stoka was more distinctive. Well, here's the thing I worry about, Mary: I have always feared that my father's genes would show up in Luke. I have never had the courage to tell Luke who his grandfather was. I try to make up for my father by help-ing anyone from the Balkans who needs help."

He didn't ask Mary to respond to his story, thinking it was best to let it sit with her. His aim was to make her think he was someone she could trust. A week later, he brought her a bottle of rakia, a customary aperitif that is drunk throughout the Balkans. "This is for hearing me out the other day. I feel so much better having told someone."

She thanked him, still holding the bottle and looking at the label. "I'm surprised you can buy this around here."

Joe smiled but did not explain how he had bought it. "Well, I'll be going." He started through the door to the porch.

"Where did you get it?" she asked.

He was not prepared for her question. He purposely mum-bled his answer as he was leaving. "A Balkan specialty shop in Portland." He left her standing in the dining room. Now, having shown he trusted her, surely she would soon divulge who she was exactly, and why she had come to the States with the men.

CHAPTER 16

SUMMER, 1997

The Frenchglen hotel was so small there was no lobby, unless you considered the front porch a lobby. When you walked in from the porch, there was the dining room with three large tables and benches. In one corner, there was a two-seater couch. Maric had a desk, more like a podium, where she checked guests in and out. There was a small alcove where Frenchglen shirts, t-shirts, and caps were displayed for sale. On either side of her desk were entrance ways: one to the kitchen and the other to a hall with a stairway going up to the guest rooms.

One night in early May, Maric made *bosanki lonac*. Things did not go well. Everybody loved the dish, including Luke, but one of the guests, a woman named Ronnie from Connecticut, got drunk. She had a strident voice, as irritating as nails scraping on a blackboard. Furthermore, her voice was so loud it was impossible for other guests to carry on conversations with each other. Even from the kitchen, Maric could hear everything Ronnie said: her last trip to Bermuda, her stint as a hostess in the Palmer House restaurant in Chicago, blah-blah-blah....

Maric decided to take matters in her own hands. She filled the water pitcher full of ice water, stood behind Ronnie and pretended to trip. Luke jumped up and offered to take the soaked Ronnie upstairs to her room. Once upstairs, he told Maric later, the woman staggered to the bathroom and tossed her cookies. (Maric loved that expression.) Fortunately the bathroom upstairs was out of earshot from the guests.

Maric apologized and cleaned up the 'spilt' water. Then she brought out small glasses and the bottle of rakia. The guests asked her to sit down at the table. By the time Luke returned, they had asked her where she was from. Hesitantly she told them she was from Bosnia. They seemed so friendly, especially this one older woman. She thought her name was Vera.

"Ah," the older woman said, "I grew up in Split, myself."

Their eyes locked. Maric thought of her parents and home. She so much wanted to talk to Vera, but she was fighting back tears. The guests finished off the plum liquor and she stood up to clear the table. Fortunately, Luke took over the conversation while Maric busied herself in the kitchen making coffee and tea.

Although he didn't cook or manage the hotel anymore, Luke still slept in a cabin at the back. That night, when he left to go to his cabin, he smiled at Maric, and for once looked her in the eye: "I see you've got some coyote in you—adaptable, opportunistic."

She guessed that was a compliment.

Ↄ

A while ago, Maric had occasion to meet Mike. He usually sat outside the Frenchglen Mercantile, a large rambling structure, a store and gas station of sorts, four buildings away from the hotel. Mike was large, both in height and girth, with muttonchop whiskers. He usually wore a dirty checkered apron and a derby hat. It seemed he spent much of the day sitting on the stoop and waiting for people to stop and possibly buy something. Always at Mike's side sat his friendly mongrel, Sniffer. Mike and Sniffer seemed mutually devoted and equally content with each other.

On her way to the school, she had to pass by the Mercantile. She always smiled at Mike and said hello, but she kept on walking quickly so she didn't have to talk with him. She was timid about striking up a conversation. He looked so different from people back home. Also, she didn't want to become friends and then feel obligated to buy his gas. She preferred to fill the Pontiac in Burns, where gas was cheaper.

She finally did talk to Mike one day when the hotel's trash bin was filled to the brim. That was a Tuesday. She was just about to make her weekly trip to the dump when she heard a commotion outside the kitchen. Sniffer was trying to topple the bin. By the time she got outside, Sniffer had accomplished his goal. "No! No!" she called out. "Stop that!" Her family had never had a dog, so she didn't really know what to do. By her second "Stop that!" Mike had arrived on the scene.

"I'm so sorry," he said picking the dog up, too late to prevent Sniffer from snatching the lamb bone from Sunday night's dinner. "Let me get him on a leash and I'll be right back to clean this up." Upon his return, Mike not only helped pick up the debris, but put the trash bags in the back of the Pontiac for Maric.

That got them to talking. Mike, she learned, was also a ranchhand for a cattle ranch in the hills south of Frenchglen. It sounded like he was as fond of the cows as he was of Sniffer. He spoke with disdain of "gentlemen ranchers," who are in it just for the money. "They come down to their ranches only on weekends, to check on the cows. I check on mine twice a day."

Mike didn't own the Mercantile, but he managed it for the owner and slept in a back room at night. The store sold a variety of practical items such as milk, eggs, bread, butter, canned goods, a few frozen meats, and ice cream. Mostly it was filled with a hodgepodge of other things that were whimsical at best: a butter churner; 1910 postcards (not of Frenchglen, but of 'Paris, France') a spinning wheel, some lathes, a three-legged stool that wobbled, and a kerosene lamp. The better stuff was placed at the front of the store. As you moved back further inside and into other rooms, the items became a jumble of junk, held together by dust and cobwebs.

Yes, you could refuel in Frenchglen. Really, all of Malheur was a place to refuel. Migratory birds loved the extensive series of shallow lakes. Maric had been told that thousands of Ross and

Snow Geese came here each spring, so many that the fields appeared to be covered in snow. Guests often spoke of the thrill of witnessing their explosive uplift, fourteen thousand of them rising together in a cacophonous harmony of honks. Maric had seen it for herself recently. She was driving to Burns when a blizzard of birds suddenly filled the sky. She stopped the car and got out to watch them.

Luke had given her a brief explanation of the ranching business. That was when she heard about Rosa, his mother, flying the helicopter up Steens Mountain. What a woman, Maric thought. She was pleased with herself now that she knew how to drive a car, but a helicopter—that was really special. Maric would love to fly up to see Steens Mountain.

Every week, when she drove by the Stoka Ranch, she thought of Joe and questioned why he changed its name. Why did he give it a Serbo-Croat name? You would think if he didn't like RR Ranch, he would have chosen a Spanish name, having spent only his first eleven years in Croatia and the rest of his early life in Argentina, and especially since the woman he married was of Mexican descent. Maybe Luke would show her the ranch someday. Her limited gas supply meant she couldn't just gallivant around. Distances were too great. She wasn't familiar enough with the area to even know what she should try to see.

Joe must have been a handsome man when he was young. Now in his mid-sixties, he showed some stiffness in his walk, but otherwise, he seemed to be in reasonably good health. His hair was gray, with some of the blond tones of his youth still showing. She thought, for sure, he was lonely, but he wouldn't admit it. She had learned that loneliness is an acceptable trait in southeast Oregon. It grooms most people for being sociable. Joe was an exception, she thought.

Luke was different from his dad, shorter and darker skinned from spending much of his day outside. His skin was already showing a somewhat leathery appearance. Maric assumed he was a few years older than she. He talked like a cowboy, but he had studied environmental issues at Oregon State University. She had noticed that he didn't talk about those interests in front of his dad, or to her, for that matter. Occasionally, she overheard him comment about such things to a guest.

"Our guests come from all over Oregon and other states. Some come to hunt and fish, but most come for the birds," Luke told her. "This part of Oregon is on the Pacific Flyway—a migration route for birds."

"What bird do most people want to see?"

"Hard to say...probably the Sage-grouse."

"I've never heard of it. Where could I see one?"

"It's not easy. You'd have to get up really early. I'll take you the next time we don't have guests spending the night. I mean when you don't have anyone to make breakfast for, let me know."

That's never going to happen, Maric thought. But a week later, five people came to dinner and didn't spend the night. She told Luke she could go the next morning.

"Go where?"

Oh brother. He doesn't remember. "To see the grouse!"

"Oh yeah.... OK, be ready to leave tomorrow morning at 5:30 A.M."

Maric had assumed they would walk somewhere, but no, Luke took her in his pickup a good 15 minutes away. For the last bit of driving she wasn't even sure they were on a road. They sat and waited in the pickup until it got light enough to see well. When Luke gave the sign, they opened the doors quietly, not bothering to shut them, and walked a short distance to get a better look.

Maric heard popping sounds and whistles—the grouse equivalent to crooning love songs—emanating from several fat birds with spiky tails, held erect like a fan. It was the strangest bird Maric had ever seen. Two to five males were strutting, each displaying its yellow neck air sacs, which they puffed out to impress the females. Their strutting stage was a barren patch of land. Luke called it a "lek."

"You know the males swallow almost a gallon of air to inflate those sacs."

"Really?"

"Then they squeeze it out to make that loud noise, those booming pops that you hear. They strut like that for about four hours, starting early in the morning. I don't know if you can see them, but there are several hens waiting around, appearing disinterested. After mating, the hen leaves the lek and walks away until she finds a good nesting site where she feels safe to lay her eggs."

As Maric and Luke walked back to the truck he added: "They eat the leaves of sagebrush and that's about it. In winter they eat the snow for water."

"Just incredible!"

"Sage-grouse are declining in number, though. It's quite a worry. They need a habitat of huge areas of unbroken sagebrush."

Maric became aware that this terrain, although static in appearance, had fascinating secrets that its barrenness camouflaged. She yawned her way through the rest of the day. Now, she better understood why people came from all over the world to see the birds.

ଔ

By mid June, Maric was in the habit of looking up the news on the school computer whenever she could leave the hotel for an hour or so. Other than that, she had little intellectual stimulus. Some days, she thought she was going to die of boredom. Nights, when there were no guests, she would have loved to use the computer, but after four, the school was locked up. Susie said she could read any of the books in the school library. Maric read *Little Town on the Prairie* by Laura Ingalls Wilder. When finished, she thought more had been going on in De Smet, South Dakota, than in Frenchglen.

She wished she could take advantage of the library in Burns.

It would be lovely to be able to take books back to Frenchglen, but she had no identification that would allow her to get a library card. She had long since buried Brenda Hines's passport, wallet, and traveler's checks. She had wrapped them in a plastic bag before hiding them in the garbage dump outside of town. She still wasn't sure if that was a wise thing to do. If they were ever found, they would definitely incriminate her. On the other hand, perhaps she may need them to get out of the country fast.

The day she discovered the history museum in Burns, her spirits picked up. Although it was open only between ten and three, four times a week, one of those days was Thursday—the day Maric went to Burns to buy groceries. Like the library, the museum had a computer and a printer for visitors to use. But unlike the library, a user didn't need identification to get on line.

On her first visit to the museum, she met the curator, Mrs. Spooner, a frail woman with white hair who was eager to point out the arrangement of the displays. "Here is the Indian section. Over here are photos of early settlers and their histories…"

Maric thanked her and walked around looking and reading captions. At last, she was able to learn about this strange and different region she found herself in. The displays were not slick, but interesting and informative. Their homemade quality was appealing to Maric. They showed an honest pride in the history and accomplishments of the people. Maric felt Mrs. Spooner's eyes following her as she moved around the large room.

She started at the Indian display. Until then, she hadn't thought that Indians might be living in Eastern Oregon. "Of course, you're in the west, you idiot," she said to herself, "cowboy and Indian country." During the week, she asked Luke about it: "I've never heard anything about Indians. Where are they?"

"There is a Paiute reservation just north of Burns."

Once she got the correct spelling of that tribe's name, she had her research topic for the following Thursday:

…The Paiutes were semi-nomadic hunter-gatherers
who relied on nuts, plants, and fish, following their

food to high and low elevations, depending on the time
of year. They made sandals, traps, fishing nets, and
wove baskets using sagebrush, willow, and tule.... Their
baskets were tight enough to carry water.

*   ...The 1860s ushered in a flood of aggressive,*
land-hungry settlers in the area, who were backed by
U.S. soldiers.... The situation eventually induced the
Paiutes to negotiate with the federal government. In
1872, President Ulysses S. Grant signed off on the 1.8
million-acre Malheur Reservation.

*   But later, the Paiutes were forced to move away.*
They were relocated elsewhere in the country, leav-
ing their Malheur Reservation empty and available
to cattlemen and homesteaders. The government
eventually allowed the Paiute to return, but gave them
marginal land that was resistant to cultivation, just
north of Burns. In this new location, the Paiutes were
well separated from the lakes—lakes that had, for cen-
turies, provided them with food and resources. Their
present reservation has about 14,000 acres, .8% of their
original area.

What a sad history, thought Maric. She wondered what
other interesting stories this barren land held. She knew that
malheur in French meant "misfortune." Why did so many features around here have *malheur* in their name: Malheur River,
Lake Malheur, Malheur Creek, etc.?

The following week, Maric learned that in the early 1800s,
a French Canadian trapper was probably the first to apply that
name to a river he was working after he discovered that Indians
had stolen his cache of beaver hides. Ever since then, that river
was known as the Malheur River. Maric wondered if there were
other tales of misfortune.

Then she got to thinking about Frenchglen. What inspired
that name? She speculated that a Frenchman came here, had

some good luck, and claimed it for his country.

Maric had put off contacting Majesira. She could get on her email account both at the museum and at the school computer, but she hadn't felt safe enough to try to contact anyone back home. It had taken her two months to build up the confidence. If her illegal status were exposed, she would be sent back to Zagreb immediately.

But it wasn't just that. There were other reasons she had not contacted Majesira yet. Some had to do with guilt. She had failed to get the tapes delivered to The Hague. A man had come all the way from the Netherlands and she stood him up.

Another source of guilt was that someone had died on account of her actions. Granted the killer had made a mistake, but if Maric hadn't done everything she had, Brenda would still be alive.

She also wondered why Majesira had suggested that she wear her turquoise rain jacket to Ljubljana. Was the jacket to be used to identify her to someone who wanted to kill her? Maric was absolutely convinced that she was the intended victim. But she just couldn't think that Majesira had wanted her dead. That would disturb her to the core.

Who was Brenda Hines? Did Majesira know Brenda? And what did Brenda want to do in Trieste? Maybe Brenda was the intended victim and there was no mistake in identity. Brenda just happened to have a jacket like Maric's. Too many coincidences! "Ayee! Enough!" she told herself. She would never figure it all out.

Also, Maric hadn't yet checked out the Harney Field Station, to see what those men were up to. If she told Majesira about it, Majesira might ask her to investigate the place, and Maric was frightened of going there.

Time to 'bite the bullet' as Luke would say. She decided to just email Majesira and not tell her where she was.

Her email stated: "I still have the evidence, but I cannot reveal where I am." She apologized for not writing sooner and asked for news. Once sent, she erased it from her sent mail folder.

Maric felt good. She had finally come to grips with her guilt and fear. Although she looked forward to Majesira's reply, she worried about what her friend would say.

CHAPTER 17

All afternoon, Luke had been driving his Ford pickup with Cooper sitting next to him. It was moments like these that Luke was happiest. This day, he was on the other side of Lake Malheur checking carp traps. When he found a carp, he had to catch it and throw it in the back of his pickup. He discovered a new diversion stream to put on the map. Its location was added to the list for which the county still needed money. Just purchasing and installing one dam and trap could cost $500 to $1,000 easily, depending on its size.

Every time he stopped the truck, Cooper jumped out and ran around as though he had never been free before. Cooper was a mixed breed with a lot of retriever in him. Now that Luke's mother had died, it was only Cooper that gave Luke unconditional love. Cooper slept at the foot of Luke's bed and made sure he got up on time in the morning. Everybody in Frenchglen knew and loved Cooper, especially Sniffer, Mike's dog. Sniffer was all heart, but undisciplined. Sniffer tried to lead Cooper astray, but most of the time Cooper knew better than to follow.

Once a week, Luke had to check on the progress of barbed wire removal for the Harney Field Station. There was still 450 miles of the fencing in the water and another 200 miles near the shoreline that needed to be taken out. Road access was nil, so inspection had to be done on horseback. Unfortunately, for that job, he had to leave Cooper at home, because, as good as he was, he chased the birds and trampled their nests.

Luke liked the work because it gave him lots of time to think. It was particularly pleasant in the summer months, but he also enjoyed it in the fall. Eastern Oregon had a continental climate: cold winters, hot summers, and four distinct seasons. He liked them all. He didn't mind the dryness, either.

Luke got to thinking about the time he had tried to explain to Mary about the rain shadow effect of the Cascade Mountains. She really tickled him.

"Humph," she said, "we have mountains in Bosnia and we have both rain in the summer and snow in the winter," she told him.

He wished she'd make up her mind. One minute she's Croatian and the next she's Bosnian. He had looked up both countries in the atlas. "They're puny! No wonder she gets confused."

Then there was the time when he taught her how to drive. For a long while, he thought that her problem was that she had no way of getting around, to see things for herself. His dad was getting tired of going into Burns to buy the groceries, so he had asked him to let the hotel use his `62 Pontiac and he'd teach Mary how to drive. "So what if she wrecks that piece of junk. It's just been sitting out behind the barn collecting blackbird poop."

"But I don't have a driver's license," Mary said, when he brought the car to the hotel.

"Who's going to care?" he asked her. "Half the people around here don't have licenses. Many are illegal. You'll fit right in." She didn't appreciate his humor.

He couldn't believe how short she was. He had to get a pillow for her to sit on so she could see over the wheel. The seat had to be pulled really close so she could reach the pedals, which meant Luke could hardly fit his legs inside. She must have seen him grimace. "Most Croatians are very tall," she said. "World famous basketball teams usually have at least one Croatian player."

He chuckled and said that he heard Croatia was famous for its shrimps. He thought she got that one. He knew he had to be nicer to her, but she was so much fun to tease. It was like having a little sister.

He remembered the sneakers she wore back then. They were too big for her, and he worried that she could trip changing from the accelerator to the brake. That wasn't safe. Then he recalled the slacks she often wore in the beginning. She had to roll up the cuffs to keep them from dragging on the ground.

It occurred to Luke that Mary probably was wearing hand-me-downs, what with the war that she had been through. She never talked about her life. He knew her parents and sister were killed only because he overheard her answering a guest's question one night.

He missed his own mother so much, but he never talked about her either. It was hard because he couldn't say anything about her to his dad. He must miss her too, but he never talked about her. She had been the warm person in the family. Most people who live around here get used to being lonely, he thought. We kind of understand that about each other. That's why we don't turn down an opportunity to chat. Mary probably came here lonely and she can't chat because she knows nothing about what's going on around here. Also, I don't think she wants to talk about her life in…in wherever.

She did speak English very well. He'd give her that. His thoughts wandered. It was certainly a good thing they had already started to make automatic transmissions back in '62. He laughed just imagining the problems he would have had teaching Mary to use a stick shift.

Actually, Mary had gotten the hang of driving pretty quickly. The day she first drove into Burns on her own, after three hours had passed, he finally saw her driving back at 15 miles an hour—her little head with the big ears barely appearing over the steering wheel.

Chapter 18

In May, 1997, Franjo Tudjman telephoned Slobodon Milošević:

T: *Slobodon? Franjo here.*

M: *I recognize your voice. To what do I owe this honor?*

T: *Well, Slobo, I have to start with an apology. Then I have to ask a favor.*

M: *I can hardly wait.*

T: *You remember how we talked about cleaning up our tapes and how I was planning to have a woman transcribe conversations that went on in my office?*

M: *O God! Why in hell didn't you just throw them away? What happened?*

T: *She did the job and finished about two months ago. You know what I had to do, she knew too much.*

M: *I'm not liking this.*

T: *Well, we had it carefully planned. One of my best men would do it in Ljubljana.*

M: *Ljubljana! Jesus to God, let me guess: he killed the wrong person.*

T: *How did you know? ...Well, never mind that. The woman we meant to do away with has disappeared. I don't know where she is and that's where I need your help.*

M: *Why should I help you? Why didn't you just throw the tapes away in the first place? That's what I did. I'll tell you why you didn't. You're an academic, a historian, a petty record keeper, an egoist! You think that whatever you do should be preserved for posterity.*

T: *Why should you help me, you ask? This is your problem too, you know. Some of my conversations were with you and involve the plans that we'll both want to deny when called before the ICTY.*

M: *Oh my God! Why did I ever communicate with you!*

T: *My mole in the ICTY tells me that the court has the tapes.*

M: *Could you claim that the conversations were fabricated?*

T: *No. No. It's our voices on the tapes.*

M: *The transcriber, whoever she is, must never testify in person to the ICTY!*

T: *Exactly. But I don't know where she is.*

M: *OK, tell me what you know about this woman.*

T: *Her name is Maric Andrich, a Bosnian Croat from Mostar.*

M: *Jesus! You couldn't have employed a Croat? Oh no, it had to be a Bosnian Croat? A Croat might have been loyal, but you chose a Croat that lives in Mostar! Ha, oh my God. How many degrees do you have?*

T: *Shut up, Slobo. Can you help me find her?*

M: *Yeah, yeah, I have some ideas. I think she may be in the States, but how will you kill her there?*

T: *Not to worry. My man won't live unless he annihilates her.*

M: *Is that Dinko—Dinko the skin head?*

T: *Yes.*

M: *You tell Dinko, if he fails, I'll get him! ...OK, I'll get back to you with details. And don't ask me how I found out. I wouldn't dream of telling you.*

CHAPTER 19

EARLY JULY, 1997

Vera and Tom had started renting a cabin on the Blitzen River, about a ten-minute drive from Frenchglen. They both loved it, but until he retired, the plan was that Vera would be spending more time there than Tom. It had one bedroom and a few appliances. There was electricity, but no telephone. The absence of a dryer was not a problem. Clothes dried quickly on a line outdoors in Eastern Oregon. Vera noticed it was easy to attract mice. She had to put the bird seed in a metal container with a tight lid. The windows and small porch were screened. She could sit out there listening to insects and frogs at night. Occasionally, deer and even pronghorn could be seen.

What she feared were rattlesnakes. She had already come across one down on the banks of the river. If bitten, she would have to drive herself to Frenchglen and call for an air ambulance. She didn't think she'd be able to get treatment in time, if she attempted to make it to Burns. She tried not to worry about it, but was extra cautious when walking outdoors.

She remembered that while flying with Luke in the helicopter, he mentioned that nature courses were taught at the Harney Field Station. HFS was a thirty-minute drive away, near Lake Malheur. She signed up for: *Ornithology in Marsh, Mountain, and High Desert*. It was not cheap, but the director of the Field Station, Steve Henshaw, was supposedly very knowledgeable. She decided she could get more out of the experience if she boarded at the Field Station during the course. They had dorms and buffet meals, which added to the price considerably.

Vera had not forgotten about the possible hideout for war criminals, something to do with *maller*. She wondered if her wild goose chase might end at the Harney Field Station. It was located about 10 miles northwest of the Frenchglen Hotel, according to the pamphlet:

> *HFS is an environmental study center which engages in activities to improve the survival of wildlife. HFS workers remove barbed wire fences that, during high water season, entangle everything from migrating birds to pronghorn. The field station is run on a shoestring by a nonprofit: the Great Basin Society.*

Vera asked someone in the Chamber of Commerce in Burns about the Harney Field Station. She was amazed that the clerk was so frank:

"Yeah, HFS pays minimum wage (at best) for work that nobody wants to do. It has several dorms, 'rustic' dorms, where the workers and guests sleep. That chumminess also goes for the communal bath houses, the kitchen, and the dining hall—everybody uses them all."

"It sounds like you've stayed there yourself," Vera commented.

"Yeah, once."

When Vera first arrived at the HFS, she checked in with Lily, the director's wife. Yes, she was here for the five-day workshop. Yes, she had already paid in full, including the meals. Lily escorted her to the women's dorm. Vera picked a lower bunk of the four made up with sheets and blankets. She was glad there was a lower still available. Her days climbing ladders were over. She put her suitcase on the bunk of her choice so no one else would claim it. Then she continued to follow Lily for a tour of other important buildings.

Lily told her that, originally, it had been a Job Corps center. Now, it was administered by an environmental non-profit group. At present, among their goals was cutting out the barbed wire surrounding the lakes, and removing the invasive carp within the lakes.

The first workshop would begin in an hour, so she had some time to explore the premises. Vera took her binoculars and started walking the perimeter of the grounds, going east from the dorms. The soil was dry, crunchy, and peppered with small tussocks of grass. The whole place had seen better days. Vera got the impression that the field station was desperate for more funding.

At the east end, she came across two men painting what appeared to be a small warehouse. Time to pretend she was bird-watching. She walked close enough to hear the men's voices, all the time looking up at the building's eaves, where there could be swallows nesting. The men were speaking Serbo-Croat, no question about it. She could understand everything they said. Unfortunately, they didn't say anything of interest. But she had five more days.

In time, she learned that Steve, the director of HFS, was very informed about the wildlife of the area, plants as well as animals. His enthusiasm was infectious and the people taking the workshop were pleased. However, the meals were sparse, the toilets were constantly backed up, and the windows that opened lacked screens. There wasn't enough ventilation in Vera's dorm. That and the snores from one woman often kept her awake.

During the day, whenever there was a break, Vera tried to move within earshot of some of the workers. Out of all the conversations she overheard, two stood out. One man named Vuk talked very crudely about a younger woman who was enrolled in the course with Vera, saying how he could show her a good time, how he could last several hours. Another man named Valdo replied: "Yeah I heard you broke all records at Omarska." Another man laughed.

This sickened Vera. She knew that Omarska was a Serb concentration camp where civilians were held, tortured, and raped during the Bosnian War. She had no doubt that the young woman that Vuk referred to was Linda, the pretty blond girl from Bend, Oregon. Vera was determined to look out for Linda during the rest of their time at the field station.

These men were Serbian War criminals, for sure. Another day, Vera heard a man whose name she thought was Josip, say quite seriously: "Yeah, well to tell you the truth, I'm ashamed. How could I have just followed orders? I even pretended I enjoyed shooting them."

"So why did you decide to come here?" another man asked.

Vera couldn't hear Josip's answer. Now, she was eager to leave HFS. She wanted to go home so she could tell Oz and Tom what she had discovered, but she wouldn't leave Linda unprotected, so Vera stuck it out for two more days. Her reward: she saw Black-throated Sparrows and her first badger.

Vera ran into Luke late one afternoon.

"Where do these workers come from?"

"I'm not sure where Dad digs them up."

"Your dad?"

"Yeah, I think he gets them from L.A. or Portland. Dad's pretty secretive about it, but I'm not complaining. For years we've been trying to find people around here to do this work. These are nasty jobs, like standing in the water cutting barbed wire in the dead of winter. He seems to have found some Serbs who are willing to do the work. I think they're Serbs." Vera almost lost her breath when she realized that Joe was involved in this nefarious business.

Later, when Luke was not around, she asked Steve, "How were you able to find these men?"

"A local rancher has made the arrangements. We are very grateful. It's so hard to get anyone to do this work."

"How can you pay them?" Vera saw nothing wrong with asking nosy questions like that.

"We have a grant."

"Do you mind my asking: how much do the men make?"

Steve, looking a little uncomfortable, answered, "The

minimum wage and, from that, we have to take money for their room and board. They clear about $80 a week. Excuse me, I have something I must tend to."

That's not much money, Vera thought. Then she wondered what they would do with it, stuck way out here, with no way to go anywhere. What will they do once they leave? They don't speak English.

Vera was sensitive to her reputation for asking a lot of questions. There were two reasons she did so. She liked to talk to people, and she was curious about a lot of things. Why was that bad? Sometimes she could tell that her probing annoyed people.

Nonetheless, when Luke showed up at lunch on the last day of the course, Vera couldn't help but ask him something about the gunfire she had heard on the way to Burns. She had spotted some White-faced Ibises and pulled off the road to get a better look. Without the engine going, she became aware that guns were being fired, lots of gunfire. It went on for the whole time she spent looking at the ibises, but she couldn't see anyone shooting. It was too far away.

"Oh yeah, were you driving by alfalfa fields?" Luke asked.

"Could be. I'm not that sure of the different crops."

"That was probably the Rat Camp."

"What's that?"

"Some people like to shoot ground squirrels using the excuse that they eat crops. They do eat the crops for three months of the year. The rest of the time they hibernate in underground colonies. They are really cute. I'm sure you've seen them. They don't store their food but fatten up to carry them through nine months of not eating."

"I have seen them. They are adorable, but probably pests to farmers, right?"

"What people around here fail to realize is that they aerate the soil, and that helps high meadows to filter and hold water so it doesn't just run off. In my opinion, ground squirrels shouldn't be killed." Luke excused himself to get some dessert from the buffet table. Vera expected he would not come back, but she was wrong. Luke took his seat again next to her and continued where he had left off: "Females are only receptive for five hours a year, but, in that short time, they will mate with many different males.... Good pie, for a change!" He downed half his serving in one bite, before continuing: "They have several alarm calls to notify the others of danger."

"Like meerkats!"

"Similar, but ground squirrels are herbivores and meerkats are carnivores. Anyway, an enterprising couple from around here, Francis and Laura Fiewiger, have devised a system of hosting shooting parties. They get permission to bring in a raised platform onto a farmer's field. People pay them money to stand on the platform so they can shoot to kill as many ground squirrels as possible. The Fiewigers call it 'Rat Camp.' They provide the shooters with a full meal afterwards."

Vera could never understand why some people enjoyed killing things. How could taking another creature's life be exciting? Not wanting to stop conversing with Luke, she quickly thought of another question to ask him. "Are they prairie dogs?"

"Prairie dogs are a type of ground squirrel." The last of the pie was eaten. Luke got up to leave, saying: "They do eat a lot of alfalfa, it's hard to convince people of their overall benefit." He stood up and turned to Vera and said, "If you can, why don't you meet with us over dinner some night at the hotel? A group of us locals, Steve, Corwin, whom you haven't met yet, and some others who are interested in the environment, we meet there on Wednesday nights to discuss projects we're working on. Please join us whenever you're around these parts, any Wednesday night at six." Luke tucked his chair in and said goodbye.

CHAPTER 20

JULY, 1997

Joe came to the hotel every Wednesday morning to check the accounts and give Maric the money needed for the next week. Normally, she looked forward to their rendering of the books, but today she was so tired she couldn't stop herself from yawning. For the last three nights, Sniffer had barked incessantly, starting at around 9:00 P.M. until about 2:00 A.M. Even Susie complained about it, and her house was on the other side of town. Mike was very apologetic.

Each morning after, Mike came over to apologize: "Normally, Sniffer sleeps on the back stoop—for years he's been doing that—never a yelp out of him."

"Must be some animal's lurking around," Luke said.

This morning, Luke staggered into the hotel dining room looking as exhausted as Maric felt. "Thank goodness, there were no guests last night," he said to Maric. "Whatever it was that bothered Sniffer bothered Cooper, or maybe Cooper was bothered because Sniffer was bothered. Anyway, Cooper, who usually sleeps next to my bed on the floor, was up pacing, looking out the window, and wimpering all night long."

Maric could hardly respond she was so tired, but roused herself enough to start making breakfast. She had cracked the second egg when Mike walked in, out of breath and quite agitated.

"I can't find Sniffer anywhere. He went quiet around two last night. I thought he had finally gone to sleep and I was so exhausted I didn't go outside and check on him. Now he's nowhere to be found." Mike collapsed on a bench in the hotel's dining area.

Thank goodness those benches are sturdy, Maric thought. She knew why Mike hadn't just brought Sniffer inside to keep him from barking. Whenever she petted the dog, she saw fleas. Then her good manners prevailed and she poured Mike a cup of coffee.

Luke immediately offered to take Cooper out and look for Sniffer. He asked Mike where he had already covered. Dog owners know how to respond to such emergencies, she thought. She listened to Mike describing the range of his search.

"If there was a bitch in heat, he wouldn't be barkin'." The man was beside himself. "Jason Mitchell said a cougar's been spotted a week ago on the lower slope of Steens."

Luke gave him a one-arm hug as best he could, Mike being a large man. "I'll go search for Sniffer. Why don't you rest here? Mary, could you scramble up some eggs for Mike?"

Maric got right on it. Not waiting for her reply, Luke went outside, saying something about Cooper and a leash. Then she heard Luke's pickup pulling out onto Highway 205. She got a glimpse of Cooper sitting upright in the passenger's seat.

An hour later, Mike left to walk home to the Mercantile, leaving Maric with just a few minutes to prepare for Joe's arrival. She didn't expect him to meticulously check her grocery list. By this time, she felt Joe trusted her. He never said much. Maric attributed that to his loneliness, since his wife had died a year ago.

After they had gone over the business for the week, she asked, squelching a yawn, if he could spare time to have a cup of coffee. She had a question to ask him. He seemed quite eager to talk. She was not eager, but this question had been brewing in her for a few weeks.

She brought out some pepper cookies with the coffee. "There is something about the Balkans I've never understood. Do you mind if I ask you your opinion?"

"No.… Go ahead."

"Well, here's something I'm confused about. Before the Ottoman Turks occupied the Balkan Peninsula, most people living there were Christian. The people living along the Adriatic Sea facing Italy were Catholic and the rest of the people living to the east were Orthodox Christian, for the most part. But they were all Christian, right?"

"Yes, I believe so," he said gazing out the window.

"Then here's my question: Why, when the Turks occupied the peninsula for 500 years, why did only Bosnians convert to Islam?"

"I have no idea. I never thought of it before," he said looking down at his coffee.

"The explanation I have heard from some Croats and Serbs is that Bosnians lacked principles, that they changed their religion to Islam so the Turks would reduce their taxes. Evidently, under the Turk's rule, if you were Muslim, you paid lower taxes."

Joe hardly looked at her. He must be bored, she thought. Maybe he's tired too. She should have stopped there, but she went on. "I just don't believe that was the reason they became Muslim." Still, he showed no interest in the topic. "To me, that explanation sounds like the Christians were trying to belittle the Bosnians for having a different religion."

"I've never thought about that before. Remember, I left Croatia when I was eleven years old," he chuckled.

"I remember some people at home had negative feelings toward Bosniaks just because they're not Christians. That's so unfortunate, don't you think?" She paused to give him time to react, but he didn't. Maric decided to bring the discussion closer to home by saying: "I like the attitude here in the States. Nobody seems to care what religion you are…"

"Well, that's not entirely true. You haven't met many people yet."

You're telling me, she thought. She wondered why he was so uninterested in the topic. She offered him another pepper cookie. Maybe he misses his wife so much he can't come out of himself. How could she broach that subject? She couldn't think of a good opening so she tackled it head on: "You must miss your wife.... Her name was Rosa?" she asked.

His eyes narrowed: "And you must miss your family." He raised his head high, so he was looking down at Maric suspiciously. "What brought you here anyway?"

"My family is all dead." She didn't want to give him a chance to follow up with another question so she immediately commented: "Luke tells me Rosa used to fly the helicopter for the ranch. You must need some help now running the ranch." He was silent. Then she had what she thought was a brilliant idea: "Can you get one of those men at the Harney Field Station to help you?"

"No, they have jobs there. Well, I'd better be going."

She could have pressed harder, but she could tell he was annoyed with her. She didn't know why.

Then, seemingly for the first time that morning, he looked at her straight in the eye. "I've always liked to help anyone who comes from the old country. We're all Slavs, aren't we? ... I wouldn't ask one of them what type of Slav he is, what his religion is, or what damn alphabet he uses."

"I'm glad you feel that way," she said feeling cowardly. She didn't know what she had said to annoy him.

"I guess when you live out here, where you're so spread out, you don't care if your neighbor goes to the same church, you're just glad to have a neighbor."

Maric certainly understood that point, but the bitterness of his tone surprised her. He terminated their discussion by simply leaving. She watched him walk down the steps. She followed him as far as the outside door. This had been a rough morning. Did Joe speak to her that way as a warning? She could tell it would be a long time before she'd ever get to see Stoka Ranch. There was so much she wanted to see and no way to do it.

Luke had been good to her. He taught her how to drive. Now that she could do the shopping herself, she didn't have to ask Susie to buy the personal items that she was too embarrassed to put on Joe's grocery list. The car had given her some freedom and privacy. She had found a secondhand store in Burns where there were good bargains, and had been able to buy sneakers and a pair of slacks that fit. Her next purchase was going to be a warm coat for winter.

Just as Joe was starting his engine to leave, Luke's pickup screeched to a stop in front of the hotel. He got out next to his father's truck. "Hi, Dad." Turning to Maric, he asked: "Where's Mike?"

"He went back home." She could see the tension in Luke's face.

"I'm afraid Sniffer was poisoned."

"What? Poisoned?"

"Yes, I just found him in a shed down the road. Good thing I had Cooper on the leash. He led me to him. I'm going to take Mike there, but first I want to put Cooper in my cabin, so he doesn't pick up the poison himself."

Having heard all this, Joe held up his hand as a goodbye gesture and drove off.

Maric was dumbfounded at Joe's lack of feeling. Her face must have shown what she was thinking, because Luke took in a deep breath, looked at her, and shook his head.

Vera had time for a quick stay at the cabin before Oz was due to arrive from Croatia. She decided to take Luke up on his invitation to join him for dinner at the hotel on Wednesday night, when he got together with his environmentalist friends for a meeting. As expected, the dinner at the hotel was marvelous. *That plucky little woman can really cook.* She hadn't had *sarma* since she was last in Zagreb, visiting Oz.

Vera got a kick out of the men. They didn't look pleased when Mary put the *sarma* dish on the table. Luke skeptically asked what was in it.

"Cabbage leaves stuffed with a mixture of rice and ground meat, put on a bed of sauerkraut."

"Hm, hum!"

"Well, always nice to try new things," Steve said.

"A bed of sauerkraut," another commented, looking at Corwin who was smirking.

When Mary cleared the table, there wasn't one cabbage roll left. Vera silently caught Mary's eye and gave her an affirming smile. All of the sudden, Vera was struck by the realization that Mary could be one of those war criminals. She remembered that during the flood, Luke said that he was the cook and manager of the hotel. "How long have you been the cook here, Mary?"

"A little more than three months," she said and disappeared into the kitchen. When she next came out, Luke suggested that she also sit down with them and join their meeting. "Leave the dishes until after we're through."

The meeting was strange to Vera, in the sense that she felt the men didn't want to be heard by the other guests at the hotel. Steve spoke in a quiet voice. "I thought we'd talk about ranching tonight."

Ranching? What does that have to do with the environment? Vera thought. "What's the problem with ranching?" she asked.

Luke broke in to say, "I think I mentioned some of them to you, Mrs. Whittier—remember when we were in the helicopter? Each cow has to have a minimum of ten acres of grazing land."

"Yes, I do remember."

Corwin said, "Our land is becoming more like a desert. Ranchers keep thinking the more land they use for cattle the better, yet it is obvious with our present system, the land is deteriorating."

Luke said, "Some people around here think we want to do away with ranching, but we don't."

"Who are the *we*?" asked Maric.

"Environmentalists," Steve said softly.

"We don't want to do away with the cattle industry, but it's been difficult to get ranchers to understand that there is a better method other than just letting the cattle loose."

"Here's the thing," said Corwin, "cattle eat grass and sage-brush until those plants are over-grazed. The land gets degraded and cows eventually need more land to feed themselves."

What Vera got out of the meeting was that open grazing is easy for the rancher, but it's not good for the land. What she really wanted to learn about was Mary. She couldn't imagine her as a war criminal. Something else kept nagging at her, but she couldn't quite figure out what it was.

Corwin was going on about how, years ago, there were many predators, wolves and cougars, who forced the animals to keep moving. Vera was losing her ability to concentrate. She heard something about herds of wild animals, like bison. Then her mind drifted.

Luke tried to summarize, "The land was healthier when we had more types of animals…."

Vera looked around. It was nine o'clock and everyone was getting tired. Further cups of coffee couldn't stop the yawns. Steve was the first to stand up. "Well, I promised Junior I would take him target shooting first thing in the morning. Guess I'd better be heading off."

Mary slipped off to the kitchen and started washing the dishes. Vera decided to give her a hand. It reminded her of times that she and Emily had cleaned up together after a meal. Just as Vera started to lapse into self-pity, Mary turned to her and gave her such a sweet smile.

"I'm glad you liked the *sarma*," she said.

"Oh, I did. Where did you learn to cook like that, your mother?" Vera immediately regretted the question because she saw Mary's eyes filling before she turned away.

"Yes," she said in a soft voice.

Mary concentrated on scrubbing a pan and didn't look up when Vera told her that her nephew was coming from Zagreb next week.

Vera thought Mary couldn't be a war criminal, few women ever were, but she couldn't neglect the fact that Joe had gotten her here, just like he did the workers at the HFS.

ଓଃ

When Vera stayed at the cabin, one way she entertained herself was to take Tom's old cane fishing pole and do some fishing herself, just like she and Fabela used to do as children in Croatia. There were a few streams outside of Split which had plenty of perch. Renewing these skills would impress Tom, she thought, and would make him more likely to want to join her for several days at the cabin. She also took pride in her attempts at self-sufficiency: digging up her own worms, cleaning and scaling the fish herself. The banks of the Blitzen were full of fat earth-worms.

The only thing Vera dreaded about her stays on the Blitzen was the long drive back to Portland, so she often allowed herself the treat of having a good breakfast at the hotel before heading out. This time, she could do one other thing to make her trip more agreeable. She could get rid of her trash before she left Frenchglen, so she didn't have to smell the rotting fish remnants during her six-hour drive. When she inquired about where she could leave it, Mary told her to follow her after breakfast and she would show her the way to the dump. She had a key to open the gate.

After a delicious French toast breakfast, Vera paid her bill and lingered on the porch until she saw Mary load her station wagon with trash bags. Vera walked out to her Honda and spot-ted Luke. She decided to say goodbye and tell him how much she enjoyed last night's discussion. She hurried back to her car when she realized Mary was waiting to lead her to the dump.

A few miles outside of town on the 205, Mary turned left onto a dirt road that was unmarked. Vera followed, but soon slowed because she thought she saw a Sage Sparrow. The bird was the correct size and she saw the dark spot on its white breast. She couldn't help herself. She stopped the car, grabbed her bin-oculars (which were always on her front seat), and got out to get a better look. It flew off. "Darn!"

She got back in the car and continued toward the dump over a washboard surface. The road ended at an outcropping of basalt boulders. Mary had told her that the boulders served as a gateway to the dump. There was Mary's station wagon. Vera pulled her car up alongside it. Another car was also there. It was gray and parked facing the road. Clever, Vera thought, with the trunk facing the dump, the trash wouldn't have to be carried as far.

Mary was nowhere in sight. Vera felt her age. Mary must have already carried her bags to the dump. Being pokey was perfectly acceptable for seniors, she thought, excusing herself. She had no sooner gotten out of the car when a man carrying a rifle came running toward her. He jumped in the gray car and drove off at a fast clip. What was that about?

Vera started down the path with her large trash bag in hand when Mary appeared smiling. "Did you see Steve and Junior on horseback? …No, I guess you can't from here. They must be out target shooting again. Didn't Steve say something last night about going target shooting?"

"Oh yes, I remember."

"Well, goodbye Mrs. Whittier. Oh, do you need help with that?"

"No. I'm fine. Thanks again for the delicious supper last night."

"Well, OK. Just follow the path. Would you please close the gate and padlock it when you're finished?"

Vera saw Mary was in a hurry, so she didn't ask her about the man with the rifle. He was too old to be Junior and Steve didn't have a chinstrap beard. After the fun of throwing her bag and seeing how it landed in the dump, she returned to her car and started her long drive back to Portland.

Vera drove toward Wright's Point, a narrow ridge with a flat top, 300 feet above the ground. What was it that Luke said about it? He had a crazy explanation of how it formed. Geology was not a subject she studied in school. Then she remembered. The top of the ridge was where a river flowed. Originally, all the land was at that height. Millions of years ago, the lava from an eruption sought the lowest path, which was the river bed. Since then, all the land has eroded away except where the lava capped the river bed. She must remember that explanation so she'd be able to impress Tom with it when she was home in Portland.

Maric considered going to Burns to be the highlight of her week, but not because the town was interesting. She loved the towns in Croatia. They were compact; intimate, with narrow, winding, and sometimes steep streets. Burns had roads wide enough to drive cattle through, yet there was no traffic. You could find a parking place anywhere. It was perfectly flat. Walking in Burns was not a charming experience. Still, when Maric learned to drive and was given the use of Joe's old Pontiac station wagon, it meant she could look forward to an adventure and some independence every Thursday, when she did the grocery shopping in Burns.

The only constraint was being restricted to ten gallons of gas a week. As Luke predicted, "Driving that old clunker, you'll be lucky to get one trip to Burns 'n back on a tank full!" He was about right: round trip to Burns and to the dump meant a minimum of 125 miles a week. At best, 'the old clunker' got 15 miles to a gallon.

When she first started driving, Maric just went to the store and drove back to Frenchglen right away. But since discovering the history museum in Burns, she was in the habit of spending her first hour there. She parked the car at the grocery store and walked to the museum.

From one of the displays, she learned of Hines, the other town contiguous with Burns. Why isn't the other town just a part of Burns? The explanation had something to do with the Hines

Lumber Company. The town was created as a company town for its employees.

One Thursday, it occurred to Maric that there may be some connection to Brenda Hines. She looked up Brenda Hines on the computer and found many newspaper articles about a woman with that name. Ms. Hines was reported to be 39 years old. That matched the information on Brenda's passport, as she remembered it. She felt ashamed to still be wearing some of Brenda's clothes. They were too big for her, but people didn't seem to take notice, thankfully.

Some of the pictures in the newspaper made Brenda look severe. Maric read that Brenda was the daughter of Marce and Edwin Hines from Portland. Her father was Edwin Hines, Jr.— 'the heir to the Hines Lumber Company fortune.'

Early articles reported Brenda missing. For weeks, her corpse had been lying unidentified in Ljubljana's morgue, before Mr. and Mrs. Hines flew to Slovenia to identify the body. Recent articles acknowledged that Brenda was dead. Maric was relieved that Brenda's family now knew about her fate. Earlier, they must have been so distressed, not knowing where she was. Maric had often thought she should go to the police and tell them what she knew about Brenda, but of course she couldn't. She feared that once the police knew she was illegal, she'd be deported immediately. She would just have to lay low. At least she was safe living in Frenchglen.

One article said the Portland police suspected that a young woman, Maric Andrich, may have killed Brenda Hines. They speculated that Andrich may have wanted to use Brenda's identity in order to enter the United States. The police had reason to believe she may be hiding out in Oregon. There was a financial reward for information leading to her whereabouts.

This report alarmed Maric. She had feared being deported, but now she realized she might be imprisoned for murdering Brenda and stealing her identity! "Oh my God, they have the death penalty in the U.S!" After a few minutes of panic, her anguish diminished. Few people knew when she had arrived in Frenchglen. Joe and Luke both wanted her to continue working for the hotel. They didn't seem to mind that she was illegal. It may occur to either Susie or Mike that 'Maric Andrich' is similar to 'Mary Andrews,' but by this time, she was fairly good friends with both of them. The others who lived in the town were day laborers who worked elsewhere. Maric rarely saw them. Thank goodness the police didn't publicize her photo, but even if they had, she now had a new hair style—a bob, short in back and longer on the sides. Her ears were covered.

She calmed down enough to check her email. At last, she had an email from Majesira:

Dear Maric,

I am so glad to hear you are alive. I have been so worried about you these last three months, but I didn't make inquiries because I figured if you were alive, you'd be in danger.

About a month and a half ago, I read in the newspaper that Brenda Hines had been murdered. I knew something had happened in Ljubljana and that was why I hadn't heard from you. You spoke of feeling guilty. Well, you can imagine how I was plagued with guilt for having possibly led you both to your deaths.

I had to find out about the tapes, if you had been able to hand them over to Bastiaan Blomme before disappearing. So I phoned the ICTY, and eventually I was connected to Bastiaan himself. He told me that you never showed up at the prearranged time on the Sunday following the opera. But then, out of the blue, three weeks later, he had received a call from the Ljubljana Police Department saying that a detective from the Zagreb Police Department was with them and wanted to turn over the tapes to the ICTY. So he went to Ljubljana again, and this time received the actual tapes. They are dynamite!

*Sorry, Maric, I've run out of time. I have much more
to tell you. I'll try to write you again in a week or two.*

Maric felt a tremendous relief. All her cloak-and-dagger
work had paid off. She sat and reread Majesira's email. It seemed
that Majesira knew Brenda Hines somehow. Had she arranged
for her to be in Ljubljana at the same time? If so, why?

Wasn't it wonderful that someone she didn't even know
was trying to help her? She would never meet this detective who
turned over the tapes, but if she ever got back to Zagreb, she
would go to the police department and try to find him. Tears
filled her eyes. She was all alone on the other side of the world,
her family dead, but there were good people trying to help her
and trying to do good things. She thought of Vesna, who had
helped her get the tapes copied, how brave and resourceful she
had been. Maric hoped she still had her cleaning job. If she ever
got her own life straightened out, she would try to do something
to help Vesna, too.

If Tudjman knew that the tapes were at The Hague, he
would still want to have her killed so she couldn't testify that
they were authentic. She was still in danger!

Maric was just going off line when she saw a man who
looked familiar enter the museum. He was tall, wearing a baseball cap and jeans. When he took off his cap Maric's heart almost
stopped beating. He was bald, just like the man at the opera
and the bus station. He had a faint chin-strap beard, not bushy.
Could it possibly be him? How would he be able to find her here?
Common sense told her she was just being unreasonable, but she
was too scared to take chances.

He hadn't spotted her. She was in a dark part of the museum, near the back exit. Before his eyes adjusted to coming
inside from bright daylight, she sneaked around the bookcases,
ducked down behind a display, and went out the back door. She
found herself in the museum's backyard, which was, unfortunately, totally enclosed by a high wooden fence without a gate.

The yard appeared to be an extension of the museum, containing several pioneer artifacts. Maric jumped up on a wagon close to the fence and used its height to help her climb over. Once on the other side, she kept going away from the museum through various yards, making sure to avoid the main road. She wound her way back to the grocery store parking lot. Forcing herself to appear casual, she walked inside, and did her shopping. Now, she wished she had bought the groceries before she had gone to the museum.

She paid the bill to the cashier and wheeled her cart out. She didn't look around, because if he was there, she didn't want him to think she had recognized him. She was definitely feeling paranoid.

Driving out of Burns, she saw no sign of him. She continued on her way to Frenchglen, driving on Highway 205 at her usual speed. She did see a car in the distance, but it never got close. She passed the Stoka Ranch and decided to slow down. The car never got closer, so it must have slowed down too, she thought. Then she increased to her usual speed, passed Lake Malheur, the road to Harney Field Station, and finally the little road leading to the dump. The car was still behind her, but when she got to Frenchglen and stopped on the far side of the hotel, no car went by; and by the time she had unloaded all the groceries, still no car had driven by.

When he first arrived at Vera and Tom's, Oz spent several days discussing with them everything that had happened in Zagreb and Ljubljana before he left. His Aunt Vera was much more interested in all the details of the murder case than Uncle Tom, of course. She was excited to tell him about her experience at the Harney Field Station, where she was sure there were Serbian war criminals hiding out.

Oz was very grateful to be able to live with them until... until what? He didn't think he'd be able to get a job, and his visa didn't really allow him to work in the U.S. He tried to take some chores off his uncle's shoulders, like mowing the lawn, filling bird feeders, sweeping the patio—whatever he could do to help. His mind was always on the case, however, and within days, he had contacted the Portland Police Department to ask if he could see Brenda Hines' apartment.

It was a hot and muggy day when Jake, an assistant detective for the PPD, accompanied Oz to Brenda's condo. Her parents knew their daughter was dead, but they still hadn't done anything about her apartment. She had lived in a swanky section of Portland, yet when they entered, Oz saw that it was simply furnished. It wasn't a crime scene, but the case was still not solved, so both men donned latex gloves.

Oz opened the drawers to her desk. Jake pointed out Brenda's address book. "There are three printed numbers we can't figure out." Oz wrote each of them down. One was 38613206955, with no spaces or dashes. He had called Edi enough to recognize the first three digits. They were the country code for Slovenia. The next digit was the city code for Ljubljana. That looked promising. He would call Edi about this as soon as he got back to his aunt's house. Another number was 99063463783. Which country used the code 990? He would investigate that. The third number was 882609104093.

Spending three hours looking through Brenda's apartment left Oz with the general impression that Brenda lived simply and dressed in plain, sensible clothes. In fact, she had few material possessions, yet her parents were quite wealthy. There was virtually no makeup and little jewelry to be found. He had heard Edi mention that she was known to be a feminist. All of his observations implied that Brenda was a serious person. Were there other reasons she did not want to flaunt herself or draw any attention? Was she a closeted lesbian, or a spy? Edi and his aunt had both told Oz that Brenda would have been the heiress of quite a fortune once her parents died.

"Was Brenda a *feminista*?" he asked Jake.

Jake hesitated, then responded, "Yes. She was a member of the IFA."

Oz was expressionless. Jake added: "The International Feminist Association."

"That's a new one for me," Oz admitted. "Did you contact them?"

"They told us surprisingly little, especially in view of the fact that she regularly attended local meetings and traveled to two of their recent international conferences."

"When and where were the conferences?"

Jake referred to his little notebook: "The first was in 1990, in Lubiana, Slovenia. Sorry, if I mispronounced the name of that city. And the second was in 1995, in Sofia, Bulgaria."

"Unusual locations!"

"That's what we thought. The IFA seems to concentrate its efforts on combating rape."

Oy! No wonder they met in my part of the world. Oz made note of what Jake had told him before going on to ask: "Is there any Balkan *organizacija* in Portland?"

"The only one we could find was a liquor store: Zoran's on 8th Avenue, downtown. Right near my favorite food truck," Jake smiled.

Zoran was a Serb name. Oz would check that out. "What did Brenda's bank account show?"

"Nothing. We didn't think anything was unusual. Of course the woman had a lot of money and she took many trips, but she came from a wealthy family."

The last thing of note that Oz found was a receipt for an anorak on top of Brenda's dresser. The price tag and little plastic attachment were left nearby. He wondered if she had been in a hurry and hadn't bothered to throw them in the wastebasket? As he remembered, one of the personal items belonging to the corpse in the Ljubljana morgue was a blue anorak—turquoise blue. Oz went into Brenda's bedroom again to look in her closet, where he thought he had seen rain gear of some kind. Yes, there was a perfectly good rain jacket hanging up. Of course, this is Portland. It rains so much here, maybe she needed to have two— one to wear and the other to dry?

"What did you find out about Ms. Hines' job?"

"She was an English teacher at a local high school. We interviewed people there. She was well thought of, diligent, and seemed to enjoy her work. No close friends among the staff."

Oz's command of English was poor, He could understand better than he could express himself, so sometimes he resorted to shortcuts: "Neighbors?" "Other friends?" "Religion?" "Hobbies?" But the Portland police had turned up nothing more. Brenda really stayed under the radar!

That next morning, Oz phoned Edi to ask him to look into the Ljubljana telephone number. Two days later, Edi called Oz back and said it was the telephone number to the Central Hotel.

By the end of the week, Oz had discovered something

about the other two series of numbers. He thought they might be scrambled in some way. So he tried writing them backward. One number turned into 390401906228. He looked up the country codes in the telephone directory and it turned out that 39 was the country code for Italy and 040 the city code for Trieste. He reversed the other number and it became 38736426099. Oz couldn't believe his luck. The country code of Bosnia was 387. This country had a smaller population, so the city code had only two digits. It matched Mostar's. Oz relayed his discoveries to Edi.

As usual, Joe drove to his hotel on Wednesday morning to go over the previous week's expenses with Mary. Typically, she showed him the receipts of her purchases and gave him whatever money was left over. In the height of the season, Joe gave her $300 for the week's expenses and $50 for her salary. So far, Mary had been able to stay within the budget he had set for her. He could tell the hotel was building up its reputation as a good place to eat. Some acquaintances even told him it was worth a drive of fifty miles to have dinner in the Frenchglen Hotel.

Joe did have one problem with Mary. What should he do with her in the winter when the hotel was closed? It's single pot-belly stove could not heat the whole hotel. That was one thing he had to discuss with her. When he hired Mary, he had told her that the job came with room and board for the entire year.

He never had this problem when Luke was the cook. Luke slept in his cabin year round. He kept warm in the winter by burning wood in its fireplace. In the past, when Rosa was alive, Luke would come home to the ranch for his evening meal. Now, Luke helped him out during hay season. He took over Rosa's work tending the herd on Steens. But other than that, Luke never came home, not even for a visit. Just as well, he thought, now he didn't have to listen to that claptrap about keeping cattle bunched up.

It wasn't that his son was a disappointment to him. He had always known he wouldn't amount to much with a mother like Rosa. The woman had no ambition. The only food she wanted to cook was Mexican. All that starch! She got fat and he farted day and night. He was glad that was over with.

Still, Joe had to figure out what to do about Mary in the winter months. He definitely wanted her to continue cooking for the hotel when it reopened.

Another thing that nagged him was that the men working at the field station had little excitement in their life. They must be depressed and homesick.

Finally, he thought of a possible solution to both problems. Before going to see Mary, he stopped off at HFS. Steve jumped on Joe's idea of hiring Mary as cook for the winter. They would provide her with a small cabin next to a dorm. As supervisor of the barbed wire removal project, Luke could keep tabs on Mary. Joe thought for sure Luke would like this plan. Just yesterday, Luke had told him that Mary would become 'unhinged' if she had to stay in the hotel with nothing to do for four months. So without consulting Luke further, Joe drove to the hotel and presented Mary with the proposition.

When he mentioned the inadequacy of one potbelly stove to heat the hotel, Mary interrupted him to say: "Well, many of us had similar problems in Bosnia when winter came. We shut off the upstairs. If there weren't doors that could be shut, we hung heavy curtains so that only a smaller section of downstairs had to be heated."

"But there's no bed to sleep on down here."

"We could easily move a single bed downstairs. That way only the kitchen, the dining room, and enough of the hall where the toilet is, needs be heated. I'll be fine. In fact, I'm used to living like that in the winter."

"Well, that's good, but I have a plan that I think would be an improvement."

Mary listened to his plan: "Hmm, that would be a change. I've never been to the field station. Is it nice?"

"Oh yes."

It was settled, Joe thought. He was relieved, but days later, after Mary talked it over with Luke, Luke had a fit.

"Dad, you can't let her stay next to that dorm. I know you think these men are poor refugees but believe me, they're the scum of the earth!"

"How do you know? You're always saying you can't understand a word they are saying. Just because they're poor, doesn't make them the scum of the earth."

"Having Mary continue to sleep in the hotel would be better for security. The phone could be answered. You can't let her stay at the field station."

Joe put off making a decision. Maybe he could come up with a better plan. He couldn't imagine how Luke could think those men were the scum of the earth. After all, they had won the war for us!

On her way to Burns, Maric mulled over Luke's warning against her working at HFS. She doubted that Joe would let her live at the hotel during the winter. If the field station wasn't good, where could she go? No restaurant would want to hire a cook during the winter months when the town had few visitors. She stopped to fill up with gas before driving to the grocery store.

Once again, her mind turned to the man that she imagined wanted to kill her. It had been a week since she saw him at the museum. If it was him and he wanted to kill her, wouldn't he have tried before this? She hadn't seen him since then, so she walked to the museum.

She got on well with Mrs. Spooner, who ran the museum. By this time, Maric knew that this sweet old lady had put up the museum exhibits herself, and done the research for them. Maric noticed, however, that they never changed, and nothing new had been added since she had been coming there. Had Mrs. Spooner lost her enthusiasm for the museum, or was she just too old to have the energy for the work, or a little of both?

As she usually did, Maric spent the first five minutes catching up on Mrs. Spooner's news. She lived alone with her cat, Peter. "Mrs. Spooner, I was wondering, does the county or the city pay for the upkeep of the museum?" Maric immediately regretted the abruptness of her question. The woman became flustered.

" Ah, ah…both, I think?"

"Do you ever want help?"

"Yes, I do. The next thing the city wants to do is to paint the inside here and spruce it up a bit."

"I would like that job. Could the city wait until mid-October to have it done, because I have another job until then?"

"My dear, don't you think you are a little bit too small to do such heavy work?"

"Oh no, not at all! If I could stay here at the museum, I could make sure it would be opened for public visits. I am well familiar with all the exhibits and where they go."

"That's true. In fact that is why I've been dreading having the work done. I'm afraid that the painters would mess everything up."

"I might take a little longer, but you could be sure nothing will be changed, unless you want it to be."

"That would be wonderful," she said smiling.

Maric didn't want to confuse Mrs. Spooner or overwhelm her with details such as where she would sleep in the museum or what pay she would receive, so she excused herself and went to the computer. She wanted to check to see if Majesira had written her. No, she hadn't. Well then, what should she look up today? If she were to help Mrs. Spooner with the museum, she should know more local history. She typed "Frenchglen, Oregon" into the computer.

> In 1872, Pete French made his way to Oregon
> with 1,200 head of cattle belonging to Dr. Glenn
> of California. His job was to locate good land for
> ranching. French settled in the Blitzen and Donner
> Valleys of Southeast Oregon. His ranch flourished
> and became known as the P Ranch. Eventually it
> encompassed 100,000 acres, on which 45,000 cattle,
> 3,000 horses and a number of mules grazed. The
> French-Glenn Livestock Company had ceaseless
> problems with homesteaders, Indians, squatters,
> and land boundary disputes. French was murdered
> for one such reason in 1897.

Everyone talked about Diamond Craters. Maric had never seen them, but she should know why they were important. She looked them up on the web and found that:

> The Diamond Craters are the best and most diverse
> basaltic features in the United States.

Maric consulted the dictionary: "basaltic: dark, fine-grained rock that solidified above ground." Before she was finished reading about the craters, she became acutely aware of how little she knew about geology. Why was geology not important to her in Bosnia? Was it because the history of the Balkans was so complicated that it consumed all of her attention? Whereas, here in Eastern Oregon, there were so few people and the history had only recently been recorded. There was another reason: the sparse vegetation here allowed the complexity of the rocks to be more apparent than in the Balkans.

> Nine million years ago, there was a volcanic vent un-
> der Burns that erupted. Rocks (pyroclastics) 30 to 130
> feet thick were deposited over a region of 7,000 square
> miles.... Diamond Craters were given that name for
> their proximity to Diamond Ranch which used a
> diamond-shaped brand.

One day, Maric hoped to see the craters, the reddish-brown layer that looked like a pancake; the fissures, the lava tubes, the bombs, the domes, the calderas—she wanted to see them all.

In early August, Oz was driving Vera's Honda from Portland to his aunt and uncle's cabin. He was glad to be alone because it gave him time to think. The route was not complicated. If he drove for six hours from Zagreb, he could get to Germany or France, going through four different countries, hearing different languages all the way. On this journey, all he had to remember were numbers: take the 5, then the 20, and finally the 205. On the 5 he passed through Salem, the capital of Oregon, but by staying on the freeway, he saw nothing of it.

He was supposed to wait for his aunt and uncle at the Frenchglen Hotel, where they would come to meet him. "We might as well have dinner there, before you follow us to the cabin," Vera had said to him back in Portland.

"She never misses a chance for that," Tom added.

Tom and Vera had driven the SUV to their cabin four days ago. By now, Uncle Tom should have been able to unwind. That wasn't a problem for his aunt. She wasn't working and she found solitude inviting. But Oz imagined Uncle Tom needing a couple of days to relax. Aunt Vera said she looked forward to seeing the 'riparian vegetation' around the river. Oz didn't know what that meant. He noticed that Vera was starting to slip fancy words about plants and the terrain into her conversations.

Oz had a lot to sort out. His aunt and uncle hadn't seemed to mind if he stayed behind in Portland for some days. He had more investigative work concerning Brenda Hines' murder to do. He took that time to go to the office of the International Feminists Association (IFA). It was not a big office. It was staffed by three seemingly dedicated volunteers.

He spoke first to a young woman named Cleo, who wore an assortment of facial jewelry but no lipstick. "We were so worried when we heard she had disappeared, then completely *devastated* by the news of her *murder*."

He chatted a bit with her and the others before he launched into his major inquiry: "Do you know what she was working on?" None of the women gave him any meaningful information.

"She was in Eastern Europe mainly as a tourist, so we're not sure what could have happened to motivate someone to kill her."

"Was she trying to connect with rape victims of the Bosnian War?" Oz noticed a woman seated at a desk in the back of the office cover up some papers in front of her.

"That wouldn't surprise me if she did, but as far as I know, that wasn't the intention of her trip," she said.

"Why did she want to return to Portland via Trieste?"

"I didn't know she was going to Trieste."

"She has been a volunteer with the IFA since 1990, is that right?"

"Yes, I guess so. I don't know when she first became involved in IFA, do you, Gloria?"

"No," the woman in back answered.

"We know she went to Trieste in June of '95, as well," Oz said.

"*We*, who's *we*? This is beginning to sound like a police interrogation. What did you say—that you are helping both the Portland Police Department and also the police in Lubiana?"

"Ljubljana", Oz corrected. He tried to explain that he was the detective assigned to a case involving the disappearance of a Zagreb woman, Maric Andrich.

"You *were* the detective? What happened?"

"I was fired."

"So why are you interested in Brenda Hines?"

Sensing their unwillingness to cooperate, he tried desperately to explain that the cases were connected: "Brenda was not the intended victim. I believe Ms. Andrich actually was."

"Is that right?" Cleo responded with seeming disinterest. "Well, I'm sorry we can't help you," she said, bringing the interview to an end.

Oz was surprised at her abruptness. He could see that further questioning would be useless. He left the office without obtaining any specific information, but his instinct was that Brenda was involved in some operation that they all took quite seriously. Also, what the women didn't say was revealing. None of them said that they felt sorry for Brenda's parents. Did they know her parents? After working for IFA for over ten years, you would think they would have met them. They seemed to want him to go away and not ask any more questions.

If he were still a police official, he would have had other options to obtain information from them, but he was limited now. He had done the best he could.

Oz had three more hours of driving ahead of him. He went over in his mind his visit to Zoran's Liquor Store. He wasn't sure how he should have handled that one. Ever since he arrived in Portland, he had not shaved. He could tell that his uncle did not approve, but over the years, Oz had learned to use a beard to his advantage. If he had a beard when he first met people and the next time they saw him he was clean shaven, they often wouldn't remember meeting him. He had used this trick many times while working undercover. He could even pretend to be a Serb.

Oz went into the liquor store and asked if he could speak to Mr. Zoran. After waiting fifteen minutes, a small man wearing a white shirt and bow tie came out of the back of the store. Oz introduced himself and asked if he was hiring. Zoran said that he wasn't. Oz pretended he was really disappointed.

"Why did you think I would be hiring," he asked.

"Well, a friend of mind told me I should ask you."

"Who's your friend?"

"I can't say. He said for sure I could get a job through you."

"Where are you from?"

"Originally? You can probably tell, right?"

"Where are you living now?"

"So you can't help me?"

"Well, I have helped people in the past, but I just can't do it now."

"When should I ask you again?"

"In a couple of weeks."

"OK, thank you. I'll be back."

An hour east of Burns still, Oz realized he had entered a gray-green ocean of sagebrush. He saw trees only around streams and up mountain slopes. This must be where the open range begins, he thought. He remembered that term from Tony Hillerman's novel. What was it called? *The Mysterious West.* The open range was land used for grazing cattle and sheep.

Still on Highway 20, Oz noticed how much dryer the terrain became. Sagebrush and juniper dominated. At Burns, Oz turned south on the 205. When he came to the lakes, he saw Sandhill Cranes and large concentrations of geese, just as his aunt told him he would. Oz's interest in the region picked up. He had never been exposed to country like this before.

Finally, he came to the town of Frenchglen. Tom had called it 'a wide spot in the road.' There were some cottonwood trees around the hotel. Had he reached an oasis? He walked through the screened-in porch. No one was around, so he picked up a brochure and started reading. There were eight rooms, none had locks, and the three bathrooms were shared.

At this point he heard someone stirring nearby. A young woman came out and asked if he would like some refreshment. She had a slight accent. She was pleasant looking, but there was something about her that was intriguing. He stared at her longer than he should have. He suddenly realized that she looked like the woman in the pictures that Mrs. Dadic had given him. My God, could it be? It's Maric Andrich! He was breathless. When he got his voice back, it cracked on the word *beer*.

She seemed relaxed and smiled: "Any particular type? We have Bud, Miller, and Negra Modelo."

"I know Bud and Miller, but what is Negra Modelo like?" He was still staring. Her eyes had narrowed. Now, it was her turn to be breathless. I've frightened her, Oz thought. It must have been something I said, or the way I said it; my accent maybe? She started backing up to the room she had come out of, not taking her eyes off him. She said slowly and methodically: "Negra Modelo is like ale. It's a dark beer."

"Well, I'd like to try it, then…. I'm a little early for dinner. I'm just waiting for my aunt and uncle. I believe they made a reservation for three for tonight."

"What's the last name?"

"Whittier: Tom and Vera Whittier."

Her attitude completely relaxed again. She smiled. "I'll get you your beer right away." When she came back with it, she said: "Yes, I remember now. Vera, I mean Mrs. Whittier, said her nephew was coming from Croatia."

"That's right. I moved in with them two weeks ago."

"Are you in the States for long?"

"I'm afraid so." He quickly realized what his comment implied, so he added: "I'm very lucky to be able to live with them. I'm out of work, you see."

"Did you have a job in Croatia?"

"In Croatia, I was a policeman, a detective actually." He couldn't help but give her a wry smile. With a twinkle in his eye he added: "I was investigating the disappearance of a young woman." Her eyes were getting watery. He continued: "Her name was Maric Andrich. I think I have found her."

Maric burst out crying. Oz teared up too. He went over and gave her a hug. "I'm so glad you're alive." Then he backed off, thinking that he must be smelly after driving that distance. He hadn't worn deodorant. In fact, he rarely put it on. But he was starting to gather that everyone wore it religiously in this country. Uncle Tom had even put a bottle of Old Spice on his breakfast plate one morning. Aunt Vera had a fit.

"What are you doing here?"

"I'm the cook for the hotel. Would you please come in the kitchen so we can keep talking? I still have to prepare some things for dinner. How did you figure out I was here?" she asked.

Oz switched to speaking Croatian. "I didn't know you were here. It's funny, my aunt has tried to get me to go bird watching for years, you know, during the Bird Festival. And here you are."

"Does she know who I am?"

"I don't think so, because she wouldn't have kept that to herself. To her, you are Mary, the cook at her favorite place to eat. How did you get here?"

"I got off the plane in Portland and followed three Serbian men outside. I didn't know what to do. I asked the man who picked them up for a job. He owns this hotel, and hired me as a cook." They were both smiling at each other. Then he noticed her getting serious again. "Did you catch the man who tried to kill me but shot that other woman, Brenda, instead? The newspapers are saying that I did it, but that's not true!"

"I know you are not a murderer, but we haven't found the real killer yet. He may still be after you, considering what was in those tapes you made, and that you are the only one who can testify about where they came from."

"Where did you find the tapes?" she asked, while peeling carrots.

"I found them inside the box on the window ledge of your bedsit."

"And what did you do with them?"

"We listened to them and then an investigator for the ICTY picked them up." She's testing me, Oz thought. He didn't blame her. He would have done the same in her shoes.

"Do you remember the name of the investigator?"

"Bastiaan Bloome."

This time she reached out to give Oz a hug. "Thank you."

Then she withdrew.

I do need deodorant, he thought.

"I'm sorry, everybody here hugs."

"I like the custom." She definitely blushed. Oh happy days!

"I'm grateful to you for handing over the tapes, not only for myself, but also for so many other people who deserve to..."

She couldn't look him in the eye—she's embarrassed, Oz thought. She's trying to formalize her 'thank you.' I love it!

"...to have justice...and for all the other people who have suffered." She tried to look at him again. "The ones responsible for those crimes must be held accountable."

He couldn't stop staring at her. "Yes, of course." Holy heaven, what a woman!

They heard some commotion outside. Maric gently pushed him out of the kitchen. "We must act like we don't know each other."

He went back into the dining room and tried to calm his emotions.

CHAPTER 27

MID-AUGUST, 1997

A week later, the Whittiers and Oz had just finished dinner at the hotel. While Maric was clearing the dinner plates from the table, Vera suggested that they all drive up Steens Mountain for the next day. "Would you be able to take the day off tomorrow, Mary? We'd love to have you come with us."

Oz noticed that she blushed, but did not look at him. "Yes, I think I could, but I'd better clear it with Luke. It'll be Saturday. Maybe I could get Susie to cover for me. She teaches in the school. She should be free and there shouldn't be much for her to do. I can have most of the dinner prepared before we go." Oz noticed she took a peek at him. "Just in case a guest strays in, Susie would be able to take a reservation or make a sandwich lunch.... I would love to go."

Oz wondered how much his aunt had picked up just from observing. Her detective skills were not limited to crimes. On the other hand, it was probably obvious that he hadn't spent much time at the cabin with them. He had thought of numerous excuses to drive off somewhere so he could come to the hotel and be with Maric.

The next morning, he used his uncle's deodorant without asking. They all had to share the bathroom and it was right there on the back of the toilet. He should have asked Tom first, but that would make him jump to conclusions. As it was, when Oz sat down at breakfast to eat with them, his uncle sniffed, then pursed his lips to suppress a smile.

Maric made them all sandwiches and packed fruit, water, and cookies for lunch. Vera brought her binoculars, of course. The night before, Maric had warned them that the summit could be quite cold, so they also brought jackets. Maric wore a lovely wool sweater that was too big for her.

Tom drove and Vera sat in the front passenger seat of their SUV. Oz and Maric sat in back. Tom turned on to the 52-mile Loop Road, a winding gravel road that gradually climbed. The first ten miles or so were rough. There was nothing much to see, only sagebrush. That was just as well, because Oz was having difficulty concentrating on anything except Maric sitting next to him. Finally he gave in to his feelings and took her hand without looking at her.

Vera said she had read that this was Oregon's highest road.

"But Steens is only the eighth-highest mountain in Oregon," Tom said.

"I was wondering about that," Maric said. "Is the height of a mountain measured relative to its base or relative to sea level? I mean, because the high desert is about a mile above sea level."

"I'm pretty sure the height of all of them is relative to sea level," Tom answered.

"Isn't there a difference between elevation and altitude?" Oz asked.

"Wait a minute," Vera said, "I have a brochure right here." She read to herself until she found the explanation: "It says it rises from the Alvord Desert which is at an elevation of about 4,200 feet to a summit elevation of 9,733 feet."

"It sounds like elevation is always relative to sea level," Oz said.

Vera mentioned that she had already seen the mountain from her ride with Luke in his helicopter. The lower part of the mountain was drier and dominated by sagebrush, but as they climbed, they went through dense stands of juniper. Climbing higher still, where there was more moisture, they saw quaking aspen.

"We have that type of tree in Bosnia—in the mountains," Maric remarked.

"I thought you were from Croatia?" Vera asked.

"I'm Croatian but I grew up in Mostar. Then, ever since the war started, I lived with my aunt in Zagreb."

"Your aunt?" Vera paused. "In Zagreb?" She turned around and looked at Oz excitedly, then turned back.

Oz could tell that his aunt had figured out who Maric was. He turned to Maric and mouthed: "She knows!" He watched Maric's expression to see how she felt about the outing of her identity. Opening his eyes wide and staring at her, he waited for a signal. Maric took a deep breath and nodded her head tentatively, affirming that it was OK.

When his aunt turned back around and stared at him, he realized he had another problem to contend with. Aunt Vera had always wanted to help him with his cases. She saw herself and her nephew as a team of detectives. Her look said: "You left me out!" As much as he didn't want to hurt his aunt's feelings, he had to be sure Maric was ready. In time, he felt sure Vera would understand that.

"Mrs. Whittier, I think you know who I am. I'm sorry for the secrecy, but no one must know I'm Maric Andrich. Oz has told me how the two of you collaborate on some of his cases, but my life and other matters are in jeopardy if my true identity gets out."

"I understand. Tom and I won't say a word."

"A word about what?" asked Tom.

"I'll explain later, dear." They were all quiet for another ten minutes, before Vera said, "I think we came at the best time of year. The aspens are starting to turn color. Look at those beautiful oranges and yellows."

"Over there, look," said Oz, "there are horses."

"Oh, they're wild mustangs. Aren't they beautiful? I read that there are about 300 roaming out here. It's thought that, originally, they were escapees from the first people here: Indians, settlers, and the like," said Vera.

Oz saw his first pronghorn. "What is it?"

"Antelope," Tom answered, but Vera said she learned from Luke that pronghorns are actually goats, not deer.

"They don't shed their horns but they do shed the outer sheath of their horns each year." (Maric translated that for Oz.) "Luke knows a great deal. You wouldn't know it to look at him," Vera noted.

Several times, Tom stopped the car so they could get out and look around. Their favorite sights were the beautiful valleys, which were more like massive gorges carved by glaciers in the classic U-shape. Kiger Gorge was the most stunning, with Wildhorse Lake nestled in its valley floor. From its overlook, they could see more than a hundred miles both to the east and west.

When they got back into the SUV, Tom commented that a car behind them seemed to be going everywhere that they were going, "…only he never catches up to us. He's probably hoping that the animals we surprise will run toward him."

Maric whipped around to look. "That gray car just coming around the bend?" she asked.

Oz heard the apprehension in her voice.

"Yes," Tom answered.

Her hand gripped Oz's more firmly and she collapsed back, facing forward.

Oz leaned over and said quietly, "What's wrong?"

"I'll tell you when we're alone." But that never happened. His aunt and uncle were always present. They ate their picnic lunch on a rock outcrop. Maric chose a spot to sit where she couldn't be seen from the road. Fortunately, there were few trees at the top. Those that were there were stunted. Someone couldn't sneak up on them without being spotted, and Oz sat at full alert, looking for the gray car.

The final view they wanted to see was from the summit. The road split in two directions. They chose the one that went to the east rim view point, as Vera had read that it was the best.

There, they got out and walked to the edge to peer over. The mountain suddenly dropped off. A mile below them they could see the white mirror of salt—the Alvord Desert. Maric said she felt dizzy and hurried back to sit in the car. Oz followed her. He knew his aunt and uncle would think they wanted to make out. They did want to make out, but first Oz wanted to hear from Maric about the gray car. Unfortunately, Vera and Tom followed them back to the car and they continued their drive.

They made it back to the hotel without incident. It had been a wonderful day, although frustrating to Oz because he wanted so much to have a chance to be alone with Maric. They dropped her off at the hotel and Oz returned with Vera and Tom to the cabin on the Blitzen River.

∝

The next morning, Oz took off in Vera's Honda for the hotel with the excuse that he had to call Edi.

"Don't you want to eat some breakfast here first?"

"I can always get some there, if I have to. But I can't be sure Edi will be home the first time I call, so I had better leave a lot of time to reach him." Oz didn't stop to hear his aunt's reply. He knew she was on to him.

He had to wait until Maric was finished handling breakfast before he could ask her more about why she was afraid of the gray car. They sat down in the dining room and talked for an hour while she told him the story about seeing this man, first at the opera, then at the bus stop, and then at the museum in Burns. Oz asked what he looked like.

Her description didn't match any of Tudjman's henchmen that Oz was aware of. That made sense. Tudjman wouldn't choose someone well-known for this job. After the war, ex-sharpshooters were looking for work. Tudjman may have found one who lacked scruples to take on the job of assassinating Maric. Oz wanted to relay Maric's description of the man to Edi, hoping he could find out the man's name. He called him immediately, but there was no answer.

It took three hours before Edi got home and answered his phone. That gave Oz and Maric more time to talk. There had been only one overnight guest at the hotel and he left for the day right after breakfast, so they had the place to themselves.

He told her about Zoran, and then that Brenda had some phone numbers in her apartment: one to Trieste and one to Mostar.

"The one for Mostar could be Majesira's number." She explained who Majesira was, and that she possibly knew Brenda Hines.

When Oz finally got hold of Edi, he learned that the Mostar number did belong to Majesira and that Edi had traveled to Mostar to talk with her. "You'd be proud of me, how safe I played it: I held up my badge in one hand and a piece of paper in the other, on which was written in Serbo-Croat: 'I am detective Edi Juric of the Ljubljana Police Department. I need to talk with you in private, but I can't take the chance that your apartment is bugged. I'll go anywhere you suggest, where you think it is safe to talk'…and she didn't laugh at me."

Always the joker, Oz thought.

"She led me to a coffee bar, Caffe Enigma. (Don't you love it?!) We sat in the back, away from the window. 'Do you know Brenda Hines?' I asked her.

"There was no answer for the longest time. Then, she said: 'Why do you want to know?'

"'She's dead.' I said, 'murdered in Ljubljana …' No comment. I went on with my explanation as to what happened to her. Still no comment. Then I asked: 'Do you know Maric Andrich?'

"'Yes, we were friends at university together,' she answered.

"'Have you heard from her in the last three months?'

"'We haven't talked since she went to Ljubljana.'

"'Do you know why she went to Ljubljana?'

"'Her boss had given her a ticket to see the opera, including dinner and a room for the night in a nearby hotel, as a way of thanking her for the work she had done for him.'

"'How did you know that?'

"'We had talked on the phone before she left for Ljubljana.'

"I'm telling you, Oz, this woman was closed-mouthed. She didn't mention the tapes. She just sat there not saying a thing. My guess is that something is going on that she doesn't want me to get wind of. So I got up to leave, excusing myself, saying I had a train to catch for Trieste.

"'Trieste! Oh no! Please don't go there,' she protested immediately.

"I asked her again and again why not, and she said she couldn't say, but that I would ruin everything if I went there. 'Please trust me. It is vitally important that you don't go there,' she insisted.

"Then it was my turn to be quiet. I just sat there. Finally she said: 'In another month it will all become clear. Promise me you won't go or call there.'

"I promised. So that's my news."

Before Edi hung up, Oz said he had another favor to ask of him. He described the mystery man. "I think this guy may be Brenda's killer, but I can't tell you why I think he's the man you're after." Oz didn't want it to get around that Maric was here in Frenchglen. "I'm pretty sure he's not one of Tudjman's body guards, but he may be a Croat ex-sharpshooter."

"I'll see what I can find, Žica."

Soon after Edi hung up, the operator rang to tell Oz the time and charges of his call, so he could pay the hotel for it. He left the money on the kitchen counter as Maric was busy. Oz decided to drive around looking for the gray car. Mystery Man would not be suspicious of Vera's Honda.

☙

Oz never saw the gray car. It occurred to him how difficult it would be to hide oneself in this terrain. It would even be difficult to follow a car without being noticed. What would he do, if he were the assassin? He'd observe Maric and learn her routine, such as going to Burns on Thursday. Why doesn't the man just pick her off while she's driving? He would have to hide somewhere close to the road and there was no hiding place that he could remember, just wide open spaces on either side, not even a ditch. Besides, she would be driving, and it's hard to hit a moving target, especially one moving fast in a car. Maybe he would keep following her, hoping she would stop so he would have a chance to shoot her. He has to do it right the first time and make sure she's really dead. Then he would try to leave the country immediately.

Why didn't the man try to kill her while she was working at the hotel? He'd have to leave the car somewhere where it couldn't be seen and walk to the hotel, hoping that he wouldn't be seen.

Maybe some of the neighbors have already spotted the gray car, Oz thought, so he walked 100 yards down the road looking for someone to question. A sizable frame building, which must have been painted white 40 years prior, had a sign over the door saying "Frenchglen Mercantile." Oz had no idea what the word mercantile meant—something to do with a merchant, maybe?

A large man was sitting outside on the stoop. They exchanged brief introductions. Mike was pleasant and seemed eager to talk to him. He wanted to know where Oz was from. Oz hated to be rude, but he couldn't take the time to chat. He asked if there had been any strange cars around town.

"Funny you should ask that," he said. "Just the other day, I found this car parked at the rear here—a man inside it. I started to walk up to him. He turned on the engine, pretended he hadn't seen me, and drove off without looking back at me. I know he saw me. The other strange thing was that he must have driven in and turned around, like he was prepared to drive off quickly."

"Do you remember what color the *altomobil* was?"

"Ah...gray...maybe light blue, I'm not sure. I wondered

what he was doing there. A little creepy, don't you think?"

"What did the man look like?"

"Well, he was wearing a baseball cap, so I didn't get a look at him. He might have had a little beard. I'm not sure, really."

Oz asked Mike to look out for this man. "We think he is likely to try to harm Maric—uh, Mary."

"Good grief! I certainly will. How could anyone want to hurt Mary?"

Oz should have had an answer ready, an explanation that would satisfy Mike's curiosity without revealing much about Maric, but nothing came to him. So he just said that he'd explain the details once the man was behind bars. "Right now, I have to hurry and try to catch him. Your description fits. Without the baseball cap, he's totally bald. He may have a chin-strap beard of some kind. Thank you for being so observant."

"Oh good grief, I wonder if that's the person who poisoned Sniffer—my dog Sniffer. About three weeks ago, Sniffer barked …." Mike gave the full story about Sniffer. "The next morning we found him dead in a shed over there, from rat poison!"

"Yes, this guy probably tried to get close to the hotel in the middle of the night. I'm sorry your dog was poisoned, but his barking probably kept Mary alive. Please keep a look out for him."

The only other person Maric had said was continually in town was the school teacher, Susie. Oz walked down the road to the school, which was on the opposite side of Route 205. He waited until he had a chance to talk with Susie alone. Oz found out that she lived in the town with her family.

"I haven't seen a car like that," Susie said, "but something peculiar happened just two days ago. I was leading my students outside to inspect our little vegetable garden. You can't assume that these kids know about plants or about growing anything but alfalfa. Their families are submerged in cattle ranching. Anyway, we walked around the side of the schoolhouse and came across this man sitting on a rickety old chair that he must have dragged over from Nelson's shack. He was just sitting there with a rifle over his knee. He had a cloth shoulder bag next to the chair. He took out a dead rabbit in an attempt, I guess, to explain what he was doing.

"What did he look like?"

He had on a baseball cap so I didn't see the color of his hair, but it was probably dark like his chinstrap beard. Anyway, he was dressed the usual way—jeans and a shirt."

"What did he have to say?"

"Humm, not much. I told him he shouldn't be hunting rabbits around the school. That would frighten the children and it's dangerous to shoot a gun around them. 'Please go away,' I said. He got up and left immediately without saying a word. I didn't want to alarm the children, so we started right in on our gardening. Actually, now that you ask, I realize he never said a word."

"Would you mind sitting in the chair the way he was sitting?" Susie sat down facing the other side of the road. "Do you usually see a lot of rabbits across the road?"

"No. Now that I think about it, he should have been turned around, facing the open country."

"Did you see his car?"

"No. I was busy with the children."

Oz asked Susie to keep a look out for the man. "We believe he is trying to kill Mary."

"Good heavens! How terrible! Why would he want to kill Mary?" she asked.

This was the question Oz didn't know if he should try to answer. He didn't want to reveal Maric's past, not without her permission, but also because the story was so long and complicated. And he was realizing his ability to speak English was stretched enough as it was. On the other hand, Susie deserved some explanation. He decided to lie. "The man is crazy, a stalker, I believe that is the word. He used to stalk her. Now we think he definitely wants to kill her."

"What about the police, can't they protect her?"

"Well, that's why I'm here."

"Oh really!" Susie looked very skeptical, her eyes narrowed and lips tightened. "You're not a policeman around here." She paused. "You're Mary's boyfriend aren't you?"

Oz mumbled, "Boyfriend?" Oh *dečko*, this is why his mom told him never to lie. "You're right. I was a policeman…" (he muttered "*drugdje*" softly, as it took him some time to make the translation.) "Ah, elsewhere, I was a policeman elsewhere, and I am Mary's boyfriend."

"Where do you come from? Your accent is a little like Mary's."

Oz didn't know what Maric had told Susie about her background, so he didn't answer Susie's question. "I have been appointed to protect her. Please help us. She is in danger. The man often wears that baseball cap so people don't notice that he's bald. He's tall. He's been an army *snajper.*"

"OK, a baseball cap. So you think he was waiting here to kill Mary? That's terrible!"

"Yes, we are sure she is in great danger."

"Why doesn't she just leave the area?"

"He would find her."

"I'll watch out for him. Oh dear, poor Mary!"

"And please tell your fellow-worker."

"My what? Oh yes, I will."

In leaving Susie, Oz couldn't help but think that people in Frenchglen must be unusually observant. Maybe that is a common characteristic of rural people. He had lived and worked in Zagreb all his life—a city more populated than Portland.

He was disappointed in himself that interviewing someone in English was so difficult. He returned to the cabin to talk to his aunt. They could speak Croatian. It took him some time to tell Vera everything.

"Oh my goodness, that poor woman! As if she hasn't gone through enough already!"

Vera made him some tea, and by the time Oz had finished

his second cup, he could tell the wheels of her puzzle-solving mind were turning.

"Do you think someone else is hiding him, someone who loaned him a car, maybe picked him up from the airport?" Vera asked.

"No. Usually, assassins make all the arrangements themselves. They want to be completely independent and leave no trace. Both Mike and Susie said he didn't say anything. He probably didn't want them to hear that he has an accent."

"Or maybe he doesn't speak English. No, he'd have to speak English to rent a car, get a motel room, that sort of thing." Vera took another tack. "He'll want to get out of the country fast, once he's killed her."

Good God, Oz thought, this is my aunt talking!

"The closest international airport would be in Boise, Idaho, but he could have flown into JFK from Zagreb. Is there any way we could find out if he flew into Boise from Zagreb? Of course, we're not sure when he came."

"She saw him only once, at the museum in Burns, sometime late in July. I wonder how he found out that Maric was here?"

"If we knew the flight and the date, then we could start looking into rental cars."

"He wouldn't book his flight under his own name. He's using false papers. He could easily get Tudjman's security office to provide him with them. So, we don't know the name he used or the date he flew, but he probably eventually flew to Boise and rented a car. But if I were him," Oz continued, "I would have another set of papers—another alias—to rent the car. He'd have an international passport. He wouldn't book the car with the flight."

"So," Vera summarized, "we think he flew from Zagreb to Boise?"

"Edi!" said Oz. "Thank God for Edi. I'm no longer a policeman, so I can't make inquiries, but Edi can. I'd better go back to the hotel and call Edi again."

"Uh huh!" she said.

Oz noticed again the twinkle in her eye.

"And don't forget to ask Luke if he saw anything unusual."

"OK, I guess I'll have to wait for him. Would you mind if I had dinner at the hotel again tonight. He may not get back until late and, you're right, I need to talk to Luke."

"Are you going to tell Maric what you found out? She'll be so frightened. I know I would be."

"She has to know. That way she'll be careful. I don't want anything to happen to her."

Oz climbed into Vera's Honda and had already started the engine when Vera came running out of the cabin. "You know, it just occurred to me that the man I saw running to get into his car at the dump was carrying a rifle. He got into a gray car." Vera explained the incident in greater detail.

When Oz finally drove off, he was short of breath and was close to having a panic attack. He realized that the incident at the dump might have just been one of several attempts on Maric's life. He hoped Edi could soon give him some information about the assassin.

CHAPTER 28

Vera and Tom drove back to Portland. Oz had asked to stay on in the cabin so 'he could work some more on the case.'

"They think we were born yesterday!" Tom said, driving the SUV.

"We *were* born yesterday, but some things never change." Vera leaned over and put her hand affectionately on Tom's thigh. The distance between passenger and driver was one of many things she didn't like about the SUV. He was so far away. She had to withdraw her hand to give her arm a rest. She thought how much more pleasant Tom was, after spending time in the country.

She was worried about Oz. He seemed to be moving fast in his relationship with Maric—too fast, she thought. She wouldn't share those thoughts with Tom, as he would easily start finding fault with Oz.

"They're probably in our bed right now," he said.

"Oh Tom!" Vera said smiling. She tried to make light of it, but actually the thought had occurred to her. "I did see them kissing down by the river, but why shouldn't they?"

"How old do you think she is?" Tom asked.

"I don't know, but I think she's close to Oz's age, maybe a few years younger."

"She never finished university, though, did she?"

"Well she hardly could during the war, could she?"

"I think she's older than Oz."

"Well even if she is, what difference does that make? You're so traditional!" They were quiet. "Oh, I forgot to tell you that Oz has read her memoir."

"Memoir?"

"Yes, she is writing it on the computer at the school. He says it's fascinating."

"Humph, I wish we could read it."

"Maybe Maric will let Oz send it to us."

"Hold it. We need to slow them down, not encourage them."

She took a turn driving. Then, when Tom had the wheel again, Vera settled into some serious daydreaming. Before they left Oz at the cabin, she had asked him if there was some 'detective' work she could do for him in Portland. He said the biggest loose end was Brenda Hines. How is she connected to all this? Why did she go to Trieste? That is quite an assignment, Vera thought. Where should she begin? Maybe she should approach Mrs. Hines, her mother.

She and Tom didn't run in the same circle as the Hines, but Vera tried to think if they had a mutual friend or a connection of some sort. Vera was a member of the League of Women Voters. Perhaps, Mrs. Hines was too. What was her first name? Marce, that's it, Marce Hines. Was she a member of a garden club, a bridge club, a church? Chances are Marce was older than Vera. If worse came to worst, she could stalk the Hines home.... Wait a minute, Vera Whittier. That's not very respectful. After all, this woman has lost her daughter to murder, just as you did several years ago. As soon as this thought crossed her mind, she realized that was her connection.

It took Vera a day to compose a letter:

> *Dear Mrs. Hines,*
>
> *I am Vera Whittier. My husband, Tom, and I live in Portland. We know what a difficult time you are going through. We lost our only child, Emily, seven years ago. She was a senior in college when someone*

raped and then murdered her. The police still haven't found the killer.

I hope you would consider coming over for tea or coffee someday so we can talk.

Vera Whittier
2246 NW Irving Street
Portland, OR 97210
(503) 555-2401

I am a good listener and would love to hear about Brenda.

Sincerely,
Vera

This Wednesday, Joe had something new to propose to Mary. He had given up on having her be the cook at HFS over the winter. Luke was dead set against that. Luke and he agreed that they definitely wanted Mary to return in the spring when the hotel reopened.

This time, Joe took a new tack. He knew that Mary was aware that the men at the Harney Field Station were Serbs. "Many of the men working at the HFS feel disconnected to their former way of life. They're in a strange country. Traditions that were so important in their homeland are not even known about around here."

"Yes," Maric said, "I can understand that. I often wondered how you were able to recruit them all the way from Trieste. They must be lonely."

"For instance, *Slava*. *Slava* probably means a great deal to each of these men. Wouldn't it be good if they could celebrate *Slava* together?"

"*Slava*? My family never found religious meaning in the day, but we always went along with our Serb neighbors in their celebration. Opening their home to everybody and offering to share their traditional food—that was a lovely tradition. I hope such feelings of goodwill are not gone forever."

Joe wasn't sure when the tradition started. He thought it was when Serbs became Christians in the 800s. As he heard it, villages or tribes took on their own saint as their protector. He

remembered if you were baptized on a saint's day, that saint became your family's patron. But he couldn't tell that to Mary. He
had already told her that he was Croatian and that he left Croatia
for Argentina when he was eleven.

Mary went on to ask: "Aren't there many different patron
saints? Which one would you celebrate? I mean, it would be difficult to choose one for a dispersed group, wouldn't it?"

"True, but since all the men have different *Slavas*, they
could just pick a day that they agree to celebrate together. I was
thinking a few days after the hotel closes for the winter."

Joe described his plan in full. He wanted Maric to teach the
men how to cook various dishes, such as *projal, ćevapi, pasulj*,
to name a few.

"That could be fun. I haven't cooked many of those treats
for years, but I guess I could do it. It would be interesting to teach
cooking, but to men? Those men, I am guessing, have probably
never cooked. That will be a challenge. I'll do it, but I don't want
to cook at the HFS for the entire winter."

Joe smiled, pleased with their agreement. "Two new men
are about to arrive, so we'll have quite a crowd."

"When are you thinking of having the celebration?"

"I'm aiming for October 5th or 6th. The hotel closes October
2nd, this year, so that would give you three days to prepare. Would
that be enough time?"

"Yes, but are the men willing to cook?"

"Yes, I think they will be."

"Did you ever help your wife, Rosa, cook?"

Joe froze and stared at Maric as if to say, "What imperti-
nence!" His eyes narrowed: "Rosa did her job and I did mine." He
couldn't look at her, he was so angry.

"I'm sorry. I was just kidding you." She got up and poured
him another cup of coffee. Eventually, she asked him: "How
many mouths will there be to feed?"

He tried to calm down before answering her. "Let's see. I
think there will be 11 workers, Steve, his wife, and Junior. That's

14. You, me, and Luke, that's another 3, so 17. Oh, and then there may be one or two coming from Portland—one who plays the *tamburica*."

"That sounds like fun."

He decided to leave his coffee and go home. He was still annoyed with her. She should be more grateful. She thinks she's so important. Without me, she'd probably be walking the streets of Portland. He couldn't smile or even look at her. He mumbled a goodbye and left the hotel.

Maric and Oz were seated in the hotel dining room, chatting over a cup of coffee. They both believed that something nefarious was going on at the HFS, and that Joe was complicit. Maric thought Luke and Steve just wanted the environmental work done. Joe was definitely helping the men get there from overseas. Other than that, she knew nothing, since she had never been to the field station.

"Oh, I forgot to tell you that Joe is planning a *Slava* celebration at the HFS. He's scheduling it for October 5th or 6th. And he said that more men, two more men, to be exact, are going to arrive at the end of September. I'm supposed to teach the men how to cook some traditional dishes."

Oz gave her the latest information from Edi. "He believes the mystery man is Dinko Knežević."

"Edi must really be a good friend to help you gather information about this."

"He is a good friend, my best actually, but it is also in Edi's interest to locate Dinko. If Dinko is after you, then he's probably the same person who shot Brenda. He doesn't get paid for killing the wrong person. It's Edi's job to bring Dinko to justice. It's the job of the Ljubljana police to find and arrest him."

"Now that you're not on a police force, you don't have access to information that Edi can acquire?"

"That's right."

She regretted her question. Maric could tell that Oz's spirits flagged at her reminder that he was no longer an official detective. "Could you read your notes again? I want to be sure I've got it straight."

"Let's see, Dinko rented a gray Nissan in Boise from Thrifty Car. It is scheduled to be returned by mid-September, September 13, I think Edi said."

"Oh my God, so Dinko's definitely planning to kill me by September 13th and then fly home to Zagreb?"

"We're not going to let that happen, don't worry! We'll find him and arrest him," Oz tried to comfort her, without knowing exactly how that could be done. "Right now, I want to concentrate on keeping Dinko from killing you. But something's also got to be done about the men at the field station."

Maric was touched. She didn't want to think of war criminals or the danger to her that Dinko posed. She wanted to relish the moment of just being with Oz. "Isn't it wonderful that you came into my life at this time of year?" Maric mused.

"You mean, if it had been May, you would have had nothing to do with me?"

She laughed. "It's just that now there are so few guests that I have lots of time to be with you."

"Let's not think of our problems right now. Where would you like to go? We can drive Vera's car—a car Dinko doesn't associate with you. And we know the color and make of his car." Oz knew how eager Maric was to see the local countryside.

"Let's see, I want to go to Hart Mountain and see the pronghorns or was it mustangs that are up there? And I'd love to see the Diamond Craters."

"Just two weeks ago we went up Steens Mountain, so let's see the Diamond Craters. What are they?"

Maric tried to remember what she had read about them at the museum. "It's an area of several square miles with many basaltic features like craters, fissures, and maar lakes. Nothing is active today, of course." She tried to explain a few terms to Oz. "The hotel has a small brochure that you can read while I clean up the kitchen."

Maric tried to concentrate on her cleaning, but then Oz came into the kitchen and said in his deep voice: "What can I do to help?" He slipped an arm around her waist and kissed her. After a minute, Maric gave up and dropped the mop on the floor. They went into the hall and climbed the stairs to her room.

Yes, they were rushing things, but Maric knew she was lucky to have found Oz. She thought of Luna, her sister, who had died so young. At least Luna had found love at the end of her short life. Some people never get that chance, which is so tragic.

Maric felt that Oz was her soulmate. Both had been through the dangers of war and political intrigue. Both were alone in the world. Both were driven to see that justice prevailed. Their pasts linked them, as did their conviction and courage to bring wrongdoers to justice. They had both been alone for so long, and had lived without experiencing the tenderness of a loved one. They were not going to let this opportunity pass. Why prolong things by going through the traditional stages of courting? They knew they loved each other. The loss of their families made them both acutely aware of how easily they could lose each other. They didn't know where they would live or what they would be doing, but they were determined to face the future together.

CHAPTER 31

In the last week, there had been few guests. If one did spend the night, Maric made sure to assign them to a room at the front of the hotel, away from hers at the rear. Oz had hardly spent any time at the cabin since his aunt and uncle went back to Portland. Maric knew he wanted to be sure she was safe. He had no weapon to ward off Dinko, so together, they decided to tell Luke of the impending threat to Maric's life, using the same "stalker" story Oz had told others. Luke was horrified that someone might try to hurt Maric and immediately offered to help protect her.

Although Luke had a rifle, he felt more help was needed. He asked Corwin, one of his environmental buddies, to help him guard the place. Maric and Oz asked both Luke and Corwin not to say anything about this to Steve—the fewer people in on it, the better.

Corwin offered to sleep on the first floor of the hotel each night. He could take the two cushions off the couch, put them on the floor, and place his sleeping bag on top. "I'm happy to help guard the place," he said to Maric and added jokingly, "You're the best cook south of Burns."

"If you'd like, please have dinner with us each night you sleep here," Maric said.

"Sleep for my meals—sounds good to me!" Corwin brought a rifle with him. That was good, Oz thought, but if Dinko tried to enter the hotel, a handgun would be a better weapon for close quarters. Oz, himself, took a sharp carving knife from the kitchen up to Maric's room. He hoped like hell he wouldn't have to use it.

The third morning that Corwin was there, Oz took Maric in his aunt's Honda to Diamond Craters, figuring if they saw the gray Nissan following them, they would abandon that plan. The brochure warned against parking in loose cinder or volcanic ash. It said to watch out for rattlesnakes and be sure to have plenty of gas and drinking water.

They went north, heading for Burns, but turned east on Highway 78 before reaching The Narrows.

"Why 'The Narrows?'" he asked Maric.

"That refers to the little strip of land that separates Lake Harney from Lake Malheur. When there's a flood, water may rise enough to cover the strip, temporarily joining the two lakes. A bridge was built to allow cars to continue to pass from one side to the other."

When they reached the craters region, Oz couldn't help but remark that the whole area resembled a giant black pancake. Maric read from the brochure:

> About 9.2 million years ago, a huge mass of hot gases, volcanic ashes, bits of pumice, and other pyroclastics violently erupted near Burns.... Much of the area known today as Diamond Craters was formed by an initial layer of very fluid lava, known as pahoehoe. In some places, the layer of basalt was pushed up to form domes. In time, the lava on the surface cooled, became brittle, and then fractured, forming fissures. Today there are fissures 9 feet wide, 40 feet deep, and as long as 250 feet.

Oz didn't want to admit it, but he still found it difficult to quickly understand distances in feet. He did a quick conversion to meters. Let's see, less than 3 meters wide, 12 meters deep. "That would be like jumping down into a glacier's crevice—very scary."

"Yes, but I'd love to see one, even if we don't go down into it. Imagine 40 feet deep!"

By reading the brochure carefully, they located a fissure close to the road. They got out. No car was in sight. It was the middle of the day. The temperature was still warm. Oz wasn't sure he'd ever get used to the dryness of this climate—unlike rainy Portland, here it was always dry. He was continually thirsty.

They ambled around the fissure's brim, peering down to see if there was an easy place to descend. They found a place where the side had somewhat eroded and caved inward. There, they could scramble down. As they started the descent, Maric said: "Oh, there's a car."

Oz checked the car, now parked not far away from their Honda. "Yeah, but it's beige, so I guess we're all right." They took their time climbing down into the fissure so they wouldn't slip. Once down on its flat floor, they explored the full length, watching out for rattlesnakes. Two jackrabbits hopped around ahead of them. "Do they ever get out of the fissure?" Oz wondered.

"Look at all the plants down here. There's grass, flowers, and bushes."

Oz was amazed. "The plants are thriving but they receive sunlight only a few hours a day. How can they get enough water?"

"They're not as exposed to wind and sun down here, so they're not as likely to dry up, probably."

Oz felt somewhat foolish that he hadn't thought of that himself. This high desert stuff was so different from any terrain he had known in Croatia.

He came up to Maric from behind, put his arms around her, and kissed the back of her neck. He couldn't resist that sassy bob. He brushed her hair back to expose her ear and kissed it. Maric turned around to face him. They pressed close in a tight embrace when a rock tumbled down from the brim above them. An owl emerged from a cavity and flew off. They froze to listen and were surprised to hear a man cursing above them on the brim. Before they had time to get scared, they heard gunshots immediately above them. Three shots, then more cursing.

Oz and Maric swiftly made their way back to where they

had descended into the fissure and started to climb out. Oz wasn't sure if that's what they should do—maybe they'd be safer in the fissure. Telling Maric to stay back and take cover, he quickly scrambled up and took a peek over the brim. He saw a man with a rifle limping quickly to the beige car. He was walking fast, but his gait was uneven, like one side of his body was heavier than the other. He finally made it to his car, turned it around, and sped off.

Oz reached down for Maric's hand to help her up.

"What was he shooting at? Was he aiming at us?"

"I don't know. Let's look around. I think he was above us when that rock fell." They started walking along the edge of the fissure to where they thought they had been standing below.

"Oh, I bet it was a rattlesnake," Maric said.

Oz tried not to show his alarm.

Generally she and Oz spoke in Serbo-Croat, but when she told him what Luke said she spoke in English: "Rattlesnakes don't bother you if you give them a wide berth."

'A wide berth' was a new expression to Oz, but he got the message. DON'T GO NEAR THEM! They're a treacherous reptile.

"Over there, look at that stack of rocks, partially covered by brush. Oh my goodness, two of them, both dead!"

Oz searched for any shell casings. He found one and put it in his pocket. While scanning the ground for another, he spotted a third rattler slithering out of a hole in the rocks. Pointing to it, he said, "There's another! Let's get out of here." They walked quickly but carefully back to the car. Oz started the motor, turned around, and headed back to Frenchglen.

Maric asked: "Did you hear what he said? I think he cursed in our language. He said something like: 'Kurvin sine!'"

"I couldn't say. It happened so fast. Anyway, he wasn't driving a gray car. It couldn't be Dinko."

When they got back to the hotel, Oz wondered about the man who appeared to have been bitten by a rattlesnake. Why did he have a rifle with him? Diamond Craters is not the type of place you would choose to go hunting. Could the man have been Dinko? After an hour, Oz figured the man, whoever he was, had had enough time to get himself to the hospital in Burns. But when Oz called the hospital, he was told that they had not treated anyone for a rattlesnake bite. The last time someone had come in for that was two-and-a-half months ago.

Thrilled with the days' adventure, except for the odd incident at the end, they asked Corwin if there was somewhere else they should go, something else they should see. "Yeah, Blitzen," he answered.

"The river?"

"No, I'm talking about a ghost town named Blitzen. It's in the Catlow Valley, west of the 205, but between Burns and Frenchglen."

"A ghost town, yes, I'd like to see that," Oz said. It sounded interesting and fairly harmless.

Corwin started to give them directions. After a minute, Maric asked him to start again so she could write them down.

"OK. Sure. Go north on the 205. Three miles north of Roaring Springs Ranch on the 205 start looking for an unmarked gravel road, turn west on it and go another 3 miles. When you come to an intersection, head south for 8 miles. Then you can't miss it. That last road is very rough and completely deteriorates when it rains."

"What do you mean by 'deteriorates?'"

"If it starts raining, you don't want to be there."

Oz and Maric smiled at each other, filled with the optimism and excitement of two people in love.

The next day, after the breakfast dishes were washed, Maric and Oz set out in the Honda.

"My God," said Oz, "how many millions of acres of sagebrush have we seen in the last few days?"

"Yes, there is no easier place to disappear, I mean really disappear, than out here."

"That reminds me of the men at the Harney Field Station. Aunt Vera is convinced that the workers are Serbian war criminals."

"She's probably right. Can't we get the police to make a raid and arrest them?"

"I think it's a job for the F.B.I., being that it's an international issue, but it would be hard to get either the F.B.I. or the police to raid the place without preliminary evidence." Maric remained silent. "I've been thinking," Oz continued, "that I may have to work there myself in order to dig up some convincing evidence to show the agency so they will consider taking action."

"If we can wait until the 5th of October, I'll be there too."

"No, that's too late. I want to go in there before you get there." He didn't say it, but he wasn't going to let Maric be there alone with those men. He could imagine what they were like. Nor would he leave her alone with Dinko still trying to kill her, so this presented quite a dilemma. For the sake of distracting her from this imminent danger, he continued: "I could go in as a new worker. I should start there at least a couple of weeks before you arrive."

"You should start working there before the arrival of the next men. Do you think they'll hire you?"

"I don't know why not. You heard Luke the other night, there is still so much barbed wire to remove. It will take at least another year to get rid of it all."

Both Oz and Maric were quiet for a while. They passed an abandoned ranch with a dilapidated sign saying "Wade's End," suspended by only one of its two chains. Oz didn't want to live in a place where there wasn't telephone service, mail delivery, or electricity. He would be lonely, even if he were with Maric. He wondered if she felt the same. The sky was cloudless, the land was barren. The only sign of human existence was a wagon trail that wandered off to somewhere.

They were now driving on the eight-mile stretch, the last road that Corwin gave in his directions. It started as a hard clay-packed road but after four miles, changed to a dusty surface that was like driving through beige talcum powder.

Finally they got to what must have been the town of Blitzen. There were a few frame structures standing, but barely. Each was atilt and missing windows and doors. One still had the stairs leading to a second story but big chunks of its walls were missing.

"It makes me sad, but in a different way than how I felt seeing Mostar after the war, when so much of it had been destroyed by shells and bullets. This is so desolate. People gave up, not because others forced them to, but because they ran out of hope."

"Didn't Corwin say the town was founded in the late 1800s? People had such courage to come all this way and try to establish a community. I think he said there was a post office. Why would they bother with a post office? I can't imagine any letters reaching here more than once a month."

"I read that there was a school, a general store, even a saloon. Why does it make me sad?" Maric asked. "I think it's because of its isolation."

Oz held her hand. "I know what you mean. Didn't Luke say that the cattle in these parts outnumber people 200 to 1?"

"I couldn't live anywhere around here, even in Burns. I suppose if you grew up here, you'd be used to it, but for me, I couldn't take it."

Oz squeezed her hand in agreement. They returned to the car and drove home to Frenchglen. Their car was completely covered in dust. At one point, they had had to use the windshield wipers to see. Oz said: "The car's now beige!" Oz and Maric exchanged a glance. Was the car that they saw the day before just covered in dust?

Oz called the hospital again to see if there had been a patient admitted with a rattlesnake bite wound, but none had.

"Do you suppose he doesn't know that he needs to be treated? It may already be too late."

Maric answered: "That could be. Also, he might want to remain hidden."

"I was thinking that Dinko wouldn't want to stay in Burns, because after a few weeks, his face would become familiar to some people. Also it would be a long way to drive everyday to get to Frenchglen. I wish Luke were here to ask him where Dinko would be likely to stay."

"Why not ask Mike at the Mercantile? He may know some likely places."

Oz walked over to the store and found Mike eager to assist. "When he left Diamond Craters, which way did he go on 205?"

"We don't know, because we were still on the 78 and didn't see which way he turned."

"Oh, of course, you were on the 78. What was I thinking!? So which way did he go on the 78?"

"I know he turned around, so I guess he went back to the 205."

"OK, that helps. The most likely place is the RV Park at The Narrows, but if he's not there, I'd try Roaring Springs Ranch. Real nice people live there. They've been known to put people up."

Oz went back to the hotel to tell Maric where he was going. "I think I remember Aunt Vera talking about the RV Park."

"Yes, now that you mention it, I heard there was one at The Narrows. I remember because I had to ask Luke what an RV park was. I don't think we have any in Bosnia."

Maric had to prepare dinner, so Oz drove off on his own. At The Narrows, a sign said to turn right on Sherman Road to get to the park. When he found it, he drove up to the office. A plaque on the counter informed him that the park manager's name was Kurt Pound.

"Are you Mr. Pound?"

"Yeah, yeah, call me Kurt."

"Hello, I'm Oz. I'm looking for a man who may be staying at your park who is from Eastern Europe."

"What's the name?"

"I don't know his name, but he probably has been staying here for some time. I saw him yesterday and I believe he was bitten by a rattlesnake."

"So, what am I to do about that? People come and go around here. This isn't a hospital."

"Well, I'm worried because I've checked and he hasn't gone to the hospital yet. He may not realize how dangerous a rattlesnake bite is. If he is here, would you please check on him?"

"Oh for God's sake, I've got a million and one things to do. My policy is to leave people alone. That's why they like to stay here. I don't ask questions, as long as they obey the rules."

If only I were still a policeman, Oz thought. "Would you mind if I looked for him? I think he might need medical attention. He may not know what to do or where to go."

"Yeah, sure! Ha! I'm supposed to give you permission to rifle through the camp sites!"

"Speaking of rifles, he has one."

Kurt laughed: "Everyone and his dog has a rifle out here." He paused, then added: "Oh, now I think I know who you mean. The guy often practices out back. Damn good shot. Yeah, he's in one of the yurts."

Oz wasn't sure what a yurt was. He associated the term with Mongolia. But he interpreted the manager's remark as giving him the go ahead to look for Dinko. "Ok, I'll see if he's in one and if he needs help."

"Likely story! I'll be watching your car. You'd better be coming back empty-handed. In fact, don't leave the park without coming in here to see me."

Oz walked around. The ground was so dusty that each step sent up puffs of the brown stuff. He finally saw what he thought were the yurts: each was a fancy round tent with a window and door. Parked to the side of one was a car covered in dust. On closer inspection, he identified the make as Nissan and he could see a gray color emerging from the dust, in places.

Oz did not want Dinko to see him, so he didn't knock on the door, but listened to see if he could tell if someone was inside. He heard nothing, so he walked quietly around to the window and cautiously peeked inside. A large man was lying on his back on a bed with one leg propped up. Oz could see his bald head and beard. It must be Dinko, and he did not look good. In fact, he hadn't moved. He must be close to death, if he's not dead already. Oz went back to the office to ask the manager to immediately call 911.

While Oz waited in his car for the fire department's emergency service to arrive, he pondered about venomous snakes. Were there any in Croatia? Dinko probably didn't realize how serious a rattlesnake bite was.

He wondered if Dinko was like some men he met in the army who came from rural Croatia or Serbia. They were tough, trained not to complain about physical pain. They were disciplined. Their upbringing taught them not to question authority: their father's in early years, their commander's later on. Showing sympathy for someone in pain was a sign of weakness. Their training included a lot, but not how to operate in a distant land with a strange ecosystem.

The emergency crew arrived fairly quickly, considering the distance they had to cover. The sheriff arrived soon after. Dinko was pronounced dead. The sheriff questioned Oz, who explained that he and his girlfriend had seen him at Diamond Craters.... "No, I've never met him before."

Oz quietly slipped off when the sheriff was occupied elsewhere. He was afraid that more questioning might lead them to discover Maric's illegal status. Driving back to Frenchglen, Oz thought it would probably take a long time for Tudjman to find out that Dinko was dead, what with all the false names he went under. We need that time, Oz thought. At least for now, Maric is safe.

CHAPTER 32

MID-SEPTEMBER, 1997

Within a few days, Oz decided it was time to try to get a job at the Harney Field Station. This frightened Maric, but he explained that he had done this type of thing many times in Zagreb for the police department.

Before going, he contacted the Portland police. He asked to speak to Sergeant Bert Norton. Unfortunately, the sergeant seemed to be in a hurry. Oz told him how he and some others had become suspicious that the Harney Field Station was being used as a hideaway for Serbian war criminals. He gave a few more details, when Norton said: "This is sounding like a job for the F.B.I."

"Yes, I understand," Oz said. "I'm going to work there undercover to try to get specific information that will hopefully convince the F.B.I. that it is their legitimate concern. Would you please contact the F.B.I. and explain the situation, so they are on the alert?" There was silence on the other end of the phone. Oz interpreted that as a lack of enthusiasm. The sergeant probably thinks it's brazen to make such a request. Nonetheless, Oz continued, "You can contact me through Mary Andrews at the Frenchglen Hotel in Frenchglen, Oregon." He gave him that phone number, as well as his aunt's in Portland.

"Well, we're awfully busy around here. I'll call the F.B.I., but I can't be sure they're going to take any of this seriously. Watch yourself! You're a long way from help, if you need it."

Oz could tell Norton was not going to press the F.B.I. Once

again, he called on Edi and explained the situation. Two days later, Edi called back to say that they (he and Chief Mlakar) had formally phoned from Ljubljana to both the Portland police and the F.B.I. "But both agencies seemed indifferent," Edi said. "Concrete evidence will help. Do be careful, Žica."

Oz had some problems to think through. The other workers at HFS would realize that Oz was Croatian. They would stop speaking freely among themselves, knowing Oz could understand everything they said. It could take weeks for them to relax their guard. Secondly, they would be suspicious if Oz drove there in Vera's Honda each day. If he had that much money, why would he work cutting barbed wire, wading in cold water? Oz would have to ask Vera if he could switch cars with Maric, so he could drive the old Pontiac to the HFS. Would his aunt mind if Maric drove her Honda? Aunt Vera was so understanding, he felt she would come through for him.

Then he had to prepare an excuse for needing a job at HFS. *I could tell them I bag groceries at the store in Burns, and I can't make enough for rent, gas, and food. By working at HFS I can make some money and get room and board free.*

Maric worried that maybe Steve, the director of the HFS, had already met Oz. They wanted to limit those let in on their plans. But there was the problem of Luke checking on how much wire had been cut once a week. He might see Oz and wonder what he was doing there. Then too, Luke would notice if the Pontiac wasn't parked to the side of the hotel.

In the end, he and Maric decided that Oz should just say honestly that he couldn't get a job anywhere and he needed to earn some money. In case someone asked him how he got out to the HFS, he would just say that his girlfriend drove him. This would take care of another problem: How would he be able to get information out? No one would be suspicious if he called his girlfriend or if his girlfriend came to pick him up. With this plan he wouldn't have to ask his aunt Vera if Maric could drive her car. Oz could hear his dad saying: "When you don't know what to say,

say the truth."

Three weeks after Tom and Vera returned to Portland, Oz started working at HFS. He hated the work and he could tell the other men were uncomfortable with his being there. They hardly said good morning and they didn't talk when he was around. When the weekend came, Maric came to pick him up in the Pontiac and they went back to the hotel.

"Did you get a call from the Portland police?"

"No."

"What about the F.B.I.?"

"No."

"What's wrong with them? Don't they realize that this is important?"

When they got to the hotel, Oz called his aunt. "I haven't heard a word," Vera said. "I hope you won't mind, but I called the PPD myself and asked if they had contacted the F.B.I. and they said they had, but the agency had nothing to say one way or another."

Both Oz and Maric were disheartened. Although they were together for the weekend, the lack of response from law enforcement had darkened their spirits. Each tried to cheer the other up.

"I just have to get some concrete evidence or they won't take me seriously," Oz observed.

The following Monday morning, Oz asked Maric to make him a large breakfast which he ate quickly. He put his small camera, which he had brought with him from Croatia, in his pocket. He prepared a mustard solution in a glass and held it while Maric drove him to the Field Station. Just before Maric dropped him off, he pinched his nose and drank the fluid. Getting out of the car he already felt whoosy. He staggered into the dining room. He didn't have to pretend he was sick. He sat down in the nearest chair he could find.

Vuk said in his loud gravelly voice. "Had yourself a good time this weekend, did you?"

Oz held his head in his hands. He pretended to give a half-hearted smile to Vuk.

"Drank and fucked, drank and fucked. Sounds like fun to me. Hey, you won't share her with the rest of us, will you Catholic boy?"

"Shut up, Vuk," said Josip. Turning to Oz: "There's some more coffee in the pot, if that will help you." Before Oz could answer, Steve walked in to round them up and drive them to where they would be working that day. The men piled into the bed of the pickup. Sick as he felt, Oz made sure to count the men to be sure they were all in the truck. Steve climbed into the cab and started to pull out of the driveway. Oz could hold it no more and vomited violently.

"Oh crap! Get him out of here."

"Hey, lean over the edge will you, for God's sake."

Pounding on the glass window to the cab, Josip called: "Hey Steve. He's sick. Stop. The new one is sick."

Steve got the message and stopped the truck. "Can you make it back on your own?"

"Yes, I think so…I'm sorry…. It must have been something I ate."

"It looks like eggs and toast. Oh, Jesus, let's get out of here before he barfs again."

Oz made his way back to the dorm slowly, in case the men were still looking at him while they drove off. Once inside, he hoped he was through vomiting. In case he wasn't, he grabbed a pan from the kitchen sink and carried it around with him. He put on the plastic gloves that he had taken from the hotel kitchen and quickly started going through the men's personal belongings. There wasn't much. Each man had flown to Portland with just a small suitcase. Oz had to collect as much evidence as he could before Steve returned. He still felt nauseous, but tried to put it out of his mind.

Vuk slept in the top bunk on the left of the dorm. Oz would start with that bastard. The men shared the spaces under the bunks for their suitcases. According to his passport, Vuk, which means "wolf" in Serbo-Croat, was Vicenzo Uberto Clemente. Oz took a photo of it. In the bottom of his suitcase, Oz found a picture of a family in front of the famous statue of Prince Michael on horseback, pointing the way for the Turks to leave Serbia, a famous bronze in a central square of Belgrade. Oz took a photo of the photo.

He tried to get through each man's possessions, taking photos of items that would indicate that the owner was not from Italy. For instance, one of the men brought a photo of his family next to their Yugo. Another had a card showing the famous fresco of Saint Sava, the first Archbishop of the Serbian Orthodox Church. Josip had brought a new suitcase, but had carelessly left the receipt in an inside pocket showing it had been purchased in Novi Sad, Serbia, a month before he flew out of Trieste as Emilio Jacobucci.

Oz only had about thirty minutes before he heard Steve's truck return. He hadn't finished, but he had to take the pan and get in his own bed. The men wouldn't be back until 5:30. He hoped to have the chance to finish the search later in the afternoon.

Steve looked in on him and asked if he was all right. Oz grunted. He heard Steve run the hose over the bed of his truck. Poor guy, thought Oz. He pretended to stagger outside and offered to help.

"No. Just get yourself well," Steve said, without any eye contact or sympathy.

"Would you mind if I telephone my girlfriend?"

Steve, gave him somewhat of a disgusted look.

"You mean Mary?"

As Oz expected, Steve escorted him to his house to make the call, knowing from overhearing filthy remarks of some of the men that Steve was very protective of his wife. While Oz called Maric, Steve stood by him. He could hear Oz's conversation. "Would you please bring me a clean shirt and some Pepto-Bismol? ...As soon as possible...thanks."

When Maric drove in to HFS, Oz walked to the car and handed her the camera. He didn't finish getting all the evidence he wanted, but he thought it best to give it to her now, in case the men became suspicious and searched him.

Maric seemed reluctant to leave him. "Are you all right?" she asked in a low voice.

"Yes, sure, just sick to my stomach." He leaned against the car, to appear weak, in case Steve was looking. "Do you think you could take the film in to Burns to have it developed?"

"Yes, of course. Here's your clean shirt and Pepto-Bismol. Please don't take any chances. Get some rest."

CHAPTER 33

MID-SEPTEMBER, 1997

A couple of weeks after she had mailed the letter to Mrs. Hines, Brenda's mother called Vera to invite her for tea. The Hines lived in a magnificent house, just as she had expected. When Marce opened the front door, Vera saw a slight woman with well-coiffed gray hair. Her greeting was polite but lacked sparkle. How well Vera could remember feeling that way.

As they talked, Vera empathized with Marce. Listening to her made Vera relive those months when she and Tom first found out about Emily's death. It was a struggle to reign in her personal feelings.

"I'm so glad you were willing to come to my house. I thought it would be easier for me to talk about Brenda here at home."

"Of course."

Marce said that she thought the den would be the best place for having tea. The room was paneled in walnut. The pine trees outside its two windows filtered the weak sunlight that entered. Marce switched on a table lamp to help out. There were a few comfortable chairs and a small couch. "Whenever I don't have command over my emotions, I come in here. This is the room where Brenda and I used to play games when she was young, and chat when she was older. I can always feel she's here with me in this room. Do you know that Brenda was adopted?"

"Yes, I had heard that."

"She came to us when she was nine. Her mother was a

single mom who worked at our company in Hines. Do you know where that is?"

"Yes, next to Burns."

"That's right. Well, a foreman in our lumberyard there told us of her mother's sudden death and asked us if we could help with finding the young girl a suitable place to live. We had no intention of adopting a child, but when we saw Brenda, both Edwin and I were so moved by her. She was grieving over losing her mother. She didn't smile for the first three months we had her. She was quiet, but a sweet little girl. Here are some early pictures of her."

They showed Brenda as a young, slightly plump girl with straight brown pigtails. In other pictures she appeared as a teenager, standing between Marce and a man, whom Vera assumed was Edwin. Brenda appeared to be short.

"Here's her graduation photo. She went to Reed University."

"Oh, she looks like a powerhouse."

Vera regretted her words immediately, but Marce laughed and said: "That she was!"

Vera thought that as a young woman, Brenda was not attractive. Her hair was severely short. Her eyes looked somewhat defiant. She hadn't smiled for the picture. Even the dimple in her chin couldn't soften the photo's impact.

"Yes, Brenda became quite a feminist during college."

Vera couldn't help but wonder if she were a lesbian. She knew that Reed had a reputation for being a liberal, counterculture college. Her thoughts raced ahead. She wondered what Brenda did after college.

"We don't know why she went to Slovenia. Edwin and I had trouble finding it on the map. I should have told you first of all that Brenda was a teacher after college. She taught high school English here in Portland. She did a fair amount of traveling during her vacations. I knew she had been to Bosnia, Serbia, even Bulgaria before the war. She attended conferences for the IFA in Eastern Europe. Do you know what the IFA is?"

"No."

"It's the International Feminist Association.

"After college, while she was teaching, about three or four years ago, Brenda became interested in finding out about her father. She knew he was Serbian, and that he lived somewhere in Oregon. The only thing she could remember was that he liked the liquor called rakia. Evidently, every six months or so, he came to visit Brenda's mother and brought her a bottle of rakia. Her mother didn't really like it that much. He never paid Brenda any attention. The last time he came, Brenda remembered her mother saying to her: 'Brenda, this is your father.' He didn't even turn to look at Brenda, he just walked out. It was soon after that her mother died. So for a long time, Brenda was heartbroken over losing her mother. Her father's rejection haunted her.

"She thought she could find out more about him through the liquor store. There was only one in Portland that imported rakia. She explained to the store owner that she was trying to locate her father, that she thought he lived in a remote area of Southeast Oregon, and that he bought rakia from the store at least twice a year. The owner had no idea who he was, but took Brenda's name, address, and telephone number.

"She never heard a word, so she decided on another tactic. She was fairly sure he came into the U.S. from Trieste, Italy. So she traveled to Trieste. There is quite a large Serb community there. Brenda was able to locate two of her father's sisters and their families. Brenda thought she recognized her father in a photograph they showed her. The sisters never got word from him after he immigrated to the United States." Marce took a deep breath.

"Brenda came home and continued teaching. She never heard from the liquor store owner, but I don't think she had given up on looking for her dad.... She was a good person. I'm sure she was not up to anything bad. Why someone wanted to kill her, I will never understand."

Vera couldn't help herself. She had to ask: "Did you ever

find out who Brenda's father was?"

"No, if Brenda knew, she didn't tell us."

Vera also wanted to know Brenda's mother's name and what caused her death, but didn't feel it was appropriate to ask.

Marce was silent for a minute, deep in thought. Then she perked up and soon asked about Emily. Vera stayed another hour while they exchanged stories about their girls.

"...I almost didn't come out of my depression."

"...Edwin and I had given up on having a child."

"...It's easier for men to divert their attention, don't you think?"

"...She was so unexpected—a gift from heaven."

When Vera left, she knew she had made a true friend.

Chapter 34

Late September, 1997

By Thursday, Oz was really tired of walking through cold water, snipping barbed wire, and dragging pieces of it to the shore—it was miserable work. In the morning, while working on the northwest side of the lake, they came across a dead pronghorn that had failed to clear the fence. Impaled and tangled so badly it was unable to free itself, it must have suffered a slow death. It reminded Oz of the reason they were removing the wire. The migratory birds had already left for the winter. Nonetheless, in the afternoon they came across a snow goose which had met the same fate as the goat.

He admired the dedication of people like Steve and Luke, who cared about making the refuge safe for the animals. One of Steve's jobs was to remove the piles of barbed wire that the workers dragged to shore. He did this work on Saturdays. It took several trips with his pickup to collect it all, as it didn't compress easily. That explained why the back of Steve's pickup was so scratched up. Every Monday, when Oz came back to work, he noticed the huge pile of the stuff behind the dorms had grown even bigger. He guessed it stayed there until there was enough to have it hauled away for scrap metal.

Oz couldn't wait for the weekend, when he could be with Maric. At the end of the day on Thursday, he and the other workers were picked up from the lake and driven back to the field station as usual. He was surprised to find that two more men had arrived earlier in the afternoon. The others were delighted and gathered around the newcomers. Oz was not included and could not hear what they said to each other. They were purposely keeping their voices low.

In spite of the occasional outbursts of laughter, Oz didn't mind being excluded. He was really tired of Vuk referring to him as 'Catholic boy.' Vuk assumed that Oz, being a Croat, was a Roman Catholic, whereas, in actuality, he was an atheist. Oz understood that for centuries, Balkan rulers and occupiers had encouraged religious intolerance as a means of extracting loyalty and a willingness to go into battle. That partially explained Vuk's attitude, but also, Oz thought, Vuk enjoyed being a bully.

At one point, some of the men laughed and turned around to look at him. Oz was slightly afraid. Were they planning something? How did the two new men get here?

Around 8:00 that night, Oz was trying to read a book on his bunk. The others were out in the dining room, talking loudly now. Oz thought he heard a helicopter fly over. About ten minutes later, he was fairly sure he heard it again. The men hadn't noticed. Oz thought they were drinking. How did they get liquor in here? It was strictly forbidden. Maybe the new men brought it with them. Oz was on edge. With alcohol in them, there was no telling what these men would do. He tried to continue reading.

His ears picked up the sound of a vehicle pulling into the driveway. He listened carefully, trying to confirm what he heard. Slowly he rose from his bunk and walked into the dining room. The men hardly noticed his presence. Then he thought he heard another vehicle pull in. Was he imagining things?

The men's voices got louder. Their slurring speech confirmed to Oz that they were getting drunk. He was the only Croat in the room. He tried to appear casual as he moved next to a window. It was so dark outside that it took him awhile to notice that there were two big vans in the driveway. Their headlights were turned off. What is happening here! Should he try to make a run for it?

A light coming from Steve's house flickered out. Men piled

out of the vans and ran in all directions. All were dressed in black and carrying rifles. Oz felt a glimmer of hope. He thought he could see Steve, Lily, and Junior being ushered into one of the vans. Three more vehicles arrived. Policemen were surrounding the dorm! They were so quiet that the men inside still hadn't noticed. Oz thought he should not keep staring out the window or the men would want to know what was holding his attention.

Just then the door flew open and five F.B.I. agents were inside, with guns at the ready, in a matter of seconds. One man slowly backed up to a distant window, probably thinking of escaping through it, until the face of an F.B.I. agent appeared outside it, ready for him. Two of the SWAT team stood between the men and their belongings. Miranda rights were read. Of course, most didn't understand what was being said. Oz could tell that they all knew what the letters "F.B.I." meant and were scared shitless.

CHAPTER 35

LATE SEPTEMBER, 1997

Maric first knew something major had happened when she went to the HFS to pick up Oz on Friday afternoon, around 4:00 P.M. The entire complex was cordoned off with yellow tape. F.B.I. agents were going in and out of the dorm, while several guarded the exterior. She was excited, thinking that the F.B.I. had raided the place, just as she and Oz had hoped. But where was Oz?

She went up to one of the agents and asked what had happened. He queried her as to who she was. After some discussion, he phoned someone and then was able to tell her: "Your boyfriend is all right. You'll probably be able to see him by tomorrow sometime." He turned away from her to talk again on his phone, then turned back toward her: "You're the cook at the Frenchglen Hotel?"

"Yes."

"There are eight of us who would like to have dinner and spend the night, both tonight and tomorrow night, can you handle that?"

"Yes, how did you know about the hotel?"

He laughed. "Ma'am, we've had the hotel, the field station, Lake Malheur, and the Stoka Ranch under surveillance for two weeks."

"Good heavens!" She was elated, breathless, and welled up with tears of relief. She got hold of herself to say: "Thank you. Yes, there's room at the hotel for eight to spend the night. What time would you like dinner?"

"Excuse me while I find out." He phoned someone again. Then turned to Maric and said: "Would between 6:00 and 6:30 be all right?"

"Yes, I may not be able to serve you dinner until 6:30, but we'll have refreshments while you wait." Maric was desperately thinking about what she could serve. She wouldn't have enough time to go into Burns to buy more groceries. She hoped Susie would be able to help. Luke and Oz weren't around. At least Oz was OK. She would have liked to have been able to talk with him.

What would she cook? With the hotel about to close and so few guests this time of year, she didn't have much food on hand. There was no time to defrost meat from the freezer. Fortunately, she had made a good batch of *cevapcici* that she planned to serve while Oz was home for the weekend. She had enough of those little pork and beef sausages to give each man two. She had some frozen asparagus tips. With those she could easily whip up some asparagus risotto. What did she have in the way of fresh vegetables? She remembered one zucchini, 4-5 carrots, two handfuls of green beans, a yellow squash, and there were some kernels of corn in the freezer. She had plenty of onions. That was enough for a vegetable salad. She better make the salad first so she could refrigerate it for an hour. Dessert was easy. She had two home-made pies in the freezer and plenty of ice cream.

She just had time to lay a fire in the potbelly stove when the men started walking in. She was plenty warm in the kitchen with the oven and burners going, but the dining room was chilly. The men didn't complain. They seemed happy to be able to relax.

They ate and drank everything she offered, which probably meant there hadn't been enough food. Although she said she was Mary, they kept calling her Maric. How did they know her real name? Maybe Oz told them, but he wouldn't do that, she was sure.

One man asked if the little sausages were Croatian. She had to answer yes, but she didn't want them to focus on her being foreign. That agent must have picked up on her hesitation. He said with a smile: "Don't worry, we're not immigration. We're only interested in criminals."

"Oh my God," Maric thought. "They know everything about me. It's just a question of time. I *will* be deported."

For a group of men, she thought, they were unusually quiet. When they did speak, it was in low voices. Maric could imagine that there was a lot of anxiety and sleep deprivation that comes with performing such a raid. They all retired to their rooms by 9:30. Maric had forgotten to say goodbye or even thank Susie for responding promptly to her plea to make up the rooms that had been stripped down for winter. Joe should give her time-and-a-half for pitching in at the last minute, she thought.

In the morning, Maric served the men French toast, as she didn't have enough eggs for any alterative. At least today she would be able to shop in Burns. After breakfast, they lingered through a second cup of coffee, before they left for the day. They took everything with them, even though they were planning on spending another night at the hotel. Of course, none of the rooms could be locked. That might explain it.

By Sunday, Oz was back and the agents were gone. Vera and Tom had driven from Portland and would join them for dinner. It was a cold fall night. The temperature outside dipped down to below freezing, but Oz kept stoking the fire so they were warm in the dining room.

Maric learned that the war criminals had been flown to a federal detention center outside of Washington, D.C. Joe had been taken to the Metropolitan Correctional Center in Seattle, where he was to be held until his trial. No one was quite sure what was going to happen to him. Luke was spending a fair amount of time at the ranch now that his father was incarcerated.

Maric hoped Luke would get back in time to join them for dinner. She had a pot roast simmering. A freshly-baked apple crumble was cooling on the counter. All that remained was to cook the potatoes and the beans. Tom had brought a couple of bottles of wine and was just uncorking one when Luke walked in. He looked tired and seemed unsure of himself. Their warm greetings could not shake off his solemn mood.

"I want you to know," he announced, "that I thought my dad collected those men from the Serb communities in L.A. and Portland. I had no idea that they were war criminals." He slumped onto one of the benches.

"We know," Maric said and handed him a glass of wine, which he left untouched for the entire evening.

Maric had already told her story to Oz, but nobody else had heard it. It felt so good to be with people she trusted enough to share it. For such a long time she had had to be careful, keeping her thoughts to herself. Even when she lived in Zagreb with Aunt Alma, she could not tell people what she was doing. (Aunt Alma wouldn't have wanted to even listen!) For so long, fear had constrained her every move and thought. Finally, she was able to share the truth with this group. She began by explaining how she had fled Slovenia to Trieste and ended up in Fernglen, following three Serbian men off the airplane to where they met Joe, and then begging him for a job, telling him she was a great cook.

Luke shook his head and said smiling: "Yeah, and I thought you were just another Serb that Dad was feeling sorry for."

She smiled at Luke: "Here's what *I* don't understand. I thought your dad was Croatian, originally. Why did he try to help Serbian war criminals?"

"Croatian! No, dad is a Serb through and through."

"But he told me his father was Ante Pavelic!"

"What?! Holy smoke, even dad's not that bad." The others were stunned, knowing Pavelic to be Croatia's version of Hitler.

"Yes, that's what Joe told me," Maric insisted. "He said after WWII, his father had escaped to Argentina."

"Oh no, no, no. He hated the Croats. He always told me that the Croats persecuted the Serbs during WWII."

"That's true," Oz put in. "The Croats were incredibly cruel during that time—worse than the Nazis."

"Dad always said his family immigrated from Krajina to

Trieste after WWII to get away from Croats."

Maric was aware that Luke knew little about the war so she explained: "Krajina is a region of Croatia that had a Serb majority. That's why Krajina tried to separate from Croatia during the Yugoslav wars."

"Well, I never got any of that straight," Luke said. "They were just names to me—Croatia, Serbia, Bosnia. I don't know anything about them, really. Anyway, what I do know is that Dad came to the U.S. from *Trieste*, not Argentina."

Maric was taken aback. "Why would he deliberately lie to me?" she asked.

"Dad always wants to be in control. He didn't like not knowing why you came to the States or where you came from. He kept at me to find out, and probably lied to you for the same reason, I guess...."

Nonetheless, it saddened Maric. At the very time Joe lied to her, she remembered thinking of him as her friend.

Finally, Vera spoke up: "I'm trying to figure out your dad's motive in all this. I'm thinking that he felt very strongly in favor of the Serbs."

"That's right," Luke said. "he felt the Serbs won the war and deserved credit."

"Did he know about the atrocities they committed during that war?"

"I don't know. I don't know if *I* know. We don't exactly stay on top of things out here. I try to be informed about environmental issues, but I rarely listen to world news. The TV and radio mention events in Idaho, but not the Balkans." Luke looked dejected. "I wish you could have known my mother. She was a kind person. They were so different."

Maric could feel Luke's loneliness. She wanted to be supportive but couldn't think of anything to say that might help him.

Vera chipped in, "When did your mother pass away, Luke?"

"In November of last year," He sighed. "She hadn't been ill, so we were unprepared."

Maric didn't have to look at Vera. She knew her well enough by now to know what she was thinking. Maric thought she'd better say something before Vera did. "What exactly did she die of?"

"The doctor thought it was a heart attack."

"Oh dear, did she have a weak heart?"

"No, not that we knew of. Evidently, women have different symptoms than men. We were unprepared. It was dreadful. I miss her very much. We were close."

"I'm so sorry. I wish we could have known her."

Maric went into the kitchen to put the final touches on dinner. She had lost everyone in her immediate family. That had been hard to bear, but at least she didn't have to suffer with disgrace, doubt, and perhaps more, like Luke.

They all settled into eating before the conversation picked up again.

"Well, what I want to know is how does Brenda fit into all this?" Vera asked.

"Brenda?" asked Luke. "Who's she?"

The others looked at each other. Then Vera continued her probing, "When your father first came to the States, where did he go?"

"The first I know is that he started working in Burns."

"So, he didn't start off as a cowboy or ranch hand?"

"No, he had a job at Hines Lumber Company first, then, some years later, he came to work for my grandfather, my mom's dad."

"That's it! I've got it."

Tom started laughing. "Oh, Vera, you love this, don't you?" Tom turned to Oz, "She should be a detective, Oz. You know that, don't you?"

Oz laughed too. "I know, and I should have gone to drama school. Tell us, Aunt Vera."

"Well, it concerns Brenda."

"WHO IS BRENDA?" Luke asked again in exasperation.

"I think she was your half sister, Luke."

"What?! Half sister?"

"Oh please, Vera. Really!" Tom said disgustedly.

"Hear me out. Oh, where to begin! Well, you all know I have become friends with Marce Hines." Turning to Luke she said, "Marce is the wife of the owner of Hines Lumber Company." Vera looked at Luke while she spoke, "Brenda had been adopted by the Hines when she was nine years old. Brenda's blood mother had lived in Hines and worked as a bookkeeper for the lumber company."

"So before Mom, my father had been married to Brenda's mother?" Luke asked.

"Well, no, not exactly. I figure Brenda was about four years older than you."

Maric cringed. Luke had had enough setbacks without spelling out new ones!

"So," Luke spoke slowly and quietly, "what happened to Brenda's mother?"

"It was thought that she killed herself because she was pregnant again, but really, no one knows for sure why she died suddenly. Brenda was left all alone, so Marce and Edwin Hines adopted her."

Elbows on the table, Luke put his head in his hands.

Maric held her breath hoping Vera would realize it would not be a good time to say anything more. She tried to give Vera a firm signal to stop, but Vera wasn't looking at her.

Vera hesitated only to take another bite of her dinner. "Delicious!...Well you see, about four years ago," (chewing and then swallowing) "Marce, Brenda's adopted mother, said that Brenda was trying to find her father. Rakia was one thing Brenda remembered about her father. When he came to visit—once or twice a year—he would bring her mother a bottle of rakia, which he liked to drink. She tried to trace her father through the store where your dad bought it."

"Rakia," said Luke. "Dad loves his rakia. I think he got it somewhere in Portland."

"Marce told me that Brenda was a teacher after college. She became determined to find out who her father was. She thought she knew his name. She knew he was Serb, but she didn't know where he lived. The rakia was her only clue. She found a liquor store in Portland that sold it."

"Zoran's," Oz interjected.

"So this Brenda is my half sister?"

"Yes, Luke, you *had* a half sister. I'm sorry to say that Brenda is dead. Maric, you had better explain this part to Luke."

Oh dear! Maric was reluctant to tell the story to Luke. He had a lot to deal with right now. He didn't need to learn about Brenda tonight. "Let's take a break so I can serve dessert." She felt sorry for Luke. Vera, who was usually more discrete, was out of line. She was becoming somewhat obsessive about solving mysteries. Now, Maric had to tell Luke that Brenda's murderer meant to kill her, but killed his half sister instead.

Midway through the apple crumble, Tom couldn't hold himself back anymore. He turned toward Vera and asked: "I want to know why you think Brenda Hines is Luke's half sister?"

Luke seemed unable to look at the others. He kept gazing at his plate.

"I don't really *know* that you, Luke, and Brenda are half-siblings. But here's the thing: both you and your father have a somewhat rare genetic trait that is visible—you both have cleft chins. Marce showed me pictures of Brenda and she had that same dimple on her chin."

"It's funny. I've always wanted a sister." He smiled faintly at Maric. "So tell me, how did she die?"

Maric could avoid the story no longer. She had a lot to explain: working for the President of Croatia, secretly collecting tapes, going to the opera in Ljubljana and escaping by using Brenda's airplane ticket. The story took over an hour to tell because of their frequent interruptions, demanding more thorough explanations. It was the story's effect on Luke that she worried about. When she finished, he got up and walked over to Maric.

"You have to stand up, little girl, so I can give you a proper hug. I'm so glad you came into my life."

Maric couldn't hold back her tears. For a few minutes, nobody talked. A cold wind was blowing outdoors. That and the persistant downpour made the indoors seem even cozier. Oz got up to add another log to the stove. Vera and Maric cleared the table.

Over coffee, Oz told them that the F.B.I. believed that the fake Italian passports and visas had been made in Belgrade. Serbs who recently arrived in Trieste with fake Italian passports were issued visas to enter the U.S. They flew to Portland and Joe picked them up at the airport and drove them to the field station. In Belgrade, they must have known about Joe and the opportunity he offered to hide war criminals in Eastern Oregon.

"Remember, Tom, I heard a ham message asking if anyone knew of a hideout called Maller? I finally realized the speaker meant Malheur," Vera said.

"Oh my God," Maric broke in, "I had asked Majesira to look into that. She must have been the one to broadcast that question.... I got it from the tapes. I think it was Milošević who said to Tudjman: 'If worst comes to worst, we always have Maller.' Vera, you heard that?"

"Yes."

"I pronounced it that way because that was how Milošević said it."

"That's an amazing coincidence," Tom said.

"But the question is, how did Belgrade know about Malheur?" Oz instinctively pronounced it the French way, not intending to correct anyone. He was deep in thought. He recounted: "First two men came into the country mid-April in 1996. Four more came in the following November sometime. Then three more came with you, Maric. That was in April of this year. Then the last two arrived just recently."

"They came knowing they would have a job and a place to live." Vera commented.

Oz pointed out that they knew so little English they were only suitable for work at the field station. "Where else would they have been hired and how would they get anywhere? It would be in their interest to learn English, otherwise they would be stuck out here forever."

"That was Steve's feeling exactly," Luke said. "He told me a woman came by the field station a couple of times expressing a willingness to teach the men English, but she wanted to do it when there were more men there. He thought she was planning to do it over the summer, but she never showed up again. Steve was disappointed."

"Oh my goodness! I'll bet you that was Brenda. I did tell you, didn't I, that Brenda was a high school English teacher? That's what Marce told me."

"Does that mean that Brenda wanted to help the men, because I don't think that was likely? She was a friend of Majesira's." Maric explained who Majesira was.

CR

The next morning, Oz and Vera suggested that Maric phone Majesira. They and Tom stood by her as she made the call. Just hearing her friend's voice made her emotional. It had only been six months since Maric last called her on a pay phone in Zagreb, but so much had happened, it seemed like years.

What Majesira told her was utterly surprising. Maric put her hand over the mouth piece so she could share the news: "Majesira knows all about catching the war criminals here."

Maric listened again as Majesira continued: "I didn't respond to your second email because it was so important to keep everything quiet. Brenda knew war criminals were being hidden in that place. She wanted me to contact Bastiaan and the F.B.I. Bastiaan was very helpful. We had to keep everything quiet. Brenda stopped talking to her parents about her search for her father. She told us the third group of men was flying to Portland in April. Then Brenda was murdered. I liked her so much, Maric! She was a wonderful person. I had known her for many years." Maric heard Majesira crying.

"I'm so sorry Majesira."

"I was devastated. Then you vanished. I became so worried about you. Bastiaan Bloome did some investigating. We figured that you used Brenda's ticket and passport to escape, but we didn't know what had happened, or where exactly you were, or even if you were still alive. I couldn't explain that in my first email to you because the Malheur trap was still being spun. More men were coming to be snared."

"That's all right. I understand, Majesira."

"Brenda never told me how Joe got involved. She said a man in Portland got Joe to pick up the new arrivals and take them to the field station."

"Did you know that Joe was her father?"

"Oh my God, no...no! She never told me that. All I knew was that she didn't like him."

Maric told her that Tudjman had sent an assassin to Oregon to kill her. "His name was Dinko."

"Really? How dreadful! You said *was*. What happened?"

"He's dead now."

"Thank God! But how?"

"A rattlesnake got him."

"A rattlesnake! How bizarre! Tell me more."

"Yes, he tried several times to kill me. And I don't think Tudjman knows yet that Dinko is dead."

"Listen, girl, you have to go to The Hague right away, 'pronto,' as they say out there. Tudjman will send someone else to kill you. Go now, before he finds out that Dinko hasn't completed his job. We've got to get Tudjman, too, you know."

"Remember the detective from whom Bastiaan picked up the tapes in Ljubljana?

"Yes."

"He's here with us now."

"How did that happen?"

"It's a long story, but he says that until The Hague indicts Tudjman publically, the court won't let it be known that there is incriminating evidence against him, so we don't think Tudjman knows yet that The Hague has the tapes."

"I wouldn't be so sure," Majesira warned.

They spent the next five minutes wallowing in the success of trapping the eleven war criminals. "Three of them were actual rapists," Majesira said, "and three more were directly involved in running the rape camps."

"How do you know who they were?"

"I'd rather not say. We were really hoping that Ratco Mladić would bite, but he didn't, that bastard!"

Maric wanted to catch up on mutual friends. She wanted to know if there was any news about Leni, or Hakim's sister, Hasiba. How far along was the repair work on Stari Most, the Ottoman bridge? Could Majesira find out about her Aunt Ada? But typically, Majesira needed to keep the conversation short. Before saying goodbye, however, she urged Maric once again to go to The Hague immediately. "You must testify to the validity of the tapes."

They hung up. Maric relayed the information to Oz, Vera, and Tom. They talked at length. Finally, Maric was convinced that she had to go to The Hague. How could she get there?

"Not to worry," Tom said. "Vera and I will drive back to Portland tomorrow. As soon as we get there, we'll buy you a plane ticket to fly to The Hague. You just tell us when you want to go."

While Joe was locked up in Seattle waiting to be tried, Luke had to oversee the ranch. He promoted one of the ranch hands who was capable of continuing Joe's procedures to be the manager, for the time being. Luke's heart had never been in it, as well Joe knew. He could hear his father ranting against him: "You idiot! All these years and you don't know one thing about ranching. I never should have sent you to the university. It was your mother's idea. I knew it was a mistake. How can you say that beef consumption is decreasing? You love steaks and so does everybody else! Cholesterol, saturated fats! Oh, for God's sake, that's just stuff they teach you at the university. We have a good business that makes money.

"And don't start mentioning water. Yes, yes, I've heard you say over and over that three-fifths of the farmland produces only 5 percent of the protein. I'm sick of your statistics. Jesus, no wonder you're a softy, you're half Mexican. Do you think statistics matter? I'll tell you what matters—making money! Stoka Ranch has continually made money, ever since I took it over."

Luke could not call his father in prison. He had to wait until Joe called him. When he did, he told Luke some things that needed special attention at the ranch. He ended the call with a plea for Luke to send him rakia. Of course, that was out of the question.

"I got a telephone call from Justin Miller, your lawyer. Do you know he wasn't aware that Mom had passed away? Didn't you let him know?"

"No, why should I?"

"Well, he wants me to stop by his office. Evidently, Mom left a will. Didn't you know?"

"Jesus!" said Joe, and abruptly hung up.

C⅊

A couple of days later, in Mr. Miller's office, Luke heard, "So you're Luke, Rosa and Joe's son. Nice to meet you, Luke. Have a seat. I didn't know your mother had passed away until a couple of days ago."

He must have read about Dad's arrest in the newspapers and then found out that Mom had died, Luke thought.

"When Rosa died...Joe never called to let me know she had passed. I think Joe didn't know that Rosa had left a will. It was mailed to me some time in November—a year ago."

"You're kidding? That's when she died," Luke said in shock.

"I see. Before I received it, she phoned me to tell me it was coming. Then she called two days later, to be sure it had arrived and was written correctly. Yes, I remember that. She was always so nice, your mother.... Well, I guess it's time to let you know what it says." He opened an envelope and started reading:

> *I inherited the RR Ranch from my father, Rudolfo Romero. My husband, Joe Gutić, changed the name to Stoka Ranch, but I am the owner. I wish to leave it, the cattle, the buildings, the house, all equipment (including the helicopter), cars, and the Frenchglen Hotel to my son Lucas Gutić....*

"My heavens!" Luke was overwhelmed. Mr. Miller gave him a minute to collect his thoughts. "I wonder why she wrote the will then? She must have died a few days later."

"So tragic!" Mr. Miller discretely waited, before continuing. "It was definitely hers to give you. I've checked the title."

Driving back to the ranch, Luke thought of something else

he should have asked Mr. Miller. He phoned the lawyer: "I'm sorry to bother you again, Mr. Miller, but could you tell me what day you received the letter with my mother's will?"

"Let's see. I still have the envelope. It's postmarked November 17, 1996, almost a year ago."

"Thanks." That meant she probably mailed it on the 16th. Luke thought that was about the time his dad had picked up the second group of workers for the HFS. He called Steve, who said those four men came in the early afternoon of the 16th. "I know your dad drove to Portland the day before and spent the night some place. He was getting too old, he said, to drive to Portland and back in one day. He started making it a two-day trip."

Mom probably wrote her will while Dad was gone, Luke thought. Maybe she had to have him away so she could get up the nerve to cut him out of it. She had had years of being somewhat abused by him. He never treated her with respect. On the other hand, Luke had never seen Joe get physical with her.

For the rest of the day, Luke was good for nothing—lost in thought. He went back and forth, wondering about his mother's death and his obligation to run the ranch. The truth was that Luke had never wanted to be a rancher. When his dad was home, Luke lived at the hotel. He didn't like to witness the dehorning, castration, and branding of the cattle. He couldn't stand to see the animals in fear. Once the calves left Stoka, they only lived six more months. In two more days, he had clarity. He could not be a rancher. His father didn't own the ranch. He did, so he decided to sell it.

One night, he started going through his mother's personal belongings. In the back of her dresser drawer he found a letter addressed to him. He cried when he saw her handwriting:

...Luke, you have a sister whose name is Brenda Hines. She came to the house yesterday, hoping to meet her father, but Joe had gone to Portland to pick up a new batch of workers for the HFS. When I opened the door, I knew immediately she was Joe's daughter. For

many years, things had not been right between your father and me. In the first years of our marriage, I was sure there was another woman. I think your grandfather knew about it also, and that might be why he left everything to me.

Brenda wanted to meet Joe. A few years ago, she had left a message at Zoran's Deli and Liquor Store in Portland for your father to get in touch with her, but he never did. (That is where your dad purchases his rakia.) She waited to hear from him until she lost hope, and then decided to go to Trieste, Italy, to look for additional family.

I don't know how she discovered that your dad was Serbian and that his family lived in Krajina. Somehow, she must have also found out that they moved to Trieste after WWII. She found your dad's two sisters living in Trieste. They were lovely to her, but very disappointed that your dad never wrote them. Their names are....

After rereading his mother's letter, he wondered what Brenda looked like. Then he recalled an incident two years ago or more. A woman came for dinner at the hotel. They had gotten into a conversation about the field station. He remembered her because she too had a dimple in her chin. It never occurred to him that she might be his sister. He wished he had known. He had always wanted a sister.

Once the war criminals were arrested, Maric was afraid she would be next. She had come into the country illegally, was living under an alias, and now her cover had been blown. Maybe they wouldn't arrest her exactly, but they would certainly force her to leave the country—probably for good.

She and Oz had talked about marriage. Oz wanted to get a job first. He hoped to be a police detective again. The Croatian police wouldn't hire him. If he applied for such a job in the United States, he and Maric would have to live in a big city where the police force would have several detectives. But who was going to hire him?

Riding in the car to Portland, Maric said to Oz: "I know I have to go to The Hague, but I'm so afraid that once I leave, I'll never get back into the country again and we'll never be together. I don't even know where I could go to be safe." She couldn't stop the flow of tears.

Oz pulled off the road so he could look her in the eye: "No matter what happens, I will find a way to be with you. No matter where you have to go, I promise we will be together again." He leaned over to give her as much of a hug and kiss as the bucket seats would allow.

After Oz resumed driving, he told her that Vera and Tom were committed to helping her obtain legal status.

A week later, Maric had given her testimony at the ICTY, guaranteeing the authenticity of the tapes. The tribunal also recorded her personal story.

"Now, that the cat's out of the bag," Bastiaan said to her, "assassinating you could not help Tudjman or Milošević escape incrimination. And they would be foolish to try to kill you out of revenge, but I'm not going to tell that to the American Embassy. I'm going to tell them that you gave invaluable evidence against two Balkans presidents who are guilty of egregious war crimes. In view of your risking your life to collect evidence against them and having suffered several assassination attempts in the last six months, the United States should grant you asylum. It would not be safe for you to return to the Balkans. It only makes sense to let you live in peace in the United States."

Bastiaan recommended that Maric stay at The Hague until a decision was made. Maric was in limbo for a week and a half. Bastiaan arranged for her to stay with a Dutch family, the de Jaagers, who kindly gave her room and board for free. They spoke English and were gracious hosts. Maric knew that, in spite of their kindness and Bastiaan's efforts to convince the embassy, it would take a miracle for her to be granted asylum. She didn't believe in miracles, but she did not get depressed either. Instead, she drew courage from several new friends she had found in the last six months, who reached out to help her. Oz, of course, was the main one, but there were others, too. Not since her parents and sister died had she felt supported. Now she did. She could get through whatever came her way.

◌॰

A month after she went to The Hague, Maric and Oz were back in Oregon, living at the Whittier's cabin on the Blitzen River. Maric had been granted asylum, but before they could move to Portland, she had an obligation to fulfill. She and Oz spent the next three weeks painting the interior of the History Museum in Burns for Mrs. Spooner. They cleared one section at a time, painted it, and then moved everything back, so that the displays were kept in order. By the time they were halfway through this project, the media became aware of their story. A photo of Maric on top of a ladder painting trim and Oz working on the ceiling with a long-handled roller was one of several pictures appearing in Portland newspapers.

Had Dinko lived, the Ljubljana Police Department could have brought him to trial. But you can't try a dead man. The best the LPD could do was to gather all the evidence against Dinko Knežević and present it to Brenda's parents to demonstrate that he was guilty of their daughter's murder. To this end, Edi flew over from Slovenia to document Dinko's actions in Eastern Oregon. When Edi was finished collecting all the relevant facts, Mr. and Mrs. Hines drove to Burns to meet him. They were given all the evidence of Dinko's crimes against Brenda and Maric. Once the Hines said they were convinced that Dinko had killed their daughter, Edi flew back to Ljubljana.

But before returning to Portland, the Hines had one request. They wanted to meet Luke. Together with Oz and Maric, they drove to Luke's ranch. Maric was surprised to see that the wrought iron arch over the driveway now read RR Ranch. While Luke served tea, Edwin and Marce kept their eyes fixed on Luke, looking for expressions and mannerisms that reminded them of Brenda. Luke asked them many questions about her.

At one point, Oz said that he thought Brenda had bought a turquoise rain jacket for the trip because she knew Maric would be wearing one. "She may have been planning to meet with Maric after Maric had turned over the tapes to Bastiaan Blomme."

"No, I disagree," Maric said. "I don't think she would have risked associating with me while the Malheur trap was in progress."

"You have a point, but why did she buy the jacket just before her trip to Slovenia, and why did she bother going to Ljubljana if she didn't want to meet you? Majesira must have told Brenda that you'd be staying in the Central Hotel, that you were going to the opera, and that you'd be wearing a blue rain jacket."

"Maybe," said Marce, "Brenda wanted to make a personal commitment of solidarity with you, Maric. It was her way of saying thank you for what you had done. Maybe she hoped, if you had both lived through this, you would remember that she was there with you."

When they were leaving, Marce gave Luke an extra long hug and told him if he ever came to Portland, they would love to have him stay with them. "There is so much we'd like to tell you about your sister."

CHAPTER 38

WRAP UP

LUKE

Aside from the ranch, Luke's other problem was the hotel. Once again, he needed to find a cook. Over the next few months, he went to many local restaurants to try to lure their cooks into taking the job at the Frenchglen Hotel. No luck. By the beginning of February, he was quickly losing hope of finding someone. The hotel was due to be reopened by March 15.

Relief came in the form of publicity—bad publicity: *F.B.I. raids Harney Field Station*; and good publicity: *Spy from Zagreb Hides as Hotel Cook*. Both stories were covered by national newspapers. By the end of February, Luke had heard that the interest in the upcoming Bird Festival greatly exceeded previous years. The Chamber of Commerce had to hire additional ornithologists, extra vans had to be found, and the demand was such that birding day trips had to be duplicated.

Luke started to receive applications from adventuresome out-of-state cooks. By the beginning of March, Luke had received four applications. He asked each to come to the hotel and cook him a meal. He was afraid that once they saw how remote the place was, they would lose interest in the job. Better to find that out right away, he figured, before the season started.

He cleaned the hotel and planted the flower boxes at the windows. Gradually, his spirits rose to the point that he could interview applicants with enthusiasm. The couple from Vermont stood out. They were in their early-sixties. The woman was a good cook, her husband was eager to help out with repairs, and they could be moved in by the second week in March. Perfect!

At last, Luke was able to find time for some of his environmental projects, and from that time forward, he took a week off each year to visit the Hines in Portland. Before his first visit, he spent a few days in the dump looking for the plastic bag of Brenda's belongings that Maric told him she had buried there. It was not a pleasant task, but to Luke, this disinterment was what he could do to honor his sister. He made a photocopy of Brenda's face from her passport picture. The Hines were grateful to receive her passport and their last letter to her. They gave him copies of family pictures of Brenda, but the one he most enjoyed looking at was the one he uncovered himself.

Oz

In January, Maric and Oz got married at his aunt and uncle's home in Portland. Luke, Susie, and Steve came from Frenchglen. Edi had gone back to Ljubljana several months before, but at least he had met Maric. His absence didn't stop him from sending a message to be read to the wedding guests. He warned Maric to be prepared for a life of drama, close calls, and intrigue. Tom laughed at that more than Vera thought was appropriate.

Oz joked about his having to suffer cutting barbed wire while standing in cold water, drinking a mustard concoction so he would throw up, and risking being caught taking pictures—all done to incriminate those men. He laughed as he said: "None of my undercover work turned out to be necessary. The F.B.I. was able to collect all that evidence and more."

However, Oz was later to learn that those very endeavors, plus his reputation in Ljubljana, convinced the Portland Police Department to hire him in February. The position included a special work permit that allowed him permanent residence in the United States. The PPD, and possibly someone in the F.B.I., put in a claim that he had special skills needed for the job. No one else could be found to do the type of undercover work that the department required. By April, Oz wore a badge that said: Detective Ozbart Zagar, PPD.

MARIC

At the age of thirty-two, Maric received a scholarship at Portland State University. She was much older than the other students (so what was new?), but happy and grateful to be able to complete her education. She and Oz spent the next two years living with Tom and Vera, until they could afford to get an apartment of their own. During that time, Maric insisted on cooking the evening meal for the family, as a way of showing her gratitude.

Vera and Maric enjoyed broadcasting messages on ham radio together. Maric had a loving husband, a new family, and was no longer living in fear. Life was good. She and Oz gradually learned American customs. They frequently reminisced about Croatia and Bosnia before the war. Once their finances stabilized, they hoped to take a trip back to the Balkans.

JOE

Joe refused to explain any of his actions, remaining silent when interrogated and during his trial. The F.B.I. had discovered, however, that he had wired money three times to a Belgrade bank. In 1996, he had opened a savings account in another bank in Burns, not his usual bank. It was from this account that the money was wired. Interrogation of one of the workers at the HFS,

Josip, revealed that there was an arrangement that this money would be deposited in a Serbian government account. According to Josip, it was to be used to give the workers' families a modest monthly income while the bread-winners were in hiding in Oregon. Joe was given a seven-year sentence.

ZORAN

Zoran, the owner of the Portland liquor store, was also arrested. The F.B.I. discovered he had been in Serbian Intelligence and came to the U.S. after Tito died. Zoran admitted to making arrangements with the Belgrade government to help some Serb 'patriots' reach Malheur to hide. He blamed the whole idea on Brenda. "That woman came into the store to find her father. I first told her I didn't know him. She came back again and again to ask me if I had found out where he lived. Each time she would tell me something else she had learned about him: he owned a ranch in one of the most isolated areas of the country, he was a devoted Serb, and he would do anything for Serbia. She did everything but arrange the hideout for our brave heroes herself. I think she set me up."

"Is that why you arranged to have her killed?" the prosecutor asked.

"No, I was not a part of that decision. I think 'Belgrade' was planning to do away with her before she went back to Trieste. She could spill the beans. She was already trying to set up English lessons with the men at the field station. That woman was a loose cannon. Ha, you can't get us for murder though. Those stupid Croats did the job for us."

Zoran got a seven-year sentence.

VERA AND MARCE

Marce and Vera became even closer friends, working together to help other parents bereaved by the loss of a child. Vera helped Majesira by translating her blog into English, and did whatever she could to further the CZ cause.

MAJESIRA

Majesira's efforts to establish a women's network of ham radio broadcasters was largely responsible for disseminating awareness of the 16 rape camps that operated during the Bosnian War. Through these broadcasts, ham operators encouraged women to come forth and share their personal experience with this type of torture. Majesira did not stop there. For another 15 years after the war, she continued to pursue Bosnian War rapists by any legal means possible. She firmly believed that impunity for these rapists would allow this gender-based torture of civilians to continue to be used as a war strategy.

Her weekly blogs are now translated into five different languages. In them, she stresses the need to honor women. The woman who has been raped should not be shunned by her husband or family members. Respect for women should be a part of every soldier's training.

Majesira still sings high praises for the International Criminal Tribunal for Yugoslavia (ICTY), as it was the first international court to identify rape as torture, a crime against humanity, and a strategy of ethnic cleansing. Long overdue!

Epilogue

Although the international community did little to prevent genocide and crimes against humanity during the Balkan wars, it did eventually try to bring war criminals to justice. In 1993, the U.N. Security Council created the International Criminal Tribunal for the Former Yugoslavia (ICTY) at The Hague, Netherlands. It was the first international tribunal since the Nuremberg Trials (after World War II), the first to prosecute genocide, among other war crimes, and the first to define mass rape as a crime against humanity in international law.

The ICTY used sealed (unpublicized) indictments to give war criminals little advanced warning, but it had to rely on the local police to make arrests. Sometimes national leaders preferred to hide the criminals, even before they were indicted, to limit national disgrace and prevent further arrests, possibly their own. In spite of these obstacles, the ICTY was able to bring 161 war criminals to justice.

As soon as the Peace Accords were signed, Franjo Tudjman began protecting indictees by hiding them, giving them new names and identities, as well as threatening war-crime witnesses with reprisals. He even planted a spy at The Hague.

For nine years, Tudjman taped all conversations in his office discussing his wartime strategies and orders for ethnic cleansing. The tapes revealed his cordial relationship with Milošević and their collusion to partition Bosnia. The tapes surfaced soon after Tudjman died of stomach cancer. He couldn't be tried posthumously, but they provided incriminating evidence. Tudjman had skillfully played into western prejudices by cloaking his quest for

Croatian nationhood as crucial to the defense of Western values, which he said conflicted with those of Eastern Orthodoxy and Islam. The ICTY appealed to his craving for Western approval by trying to convince him that Croatian membership in both the EU and NATO would be denied if indicted criminals were not arrested.

The story of *Malheur* ends before Serbia's War in Kosovo (1998-1999). Resisting diplomatic solutions, Milošević refused to allow NATO peacekeepers into Kosovo. Without U.N. authorization, NATO bombed Belgrade, expecting Milošević to immediately capitulate. Instead, he spent three months forcing a million Albanians in Kosovo to leave. Milošević finally relented when he lost the Serbian election in 2000. By 2001, Milošević was imprisoned at The Hague, where he insisted on serving as his own defense lawyer. His poor health led to long delays in the trial. In 2006, he died of heart failure in his prison cell. He was never sentenced, but he was the first acting head of state to ever be indicted for war crimes.

Although they do not appear in the story of *Malheur*, two other war criminals may be familiar to the reader. Radovan Karadzic was the President of the Republic of Srpska. After the war, he was on the run for 13 years. Karadzic hid in plain sight, under the assumed identity of a new-age healer. He was arrested in Belgrade in July, 2008, and was sentenced in March, 2016, to 40 years in prison.

Ratko Mladic orchestrated the siege of Sarajevo and was responsible for the genocide at Srebrenica. He remained at large for years after the war, much of that time hidden by the Serbian Security forces. Since 2006, he has been in prison at The Hague. Sentencing has been delayed due to his health and technicalities with the trial. Final sentencing is expected in 2017.

Whether or not the West was afraid of promoting a Muslim presence within a "Christian" Europe, they did not give as much support to Bosnia as they gave to Croatia. During the wars of secession, Bosniaks suffered far worse than Croats or Serbs. Most of the fighting took place in Bosnia. Eleven thousand civilians who lived in Sarajevo were killed during the four-year siege. The majority of the victims of genocide, rape, and other forms of torture were Bosniaks.

Many think that the wars were driven by political leaders who used religious differences to sanctify aggression and brutality. They produced circumstances which allowed psychopaths and sadists the freedom to kill and torture. But to Bosnian women, longstanding gender inequality also played a major role. Many families and husbands would not accept a raped woman back into the home. Dishonoring women helped to destroy families and communities. Too many soldiers did not see women as their equals and followed orders to rape. Allowing rapists impunity, not showing rape for what it is—a means of torture and ethnic cleansing exerted on civilians—would have destabilized the peace.

The ICTY provided victims a voice. Many gave testimonies about their abuse and suffering. The tribunal established crucial facts which ensured a correct historical record. The court held senior individuals like Milošević accountable. Its work has helped to greatly expand international humanitarian law and, at last, to establish rape as a crime against humanity.

Originally, there were six republics in Yugoslavia. The story of *Malheur* only discusses the fate of Slovenia, Croatia, Serbia, and Bosnia. Macedonia did not have to fight to gain statehood. When it declared its independence in 1992, Yugoslavia let it go, probably because it was poor and landlocked. However, Greece would not accept its name. For centuries, "Macedonia" was an important region in Greek history. To placate the Greeks, the country of Macedonia is now called the Former Yugoslav Republic of Macedonia—FYROM.

Montenegro had always been closely allied to Serbia. It stayed in Yugoslavia until 2006. From 1995 until 2006, Yugoslavia consisted of only two republics, Serbia and Montenegro, as the other four had already seceded. In 2006, Montenegro peacefully left Yugoslavia and became an independent nation, marking the end of the grand experiment to unify southern Slavs.

ơ   ơ   ơ

Image of the Stari Most Bridge, Mostar, Bosnia
adapted from a photo by Ramirez Hun, used under the Creative
Commons Attribution-Share Alike 3.0 Unported license

*Image of the Frenchglen Hotel, Oregon
adapted from a photo by Cacophony, used under the Creative Commons
Attribution-Share Alike 3.0 Unported license*

ACKNOWLEDGEMENTS

I was living in Washington, D.C. when Yugoslavia first started to break up. The ensuing wars of secession involved people of the same ethnicity, who spoke the same language, and lived in a region the size of Oregon, yet who resorted to genocide, ethnic cleansing, and systematic rape. In spite of almost daily media coverage throughout the early 90s, I had difficulty following events and understanding the causes of such brutality.

Twenty years later, my husband Ken and I went on a Road Scholar (formerly Elderhostel) trip to the Western Balkans. After reading numerous books and articles, I finally felt I understood enough to attempt to write a novel set in the region. It seemed that people were too quick to blame the Serbs, so it was fundamental for me not to take sides. My studies taught me that the Croats had also committed despicable acts, and Balkan history was rife with self-serving interference from foreign powers.

In spite of extensive reading, it was risky to set the story in a foreign land that I had only been to once. Before I started writing, Ken and I happened to take a five-day trip to Eastern Oregon to go to the bird festival in Burns. We stayed at the Frenchglen hotel in a town of just eleven people. This region of dispersed cattle ranches is the most remote area of the lower forty-eight states. I loved it, and became committed to having the story also take place in Eastern Oregon. My challenge was devising a plot that included these two distinct settings. I would like to make clear that there were no actual Sebian war criminals ever sent to the Malhuer Field Station, which I called the Harney Field Station in the book, and it should not be confused with the Malheur

Natural Wildlife Refuge, which was occupied by a group of militant anti-government activists for 41 days in early 2016.

I appreciate the advice from John Ross, manager of the Frenchglen Hotel and Duncan Evered, co-director of the Malheur Field Station. A special thanks to Roger Rouvola for guiding me through the references to ham radio. Roger is an Extra class licensed ham (NA6DX) and an electrical engineer. Most importantly, he gave up much time explaining to me the legalities and customs of ham radio use. I also owe thanks to several friends who gave advice and pointed out errors in the text during pre-reading of the manuscript.

The personal testimonies of victims of torture during the Bosnian War were taken from the internet.

As always, I am most grateful for the editing care and encouragement of my publishers at Plowshare Media. Lastly, I appreciate the patience and advice of Ken, to whom I have dedicated this work.

ABOUT THE AUTHOR

Pamelia Barratt now lives in San Diego. She grew up in Chicago and taught high school chemistry, math, and physics in the Washington D.C. area. Retirement finally gave her the opportunity to write. *Malheur* is Pam's fourth mystery novel. The others are: *Blood: The Color of Cranberries* (2009), *An Ostentation* (2011), and *Gray Dominion* (2013). All her books have been published by Plowshare Media in La Jolla, California.

For additional information, please visit her website at:
http://pameliabarratt.com/

www.ingramcontent.com/pod-product-compliance
Lightning Source LLC
Chambersburg PA
CBHW070323260626
47160CB00003B/935